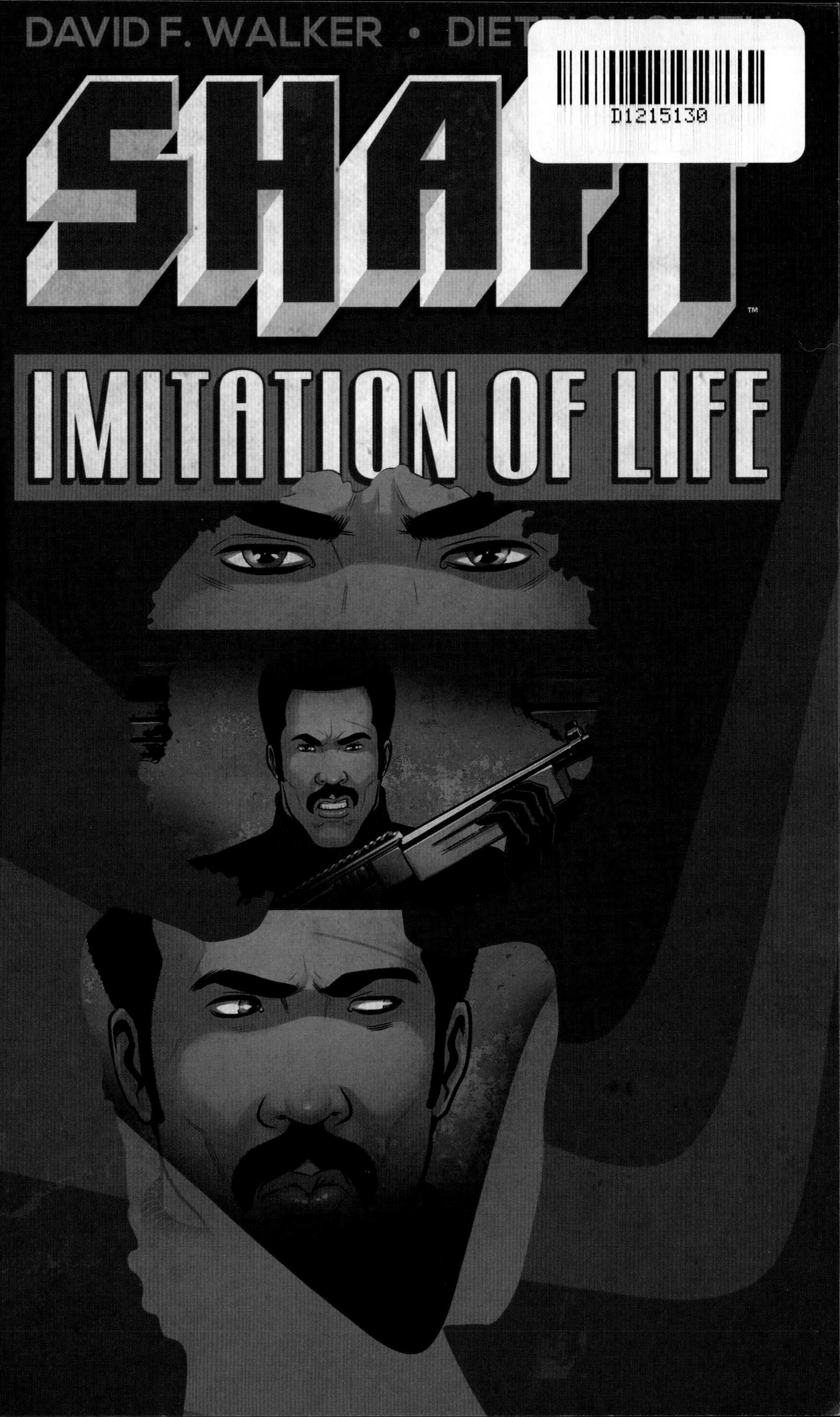
DAVID F. WALKER •
SHAFT™
IMITATION OF LIFE

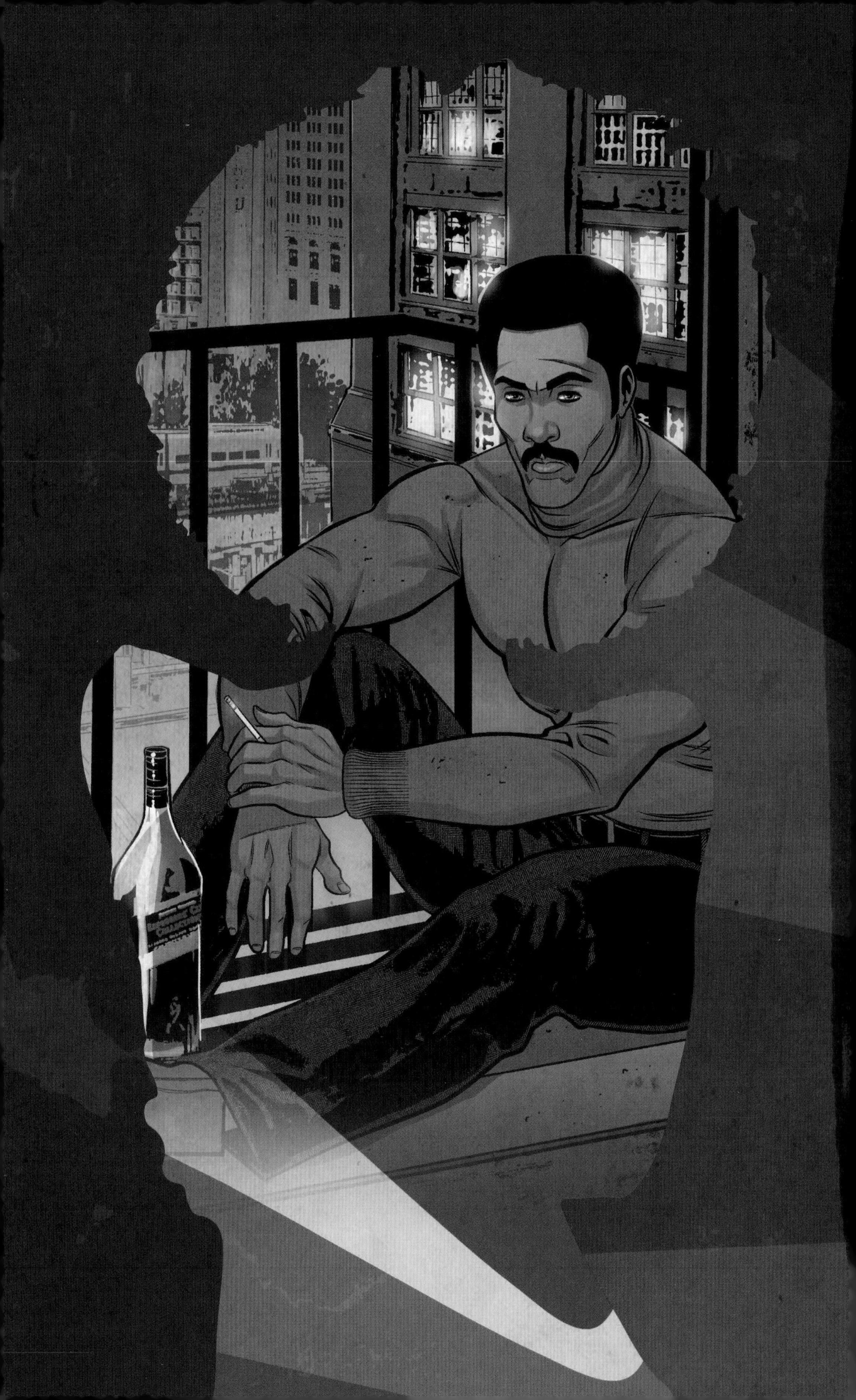

SHAFT
IMITATION OF LIFE

SHAFT CREATED BY **ERNEST TIDYMAN**

WRITTEN AND LETTERED BY **DAVID WALKER**

ILLUSTRATED BY **DIETRICH SMITH**

COLORED BY **ALEX GUIMARÃES**

COVERS BY **MATTHEW CLARK**

COVER COLORS BY **VINICIUS ANDRADE**

COLLECTION DESIGN BY **CATHLEEN HEARD**

SPECIAL THANKS TO **STEVE KASDIN**

DYNAMITE®

Online at www.DYNAMITE.com
On Facebook /Dynamitecomics
On Instagram /Dynamitecomics
On Tumblr dynamitecomics.tumblr.com
On Twitter @dynamitecomics
On YouTube /Dynamitecomics

Nick Barrucci, CEO / Publisher
Juan Collado, President / COO

Joe Rybandt, Executive Editor
Matt Idelson, Senior Editor
Anthony Marques, Associate Editor
Kevin Ketner, Editorial Assistant

Jason Ullmeyer, Art Director
Geoff Harkins, Senior Graphic Designer
Cathleen Heard, Graphic Designer
Alexis Persson, Production Artist

Chris Caniano, Digital Associate
Rachel Kilbury, Digital Assistant

Brandon Dante Primavera, V.P. of IT and Operations
Rich Young, Director of Business Development

Alan Payne, V.P. of Sales and Marketing
Keith Davidsen, Marketing Director
Pat O'Connell, Sales Manager

ISBN-10: 1-5241-0260-9 | ISBN-13: 978-1-5241-0260-9
First Printing 10 9 8 7 6 5 4 3 2 1

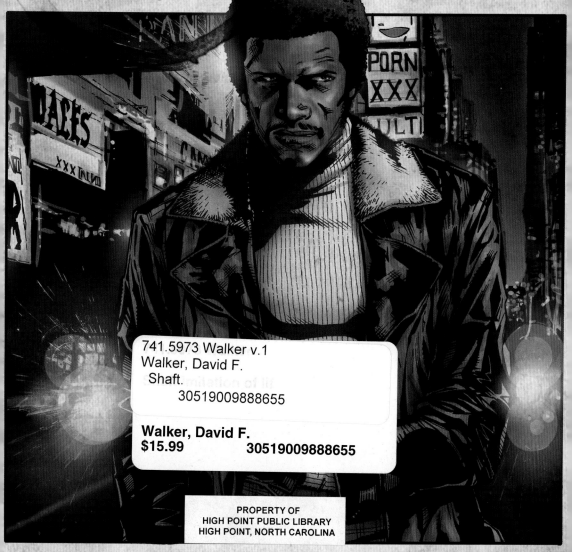

DAVID F. WALKER • DIETRICH SMITH

SHAFT

IMITATION OF LIFE

A DYNAMITE COMIC • $3.99

Part One: BEFORE AND AFTER

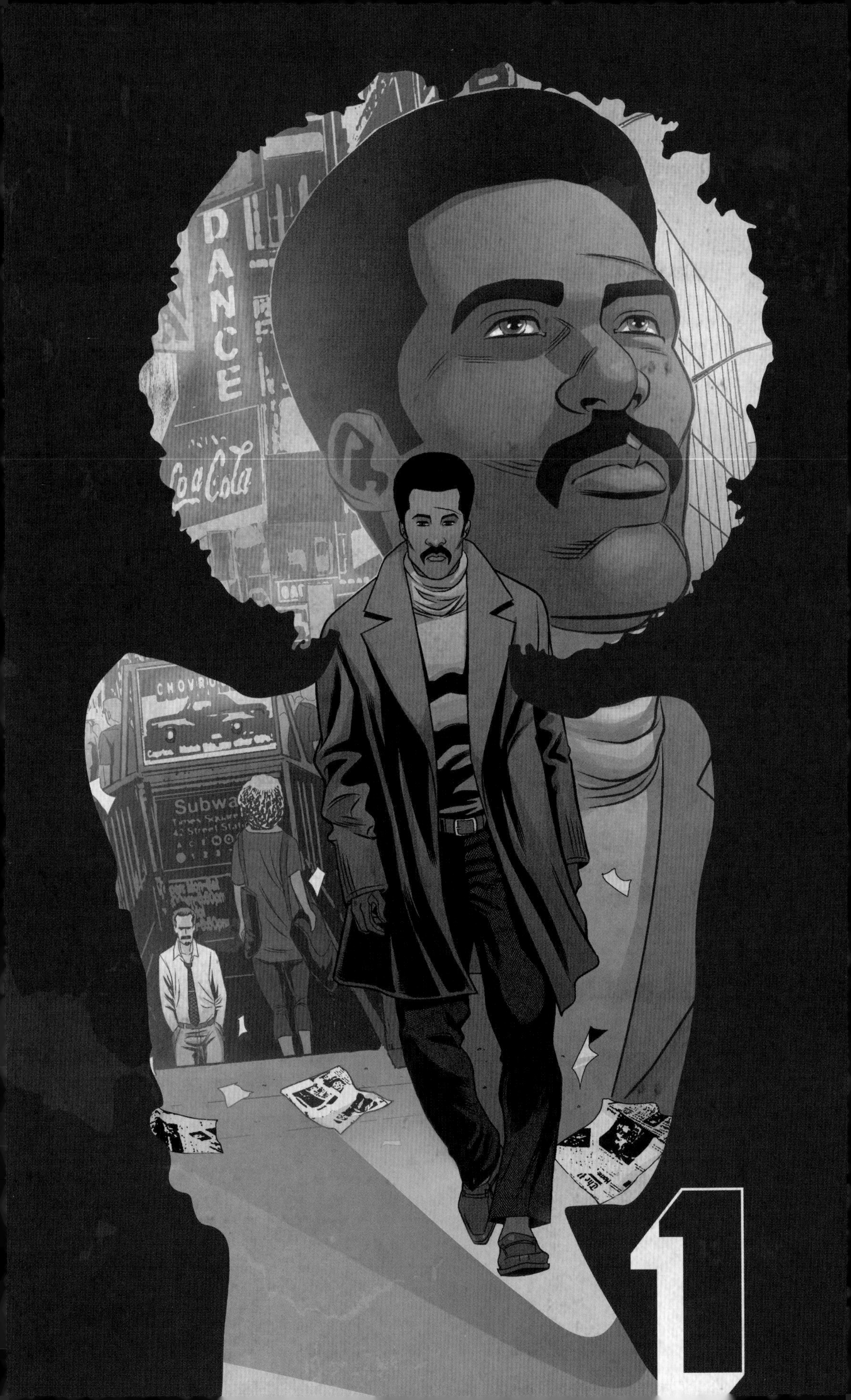
DANCE
1

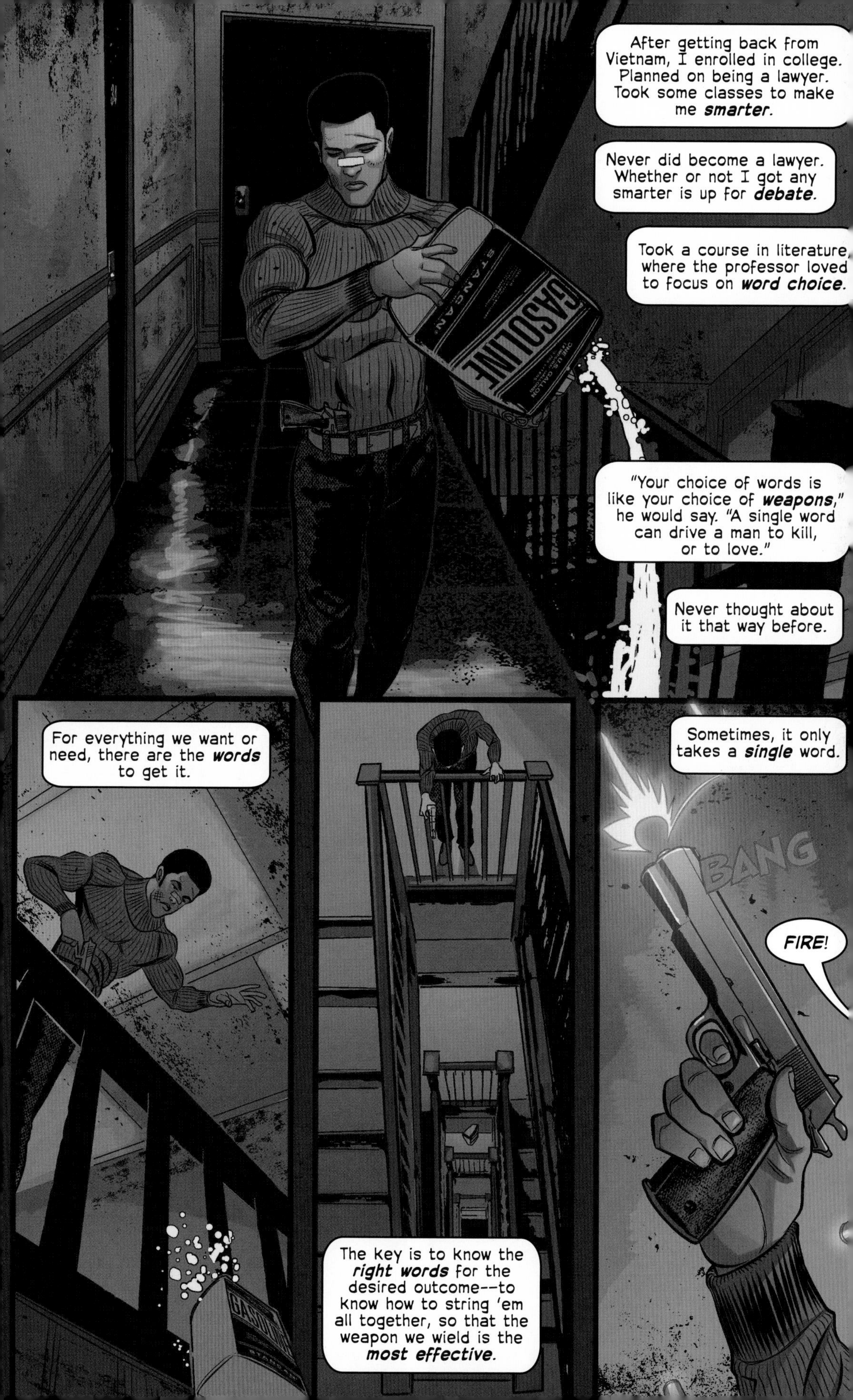
After getting back from Vietnam, I enrolled in college. Planned on being a lawyer. Took some classes to make me *smarter*.
Never did become a lawyer. Whether or not I got any smarter is up for *debate*.
Took a course in literature, where the professor loved to focus on *word choice*.
GASOLINE
"Your choice of words is like your choice of *weapons*," he would say. "A single word can drive a man to kill, or to love."
Never thought about it that way before.
For everything we want or need, there are the *words* to get it.
The key is to know the *right words* for the desired outcome--to know how to string 'em all together, so that the weapon we wield is the *most effective*.
Sometimes, it only takes a *single* word.
BANG
FIRE!

THE GODDAMN BUILDING IS ON FIRE!

FIRE!

BANG

Went into the Marines when I was **seventeen**. The judge gave me a **choice**--prison as an adult, or join the military.

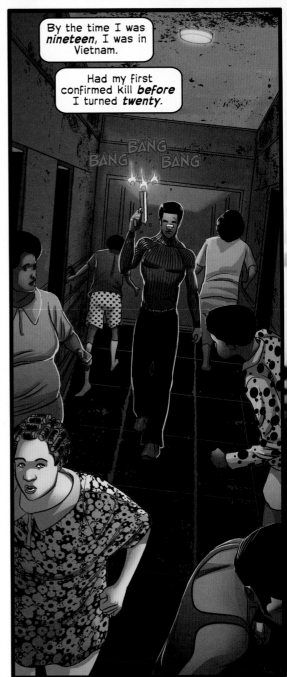

By the time I was **nineteen**, I was in Vietnam.

Had my first confirmed kill **before** I turned **twenty**.

BANG BANG BANG

Killing came a little too **easy** for me.

OUTTA THE WAY!

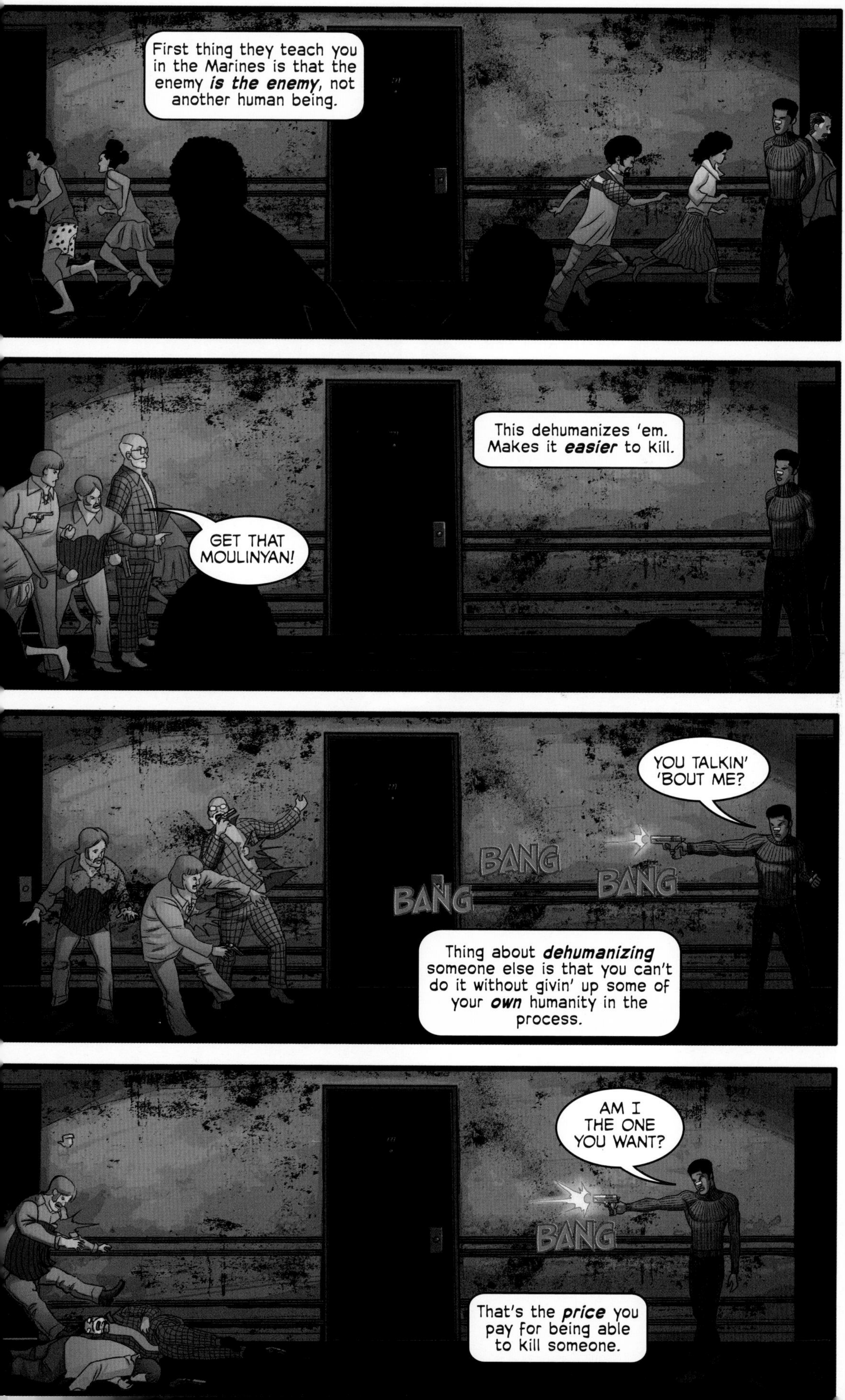
First thing they teach you in the Marines is that the enemy *is the enemy*, not another human being.
This dehumanizes 'em. Makes it *easier* to kill.
GET THAT MOULINYAN!
YOU TALKIN' 'BOUT ME?
BANG
BANG
BANG
Thing about *dehumanizing* someone else is that you can't do it without givin' up some of your *own* humanity in the process.
AM I THE ONE YOU WANT?
BANG
That's the *price* you pay for being able to kill someone.

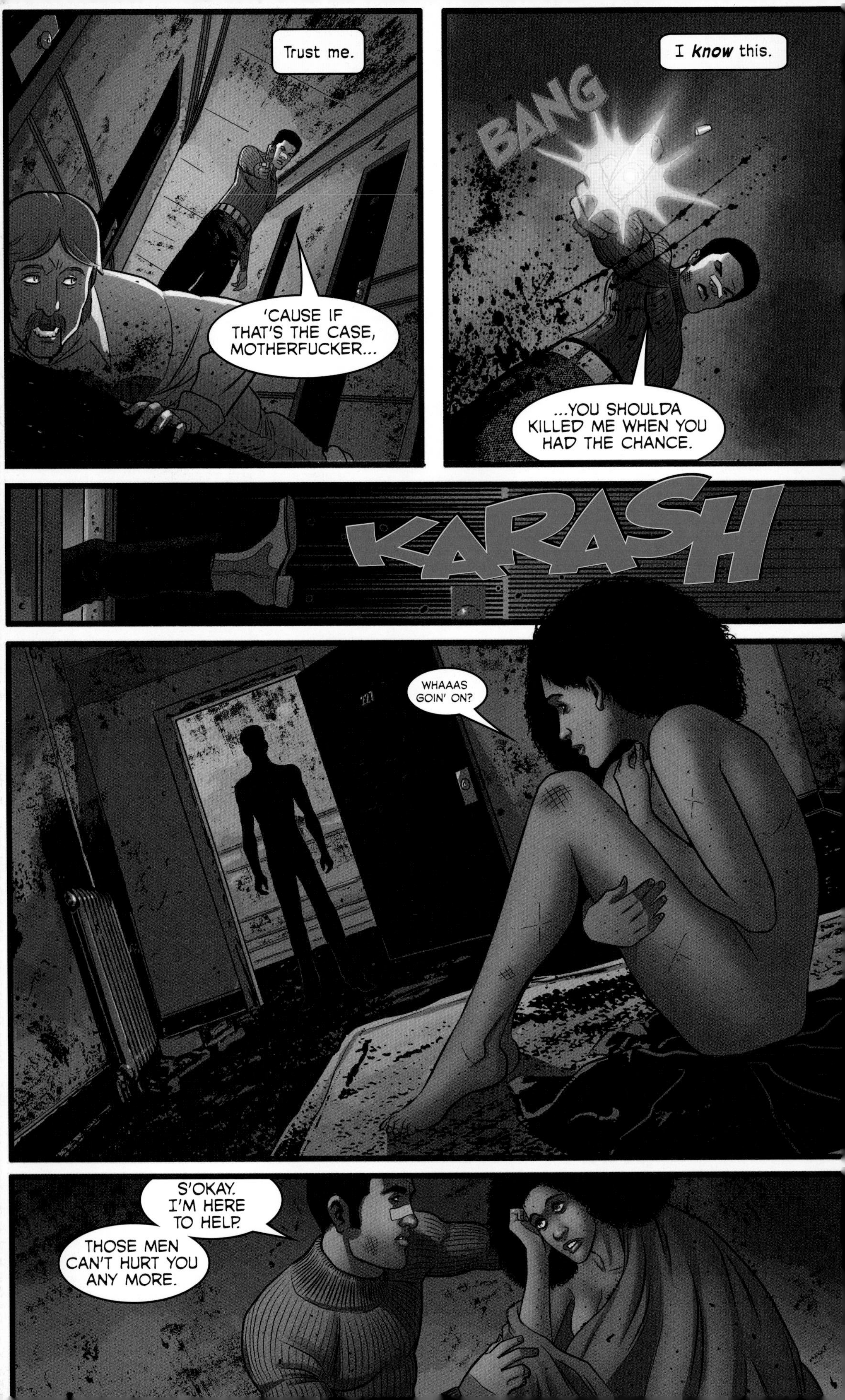
Trust me.
'CAUSE IF THAT'S THE CASE, MOTHERFUCKER...
I *know* this.
BANG
...YOU SHOULDA KILLED ME WHEN YOU HAD THE CHANCE.
KARASH
WHAAAS GOIN' ON?
S'OKAY. I'M HERE TO HELP.
THOSE MEN CAN'T HURT YOU ANY MORE.

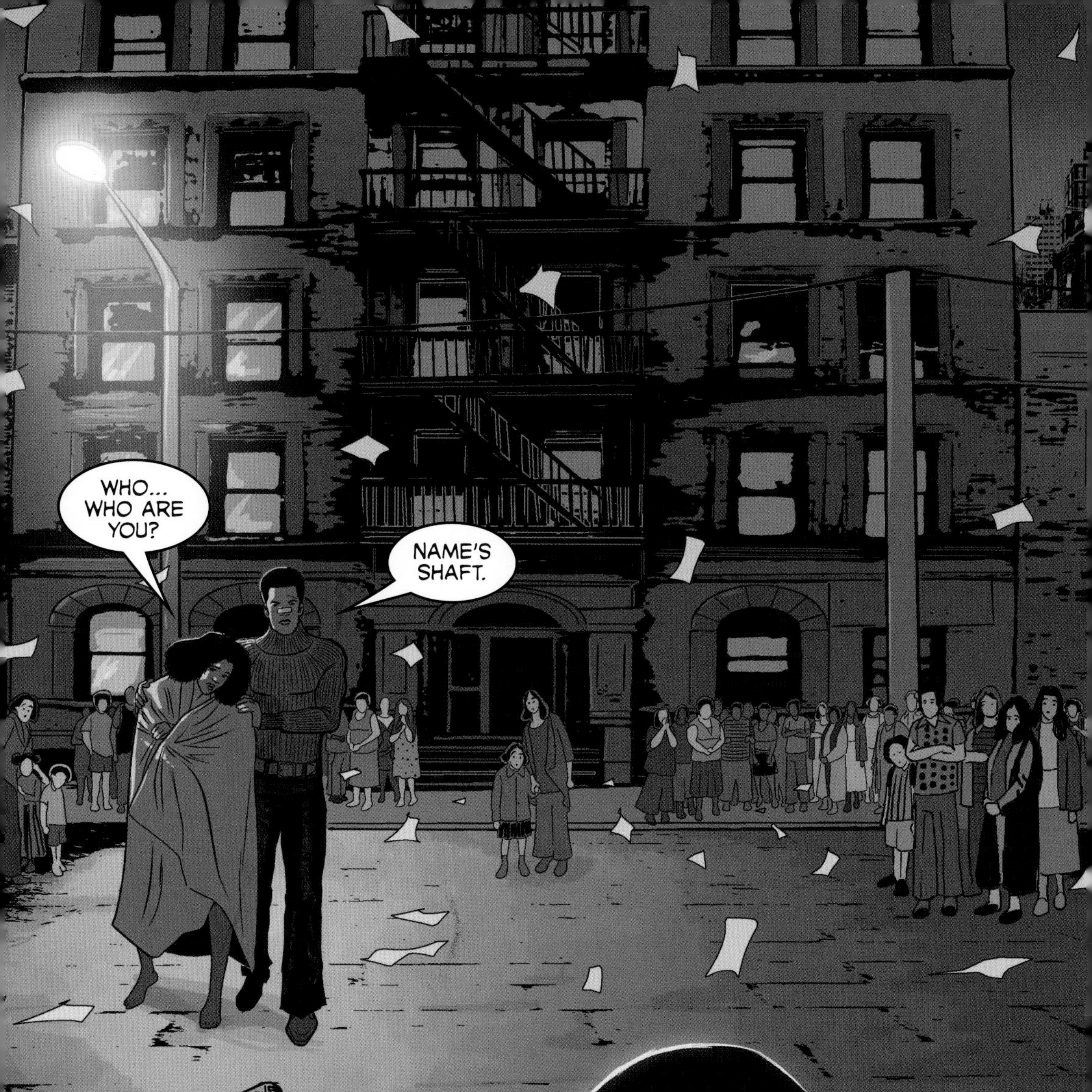
WHO... WHO ARE YOU?
NAME'S SHAFT.

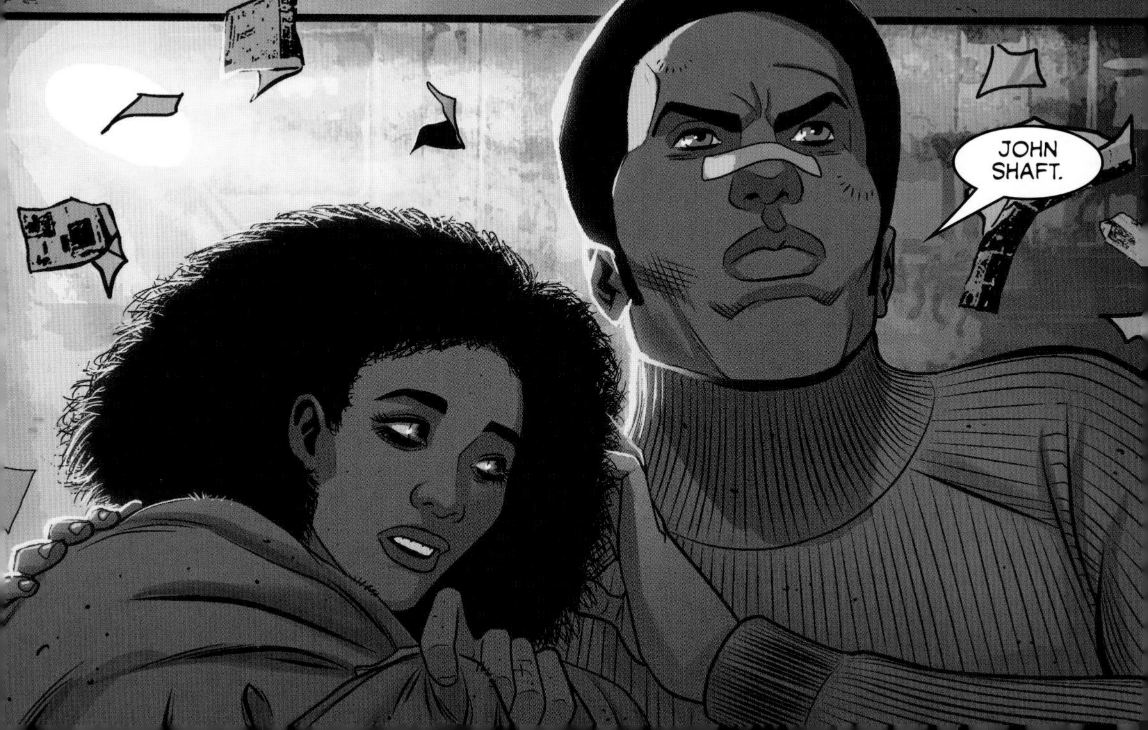
JOHN SHAFT.

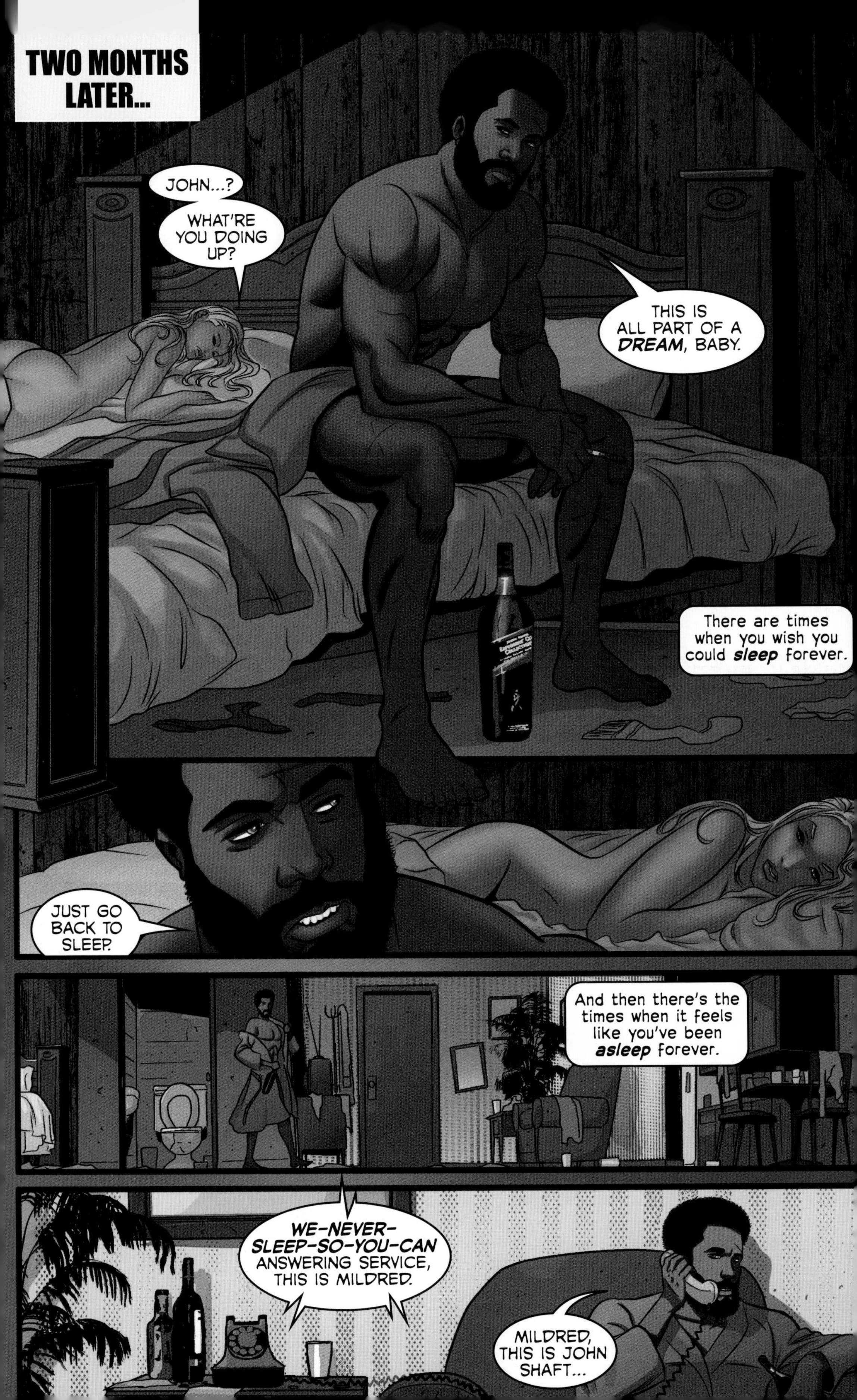
TWO MONTHS LATER...
JOHN...?
WHAT'RE YOU DOING UP?
THIS IS ALL PART OF A DREAM, BABY.
There are times when you wish you could sleep forever.
JUST GO BACK TO SLEEP.
And then there's the times when it feels like you've been asleep forever.
WE-NEVER-SLEEP-SO-YOU-CAN ANSWERING SERVICE, THIS IS MILDRED.
MILDRED, THIS IS JOHN SHAFT...

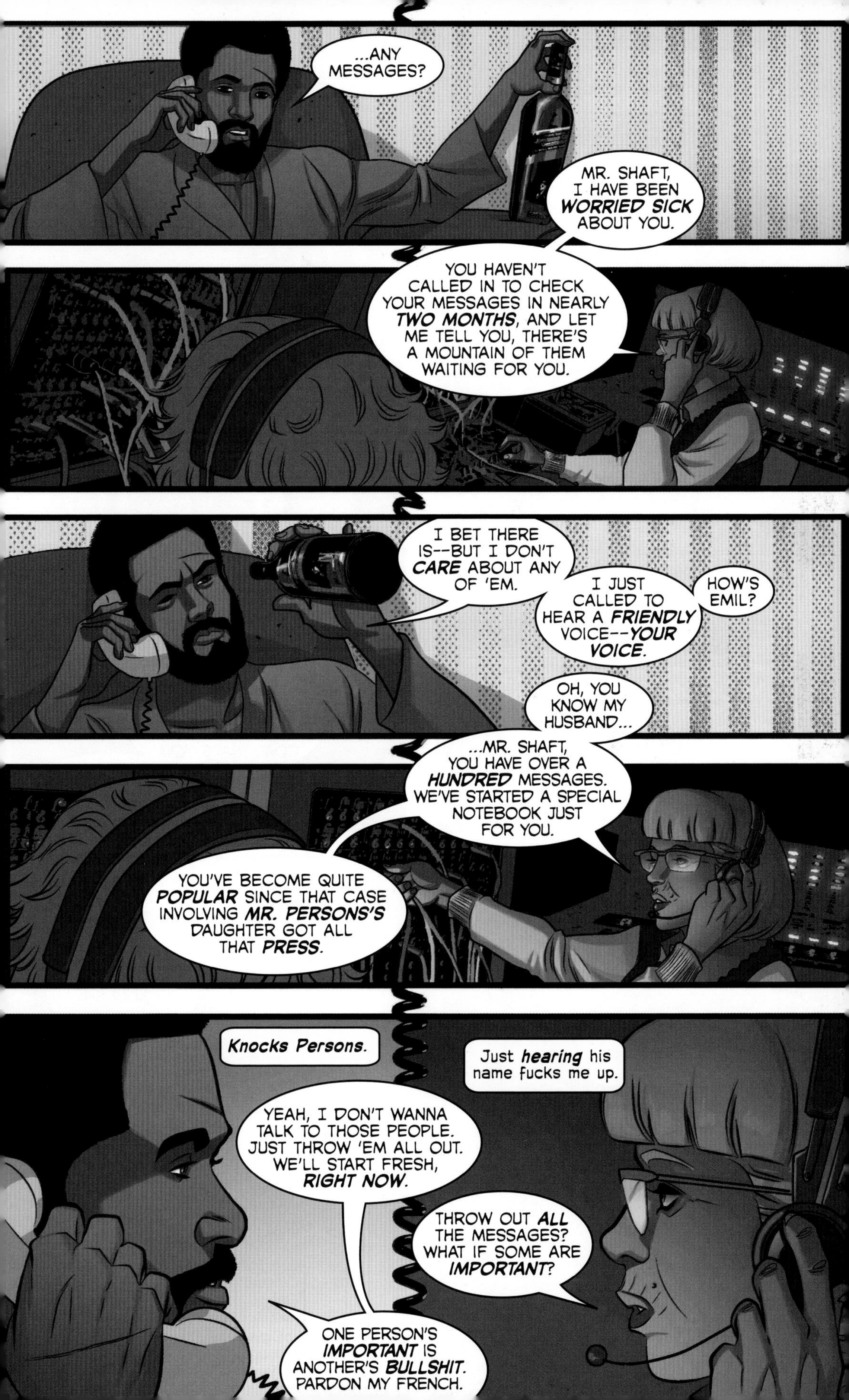
...ANY MESSAGES?
MR. SHAFT, I HAVE BEEN WORRIED SICK ABOUT YOU.
YOU HAVEN'T CALLED IN TO CHECK YOUR MESSAGES IN NEARLY TWO MONTHS, AND LET ME TELL YOU, THERE'S A MOUNTAIN OF THEM WAITING FOR YOU.
I BET THERE IS--BUT I DON'T CARE ABOUT ANY OF 'EM.
I JUST CALLED TO HEAR A FRIENDLY VOICE--YOUR VOICE.
HOW'S EMIL?
OH, YOU KNOW MY HUSBAND...
...MR. SHAFT, YOU HAVE OVER A HUNDRED MESSAGES. WE'VE STARTED A SPECIAL NOTEBOOK JUST FOR YOU.
YOU'VE BECOME QUITE POPULAR SINCE THAT CASE INVOLVING MR. PERSONS'S DAUGHTER GOT ALL THAT PRESS.
Knocks Persons.
Just hearing his name fucks me up.
YEAH, I DON'T WANNA TALK TO THOSE PEOPLE. JUST THROW 'EM ALL OUT. WE'LL START FRESH, RIGHT NOW.
THROW OUT ALL THE MESSAGES? WHAT IF SOME ARE IMPORTANT?
ONE PERSON'S IMPORTANT IS ANOTHER'S BULLSHIT. PARDON MY FRENCH.

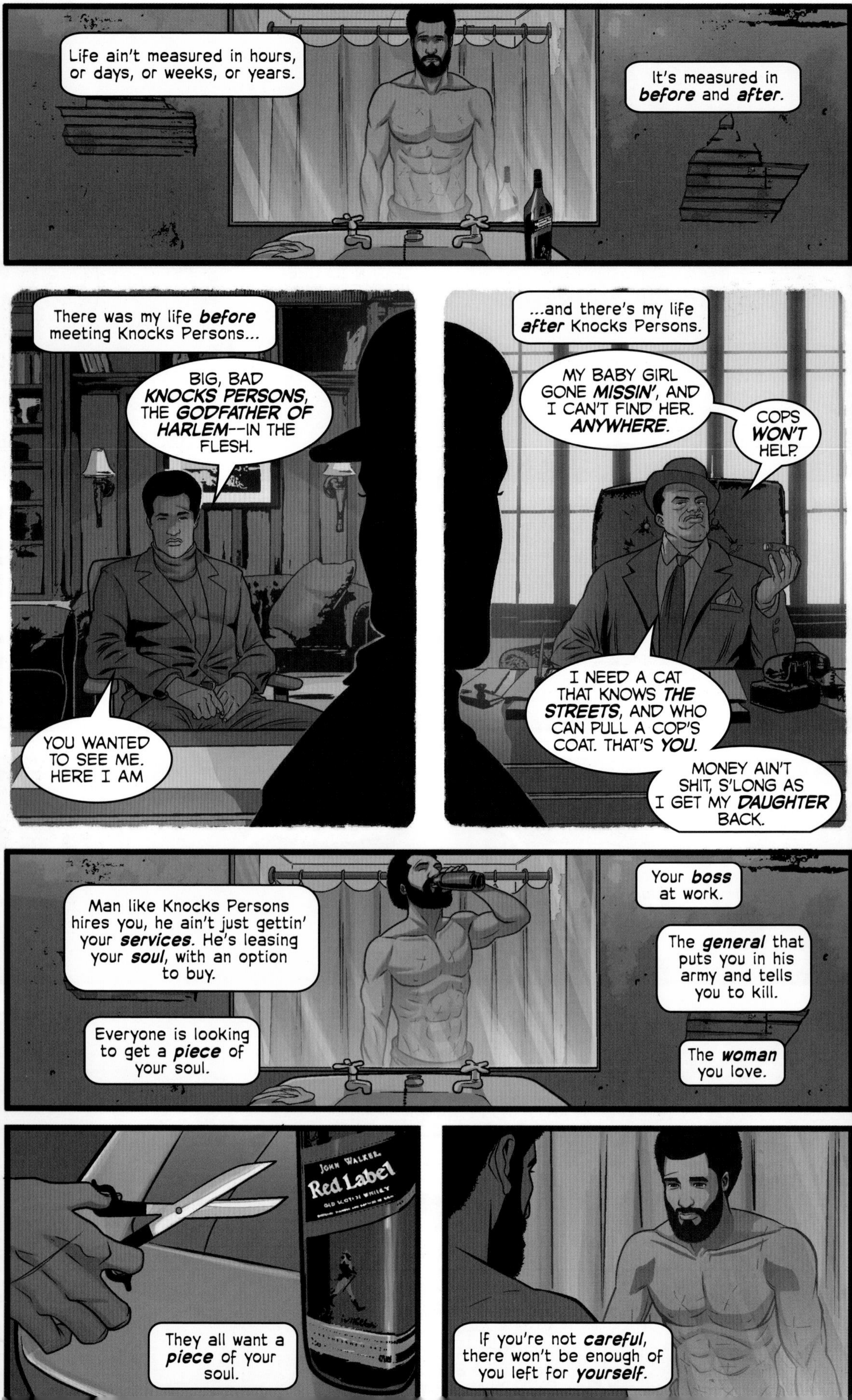

Life ain't measured in hours, or days, or weeks, or years.
It's measured in *before* and *after*.
There was my life *before* meeting Knocks Persons...
BIG, BAD *KNOCKS PERSONS*, THE *GODFATHER OF HARLEM*--IN THE FLESH.
YOU WANTED TO SEE ME. HERE I AM
...and there's my life *after* Knocks Persons.
MY BABY GIRL GONE *MISSIN'*, AND I CAN'T FIND HER. *ANYWHERE*.
COPS *WON'T* HELP.
I NEED A CAT THAT KNOWS *THE STREETS*, AND WHO CAN PULL A COP'S COAT. THAT'S *YOU*.
MONEY AIN'T SHIT, S'LONG AS I GET MY *DAUGHTER* BACK.
Man like Knocks Persons hires you, he ain't just gettin' your *services*. He's leasing your *soul*, with an option to buy.
Everyone is looking to get a *piece* of your soul.
Your *boss* at work.
The *general* that puts you in his army and tells you to kill.
The *woman* you love.
JOHN WALKER
Red Label
They all want a *piece* of your soul.
If you're not *careful*, there won't be enough of you left for *yourself*.

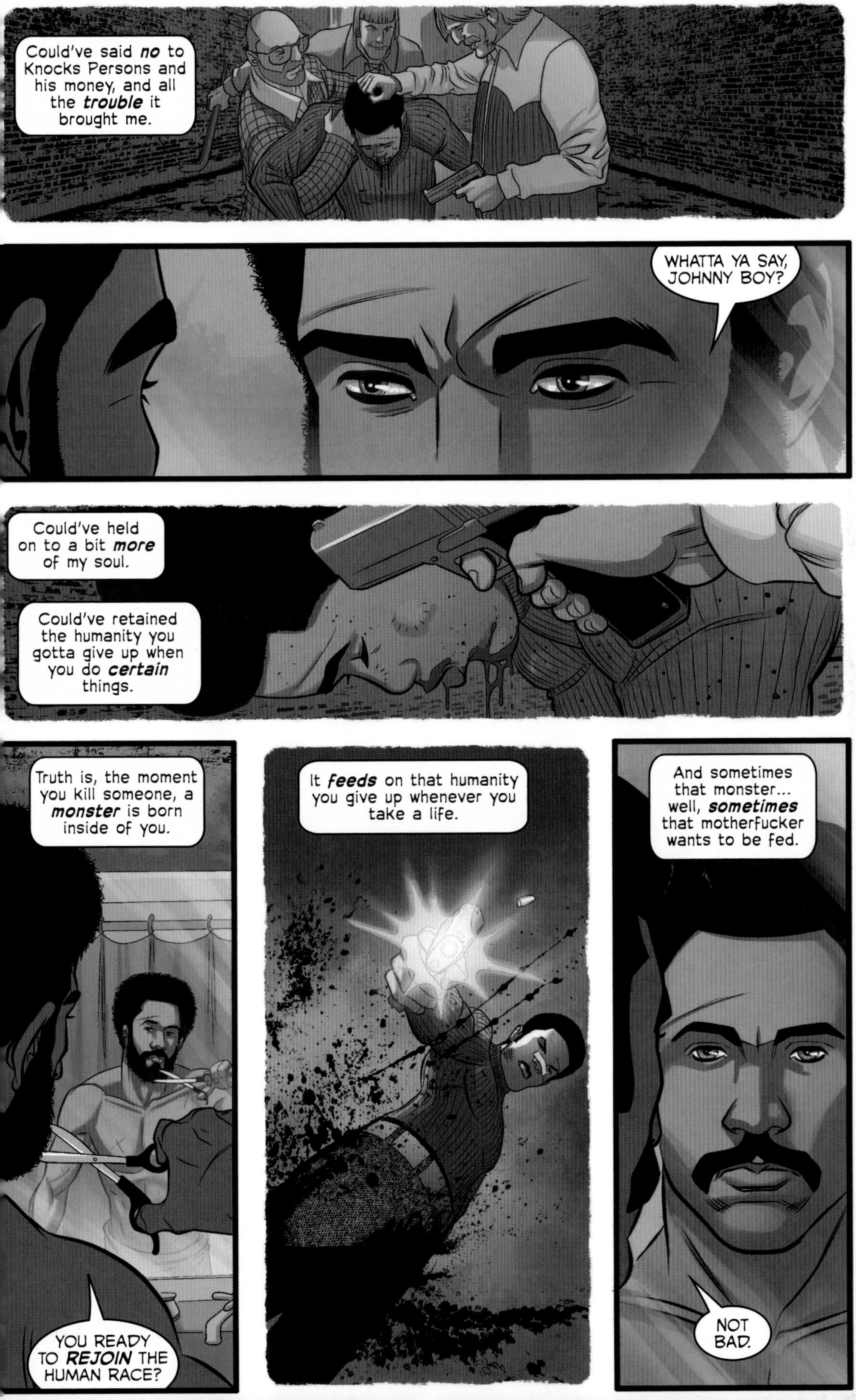
Could've said no to Knocks Persons and his money, and all the trouble it brought me.
WHATTA YA SAY, JOHNNY BOY?
Could've held on to a bit more of my soul.
Could've retained the humanity you gotta give up when you do certain things.
Truth is, the moment you kill someone, a monster is born inside of you.
YOU READY TO REJOIN THE HUMAN RACE?
It feeds on that humanity you give up whenever you take a life.
And sometimes that monster... well, sometimes that motherfucker wants to be fed.
NOT BAD.

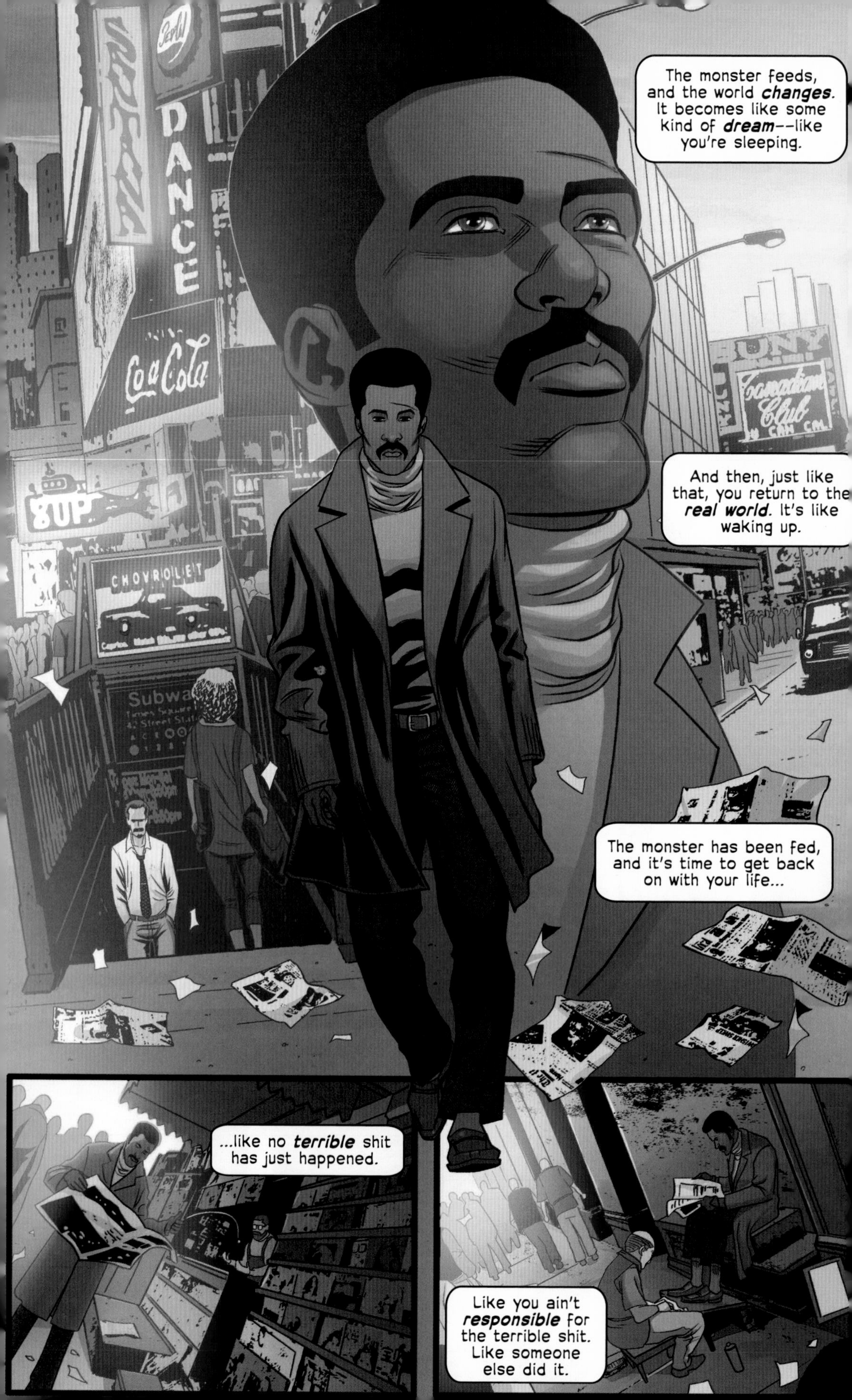
The monster feeds, and the world *changes*. It becomes like some kind of *dream*--like you're sleeping.
And then, just like that, you return to the *real world*. It's like waking up.
The monster has been fed, and it's time to get back on with your life...
...like no *terrible* shit has just happened.
Like you ain't *responsible* for the terrible shit. Like someone else did it.

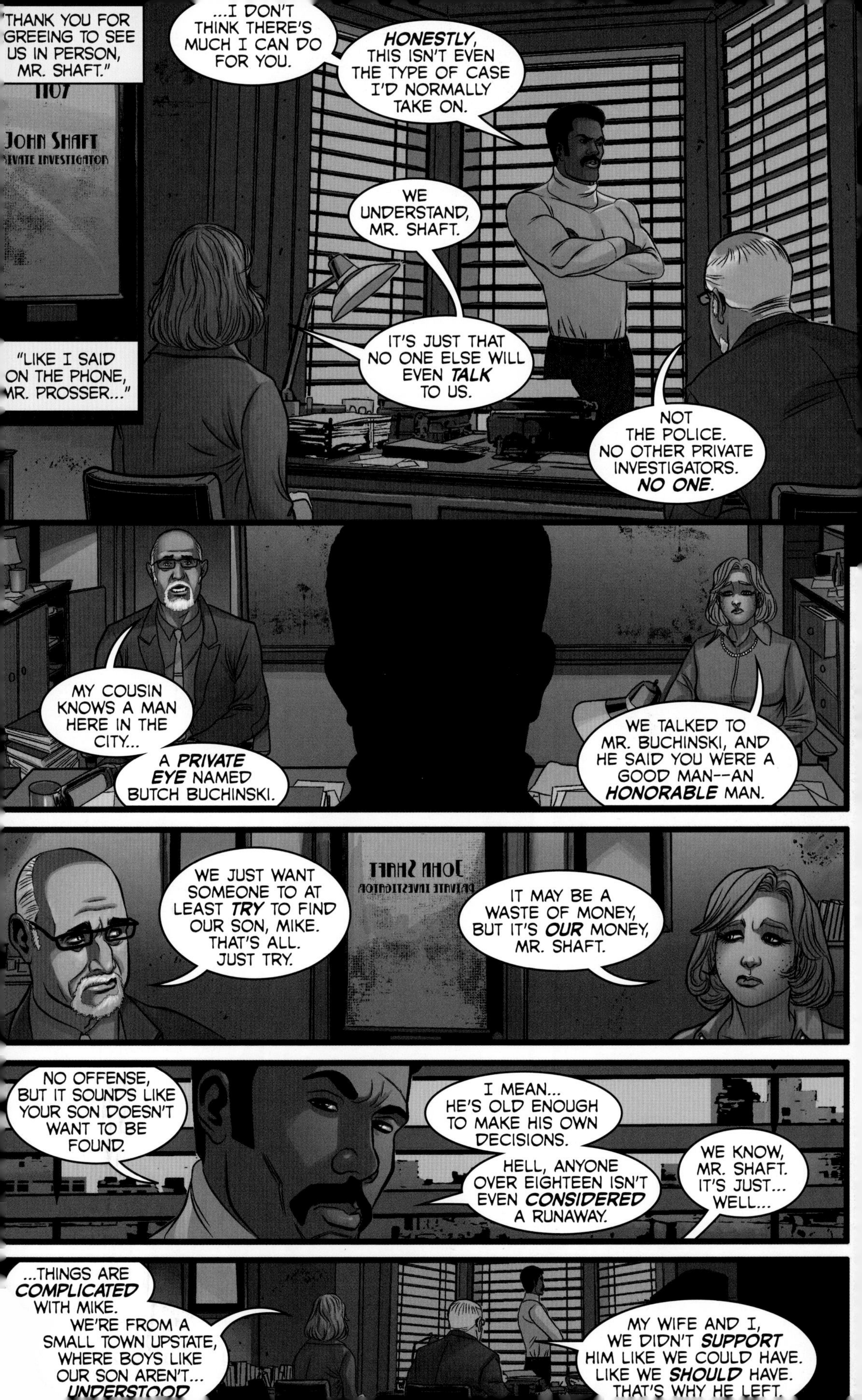
"THANK YOU FOR AGREEING TO SEE US IN PERSON, MR. SHAFT."
...I DON'T THINK THERE'S MUCH I CAN DO FOR YOU.
HONESTLY, THIS ISN'T EVEN THE TYPE OF CASE I'D NORMALLY TAKE ON.
1107
JOHN SHAFT
PRIVATE INVESTIGATOR
WE UNDERSTAND, MR. SHAFT.
"LIKE I SAID ON THE PHONE, MR. PROSSER..."
IT'S JUST THAT NO ONE ELSE WILL EVEN TALK TO US.
NOT THE POLICE. NO OTHER PRIVATE INVESTIGATORS. NO ONE.
MY COUSIN KNOWS A MAN HERE IN THE CITY...
A PRIVATE EYE NAMED BUTCH BUCHINSKI.
WE TALKED TO MR. BUCHINSKI, AND HE SAID YOU WERE A GOOD MAN--AN HONORABLE MAN.
WE JUST WANT SOMEONE TO AT LEAST TRY TO FIND OUR SON, MIKE. THAT'S ALL. JUST TRY.
JOHN SHAFT
PRIVATE INVESTIGATOR
IT MAY BE A WASTE OF MONEY, BUT IT'S OUR MONEY, MR. SHAFT.
NO OFFENSE, BUT IT SOUNDS LIKE YOUR SON DOESN'T WANT TO BE FOUND.
I MEAN... HE'S OLD ENOUGH TO MAKE HIS OWN DECISIONS.
HELL, ANYONE OVER EIGHTEEN ISN'T EVEN CONSIDERED A RUNAWAY.
WE KNOW, MR. SHAFT. IT'S JUST... WELL...
...THINGS ARE COMPLICATED WITH MIKE.
WE'RE FROM A SMALL TOWN UPSTATE, WHERE BOYS LIKE OUR SON AREN'T... UNDERSTOOD.
MY WIFE AND I, WE DIDN'T SUPPORT HIM LIKE WE COULD HAVE. LIKE WE SHOULD HAVE. THAT'S WHY HE LEFT.

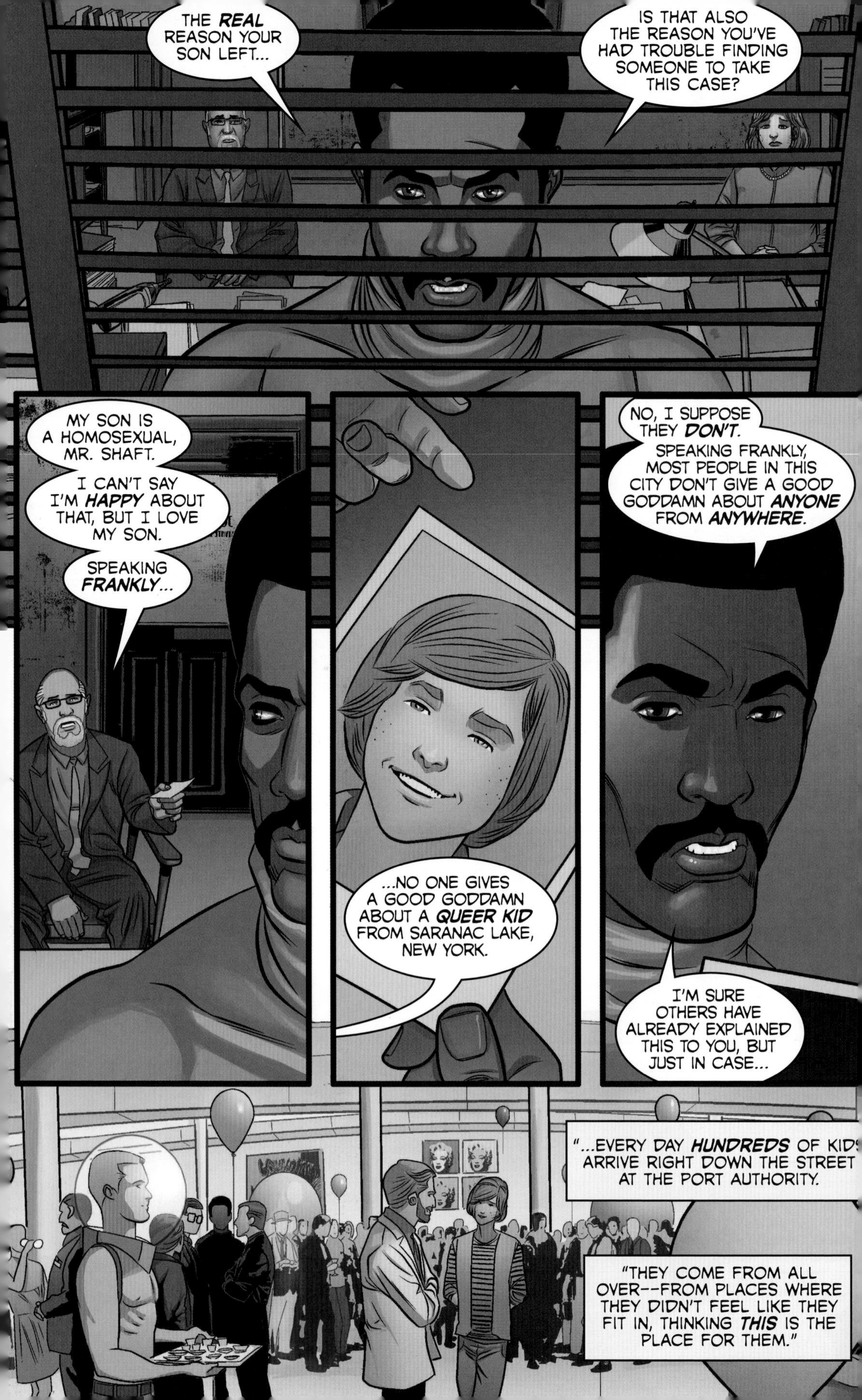
THE REAL REASON YOUR SON LEFT...
IS THAT ALSO THE REASON YOU'VE HAD TROUBLE FINDING SOMEONE TO TAKE THIS CASE?
MY SON IS A HOMOSEXUAL, MR. SHAFT.
I CAN'T SAY I'M HAPPY ABOUT THAT, BUT I LOVE MY SON.
SPEAKING FRANKLY...
...NO ONE GIVES A GOOD GODDAMN ABOUT A QUEER KID FROM SARANAC LAKE, NEW YORK.
NO, I SUPPOSE THEY DON'T.
SPEAKING FRANKLY, MOST PEOPLE IN THIS CITY DON'T GIVE A GOOD GODDAMN ABOUT ANYONE FROM ANYWHERE.
I'M SURE OTHERS HAVE ALREADY EXPLAINED THIS TO YOU, BUT JUST IN CASE...
"...EVERY DAY HUNDREDS OF KIDS ARRIVE RIGHT DOWN THE STREET AT THE PORT AUTHORITY.
"THEY COME FROM ALL OVER--FROM PLACES WHERE THEY DIDN'T FEEL LIKE THEY FIT IN, THINKING THIS IS THE PLACE FOR THEM."

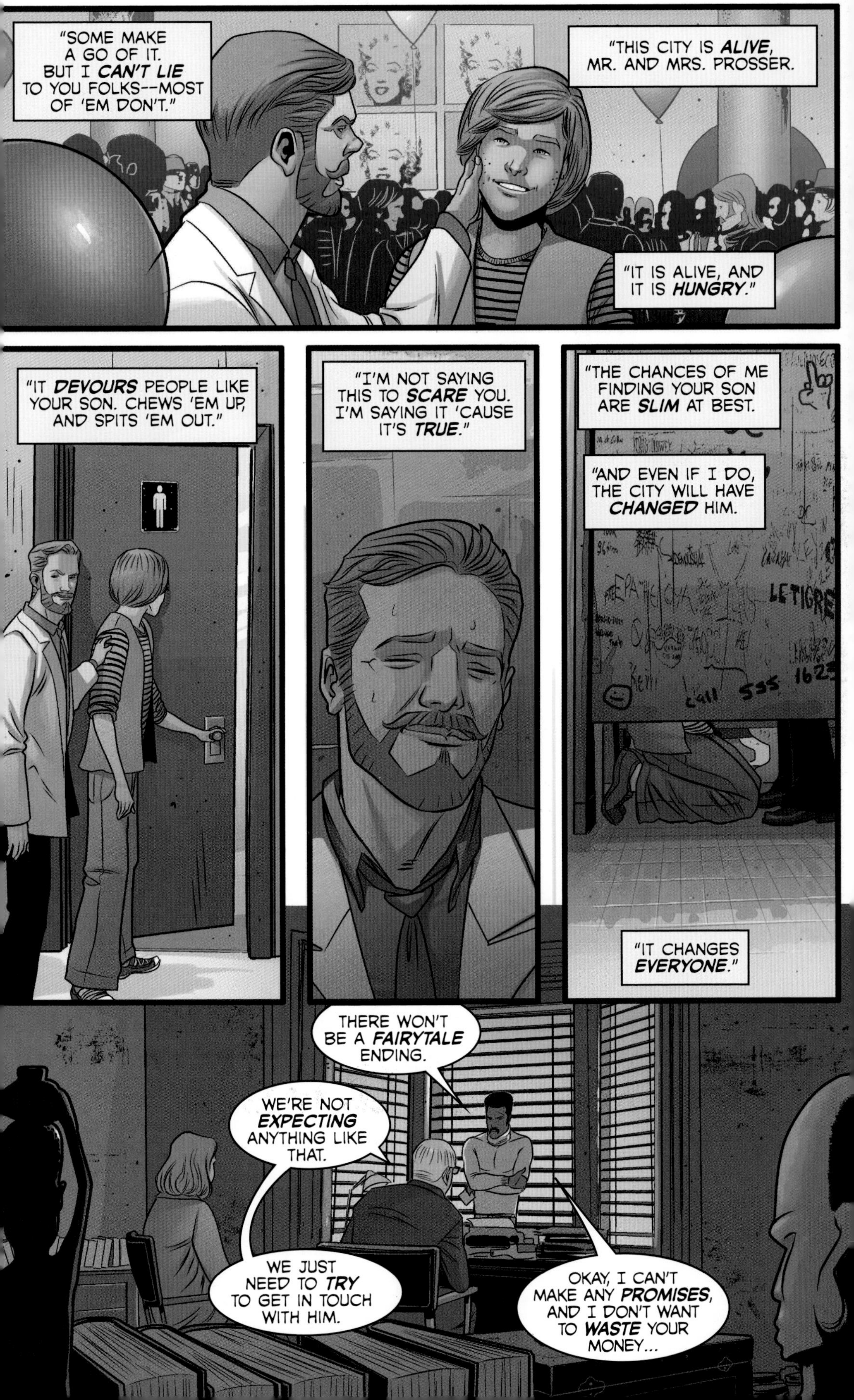
"SOME MAKE A GO OF IT. BUT I CAN'T LIE TO YOU FOLKS--MOST OF 'EM DON'T."
"THIS CITY IS ALIVE, MR. AND MRS. PROSSER.
"IT IS ALIVE, AND IT IS HUNGRY."
"IT DEVOURS PEOPLE LIKE YOUR SON. CHEWS 'EM UP, AND SPITS 'EM OUT."
"I'M NOT SAYING THIS TO SCARE YOU. I'M SAYING IT 'CAUSE IT'S TRUE."
"THE CHANCES OF ME FINDING YOUR SON ARE SLIM AT BEST.
"AND EVEN IF I DO, THE CITY WILL HAVE CHANGED HIM.
LE TIGRE
"IT CHANGES EVERYONE."
THERE WON'T BE A FAIRYTALE ENDING.
WE'RE NOT EXPECTING ANYTHING LIKE THAT.
WE JUST NEED TO TRY TO GET IN TOUCH WITH HIM.
OKAY, I CAN'T MAKE ANY PROMISES, AND I DON'T WANT TO WASTE YOUR MONEY...

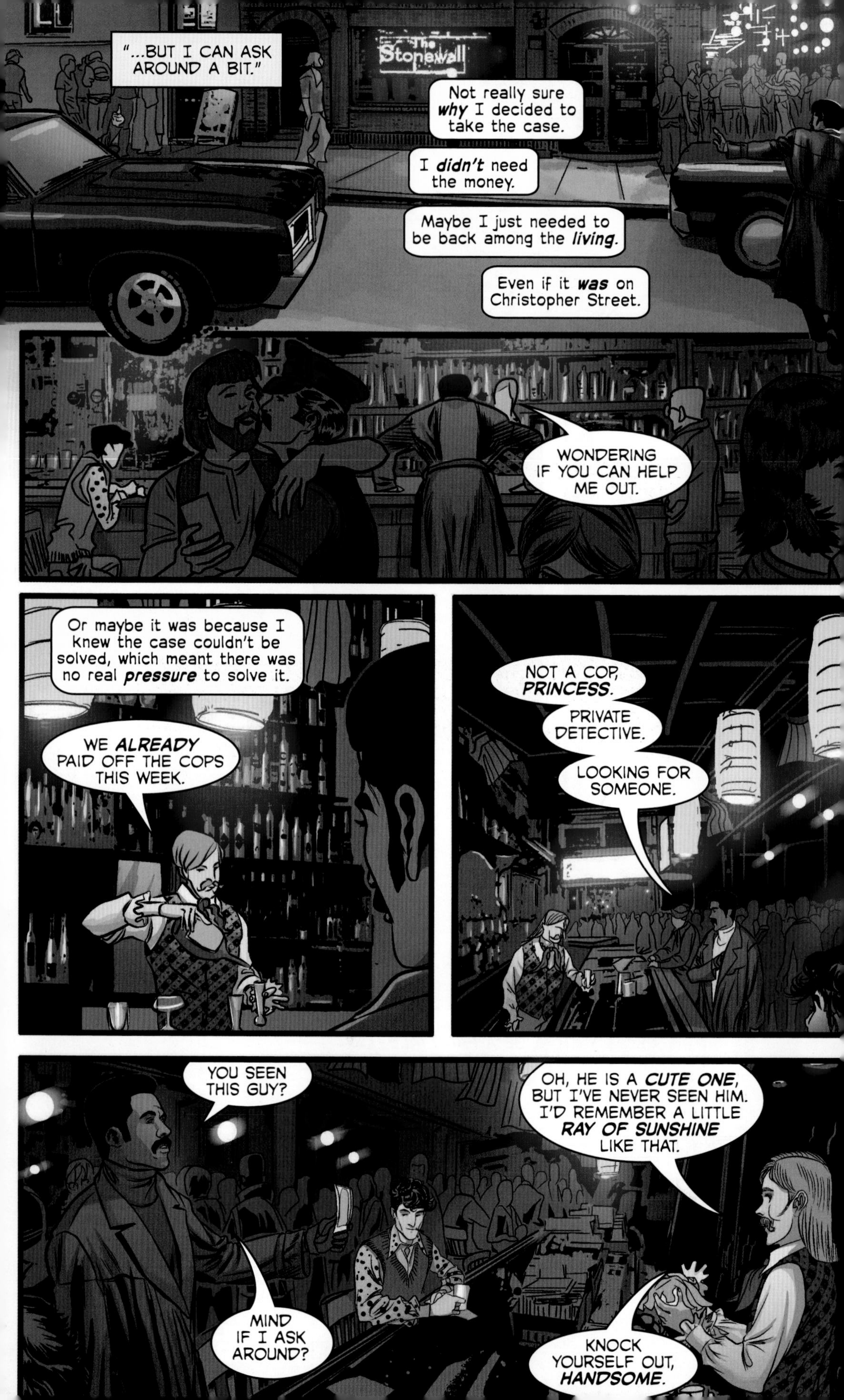
"...BUT I CAN ASK AROUND A BIT."
Stonewall
Not really sure *why* I decided to take the case.
I *didn't* need the money.
Maybe I just needed to be back among the *living.*
Even if it *was* on Christopher Street.
WONDERING IF YOU CAN HELP ME OUT.
Or maybe it was because I knew the case couldn't be solved, which meant there was no real *pressure* to solve it.
WE *ALREADY* PAID OFF THE COPS THIS WEEK.
NOT A COP, *PRINCESS.*
PRIVATE DETECTIVE.
LOOKING FOR SOMEONE.
YOU SEEN THIS GUY?
OH, HE IS A *CUTE ONE*, BUT I'VE NEVER SEEN HIM. I'D REMEMBER A LITTLE *RAY OF SUNSHINE* LIKE THAT.
MIND IF I ASK AROUND?
KNOCK YOURSELF OUT, *HANDSOME.*

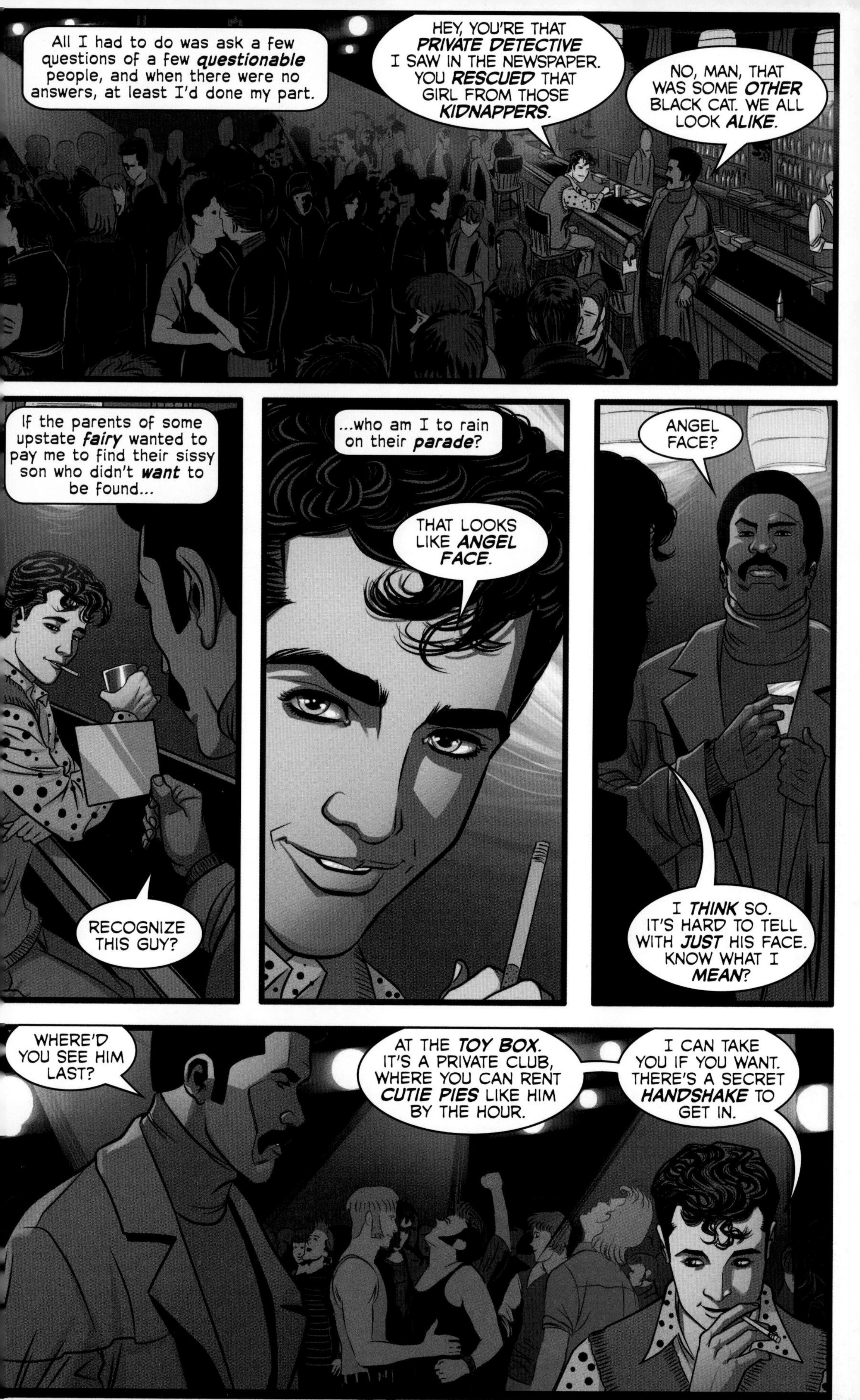
All I had to do was ask a few questions of a few questionable people, and when there were no answers, at least I'd done my part.
HEY, YOU'RE THAT PRIVATE DETECTIVE I SAW IN THE NEWSPAPER. YOU RESCUED THAT GIRL FROM THOSE KIDNAPPERS.
NO, MAN, THAT WAS SOME OTHER BLACK CAT. WE ALL LOOK ALIKE.
If the parents of some upstate fairy wanted to pay me to find their sissy son who didn't want to be found...
RECOGNIZE THIS GUY?
...who am I to rain on their parade?
THAT LOOKS LIKE ANGEL FACE.
ANGEL FACE?
I THINK SO. IT'S HARD TO TELL WITH JUST HIS FACE. KNOW WHAT I MEAN?
WHERE'D YOU SEE HIM LAST?
AT THE TOY BOX. IT'S A PRIVATE CLUB, WHERE YOU CAN RENT CUTIE PIES LIKE HIM BY THE HOUR.
I CAN TAKE YOU IF YOU WANT. THERE'S A SECRET HANDSHAKE TO GET IN.

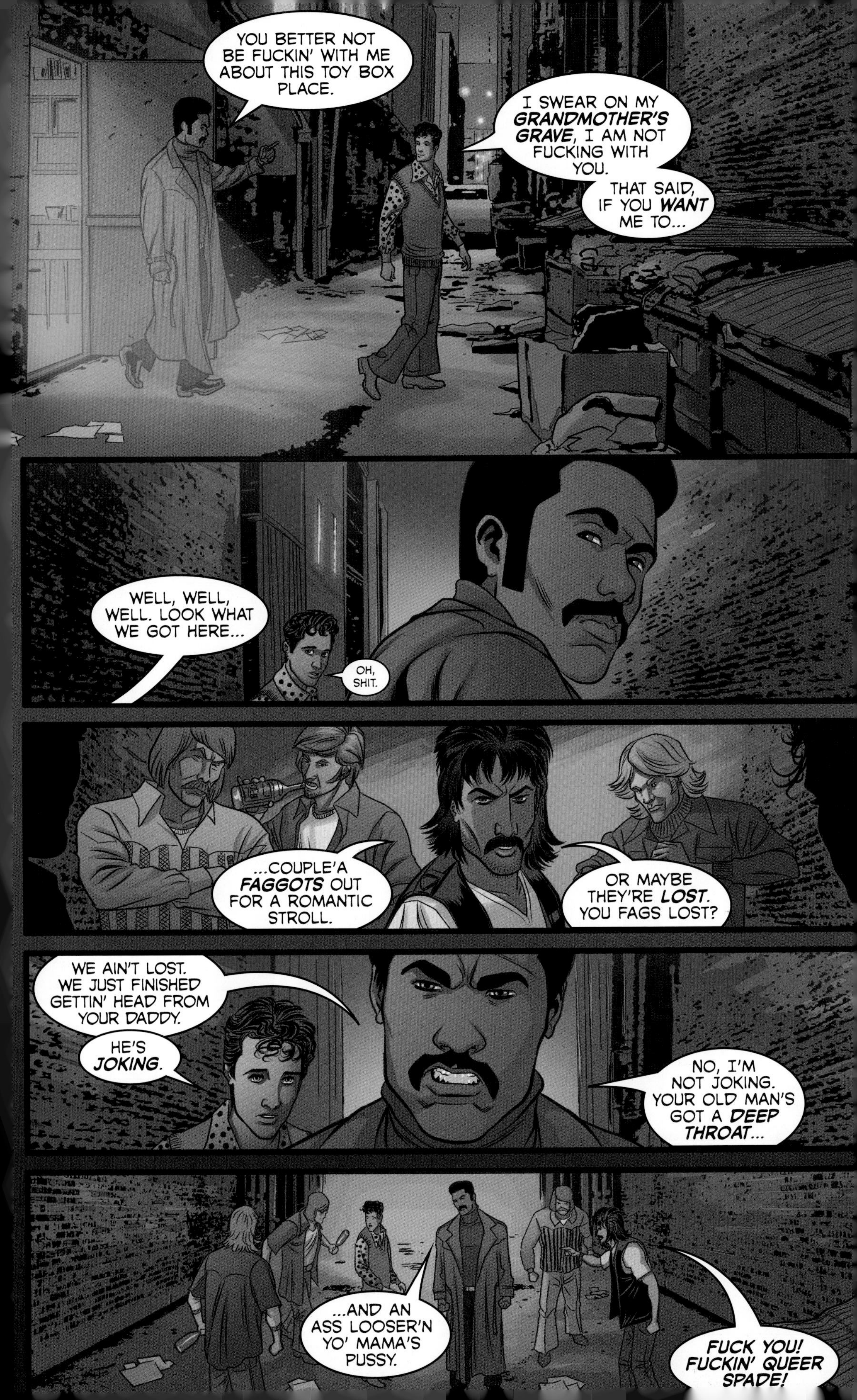
YOU BETTER NOT BE FUCKIN' WITH ME ABOUT THIS TOY BOX PLACE.
I SWEAR ON MY GRANDMOTHER'S GRAVE, I AM NOT FUCKING WITH YOU.
THAT SAID, IF YOU WANT ME TO...
WELL, WELL, WELL. LOOK WHAT WE GOT HERE...
OH, SHIT.
...COUPLE'A FAGGOTS OUT FOR A ROMANTIC STROLL.
OR MAYBE THEY'RE LOST. YOU FAGS LOST?
WE AIN'T LOST. WE JUST FINISHED GETTIN' HEAD FROM YOUR DADDY.
HE'S JOKING.
NO, I'M NOT JOKING. YOUR OLD MAN'S GOT A DEEP THROAT...
...AND AN ASS LOOSER'N YO' MAMA'S PUSSY.
FUCK YOU! FUCKIN' QUEER SPADE!

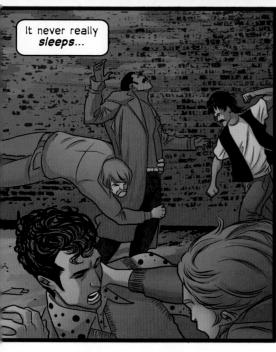

It never really *sleeps...*

...this *monster* inside of me.

It first *woke up* when I was still a kid.

It developed a *taste for blood* while I was in Vietnam.

I don't *control* it so much as I have an un*derstanding* with it.

I don't *like* the monster...

...but I understand what it *is*.

Understand its *purpose*.

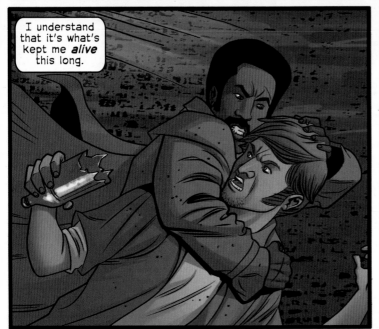

I understand that it's what's kept me *alive* this long.

It's part of *me*.

It *is* me.

And god help any sonovabitch stupid enough to get in *our* way.

YOU OKAY?

I DON'T THINK SO.

MY PLACE IS PRETTY CLOSE. I'LL GET YOU *PATCHED* UP.

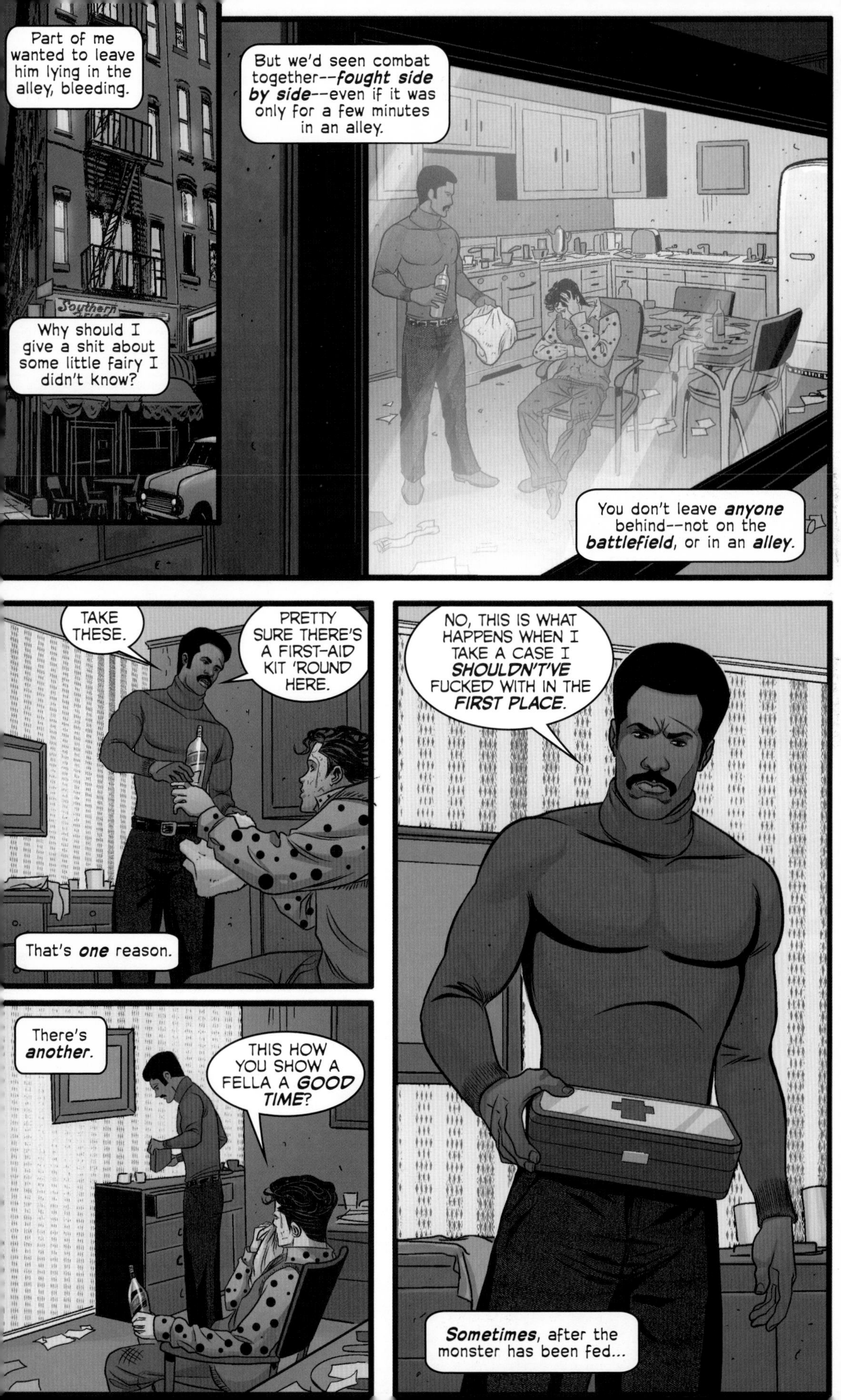

Part of me wanted to leave him lying in the alley, bleeding.
Why should I give a shit about some little fairy I didn't know?
But we'd seen combat together--*fought side by side*--even if it was only for a few minutes in an alley.
You don't leave *anyone* behind--not on the *battlefield*, or in an *alley*.
TAKE THESE.
PRETTY SURE THERE'S A FIRST-AID KIT 'ROUND HERE.
That's *one* reason.
There's *another*.
THIS HOW YOU SHOW A FELLA A *GOOD TIME*?
NO, THIS IS WHAT HAPPENS WHEN I TAKE A CASE I *SHOULDN'T'VE* FUCKED WITH IN THE *FIRST PLACE*.
Sometimes, after the monster has been fed...

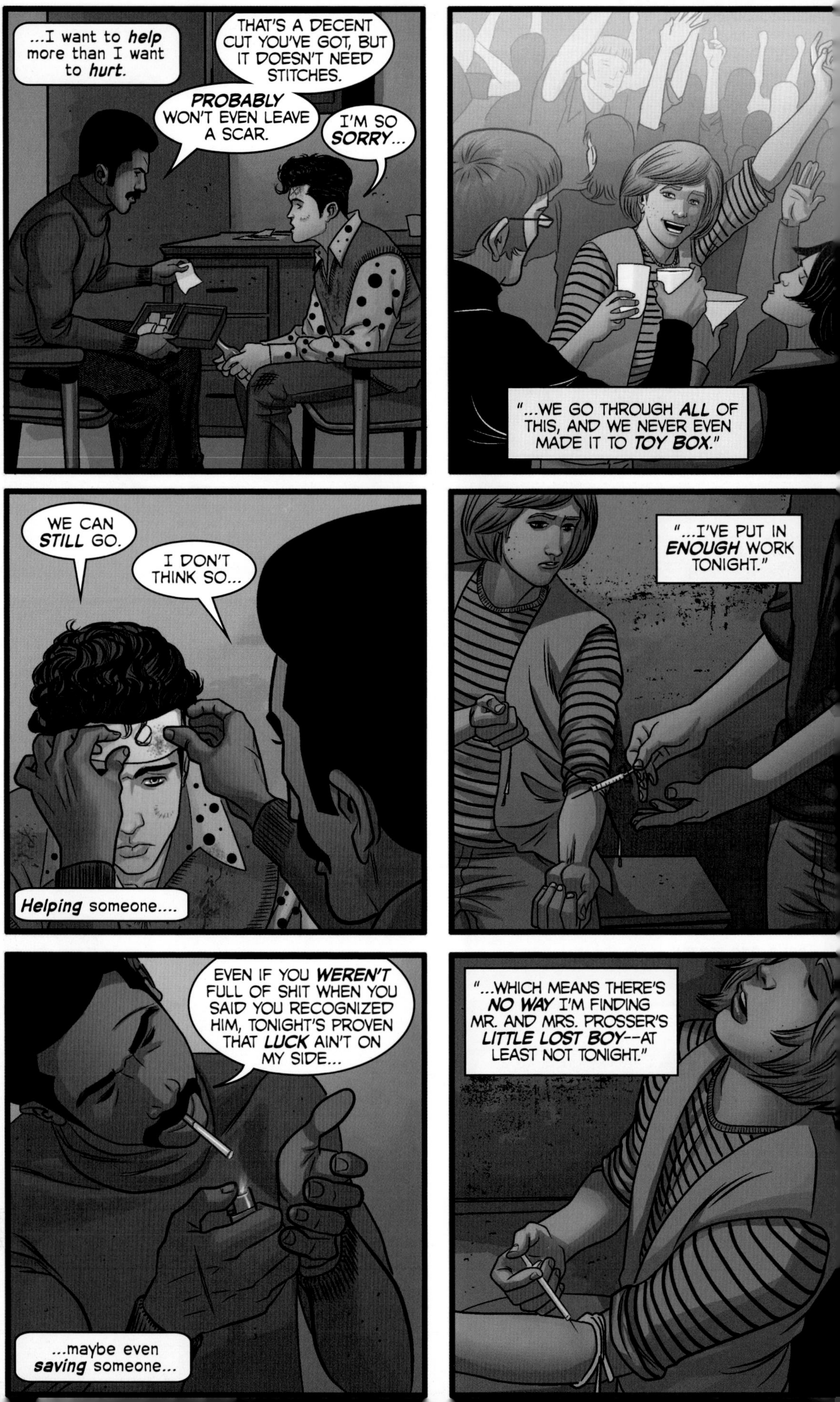
...I want to *help* more than I want to *hurt*.
THAT'S A DECENT CUT YOU'VE GOT, BUT IT DOESN'T NEED STITCHES.
PROBABLY WON'T EVEN LEAVE A SCAR.
I'M SO *SORRY*...
"...WE GO THROUGH *ALL* OF THIS, AND WE NEVER EVEN MADE IT TO *TOY BOX*."
WE CAN *STILL* GO.
I DON'T THINK SO...
Helping someone....
"...I'VE PUT IN *ENOUGH* WORK TONIGHT."
EVEN IF YOU *WEREN'T* FULL OF SHIT WHEN YOU SAID YOU RECOGNIZED HIM, TONIGHT'S PROVEN THAT *LUCK* AIN'T ON MY SIDE...
...maybe even *saving* someone...
"...WHICH MEANS THERE'S *NO WAY* I'M FINDING MR. AND MRS. PROSSER'S *LITTLE LOST BOY*--AT LEAST NOT TONIGHT."

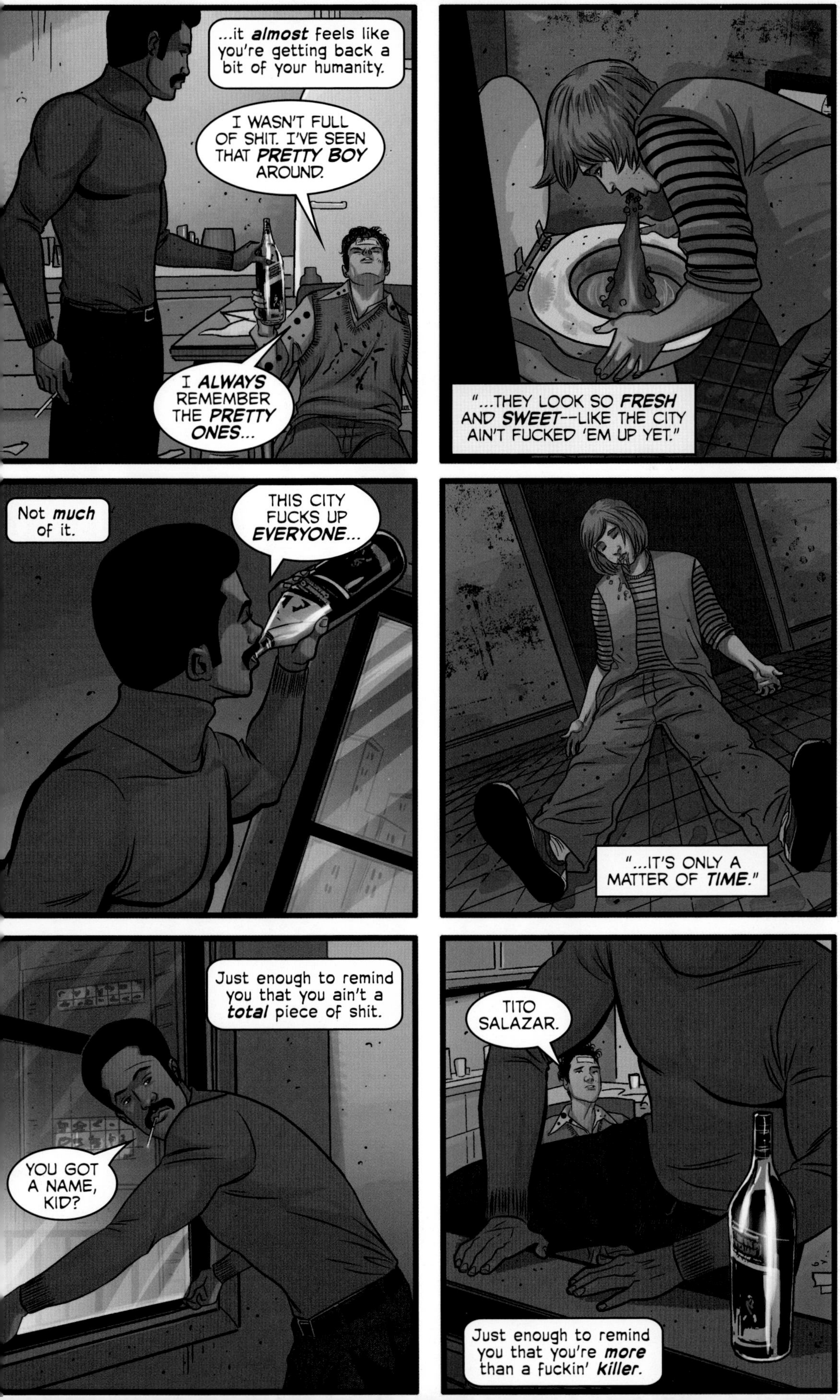
...it almost feels like you're getting back a bit of your humanity.
I WASN'T FULL OF SHIT. I'VE SEEN THAT PRETTY BOY AROUND.
I ALWAYS REMEMBER THE PRETTY ONES...
"...THEY LOOK SO FRESH AND SWEET--LIKE THE CITY AIN'T FUCKED 'EM UP YET."
Not much of it.
THIS CITY FUCKS UP EVERYONE...
"...IT'S ONLY A MATTER OF TIME."
Just enough to remind you that you ain't a total piece of shit.
YOU GOT A NAME, KID?
TITO SALAZAR.
Just enough to remind you that you're more than a fuckin' killer.

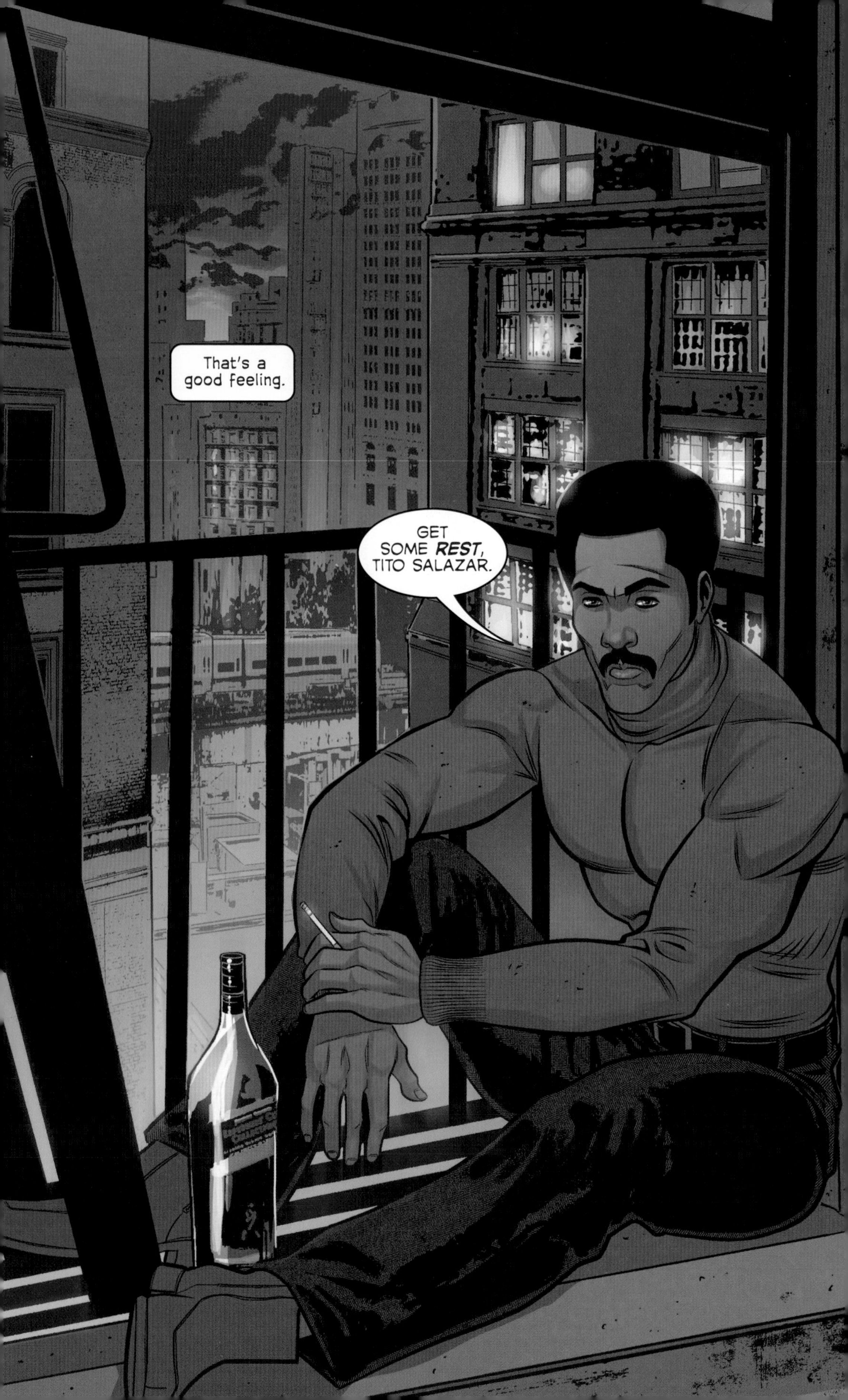
That's a good feeling.
GET SOME REST, TITO SALAZAR.

DAVID F. WALKER • DIETRICH SMITH

SHAFT

IMITATION OF LIFE

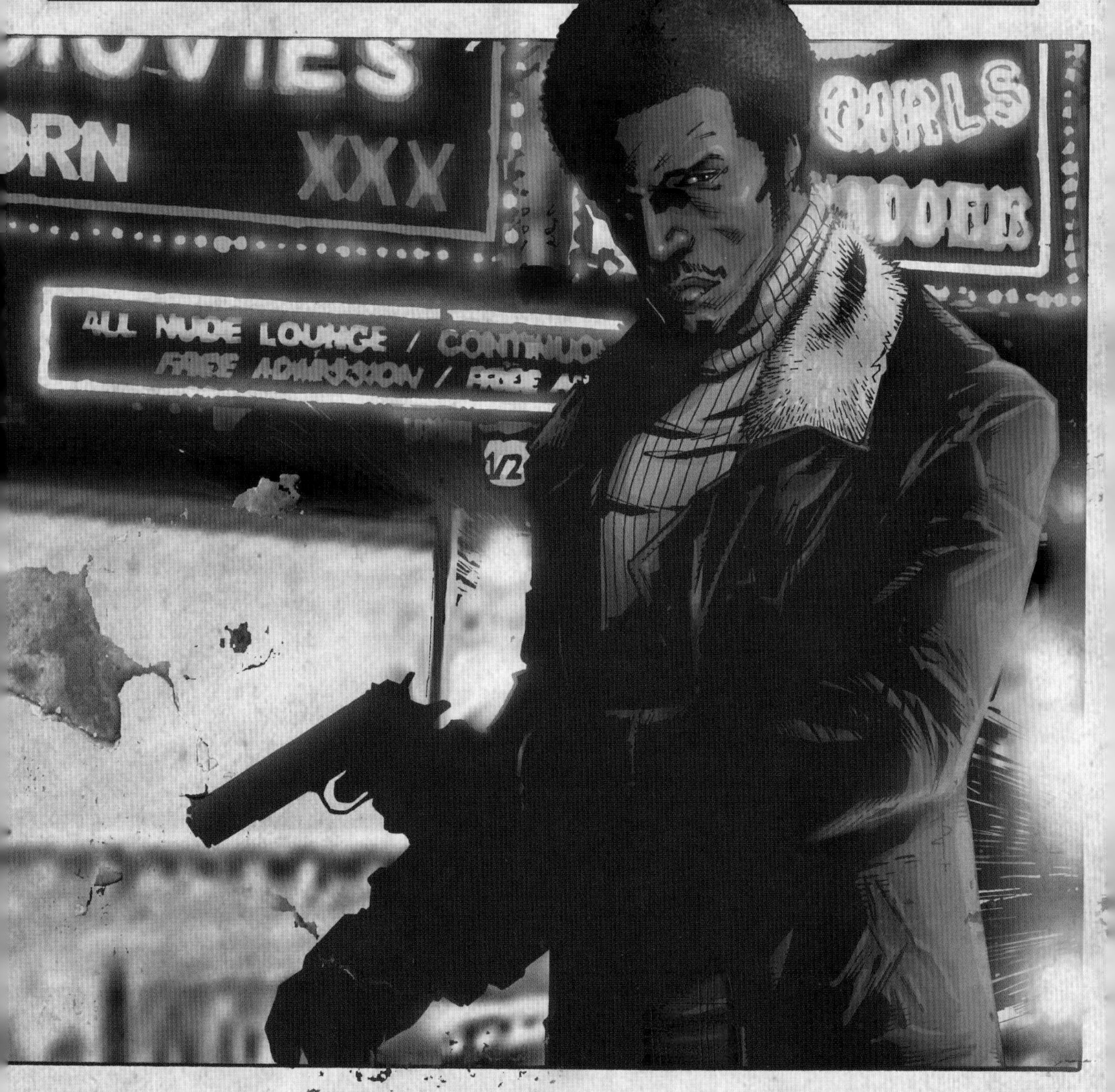
XXX
ALL NUDE LOUNGE /
FREE ADMISSION /
1/2

Part Two: EASY MONEY

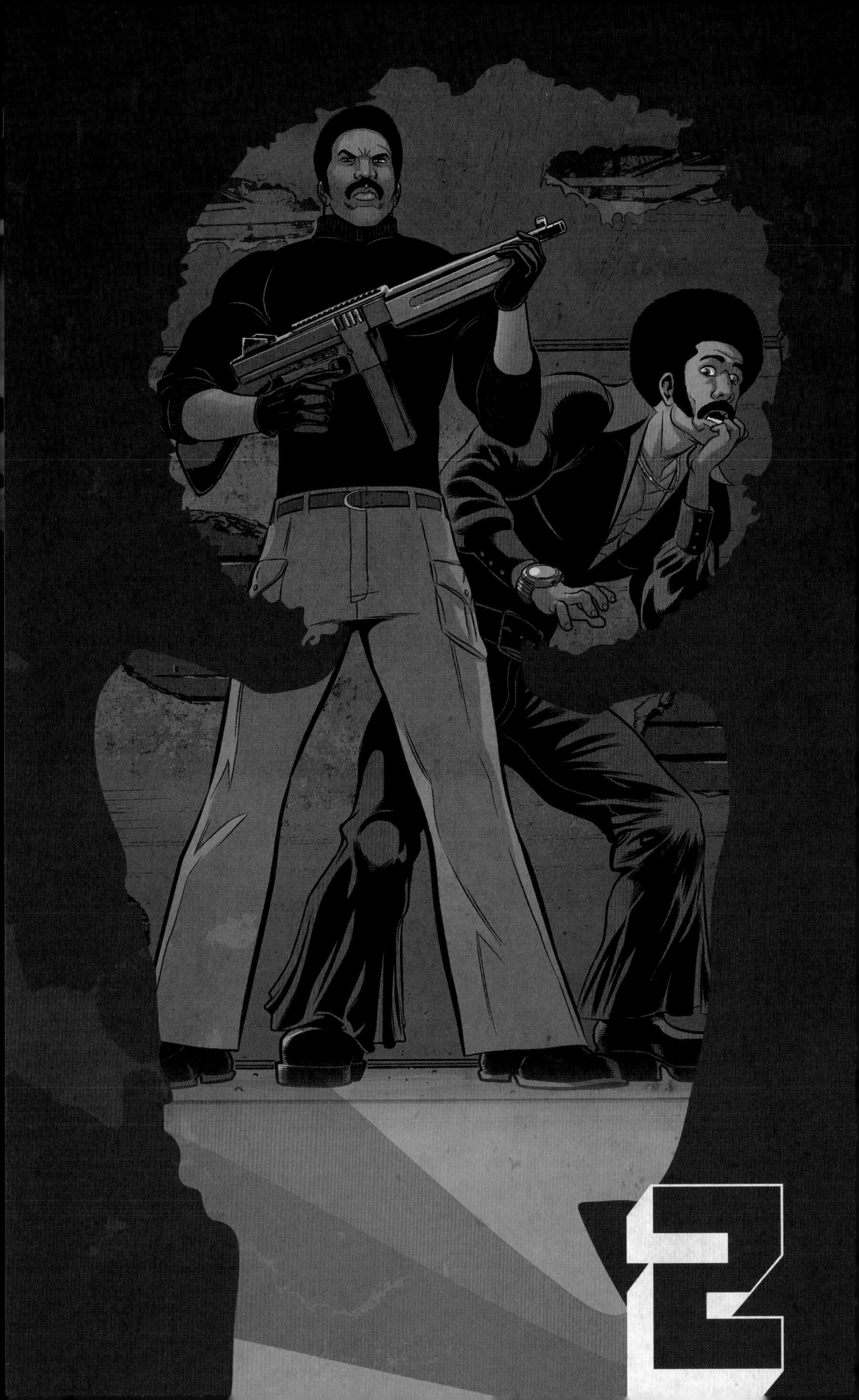
2

My name is John Shaft.

I'm a private investigator.

Most of my cases are *boring*.

Divorces. Insurance claims. Crap like that.

Easy money.

I NEED YOU TO *FOCUS*. HEAR ME?

I...I DON'T THINK...

Had a few high profile cases that made headlines, but really, it's mostly boring stuff.

But every once in a while...

DIDN'T TELL YOU TO *THINK*, MOTHERFUCKER. I TOLD YOU TO *FOCUS*.

I...I... *CAN'T*...

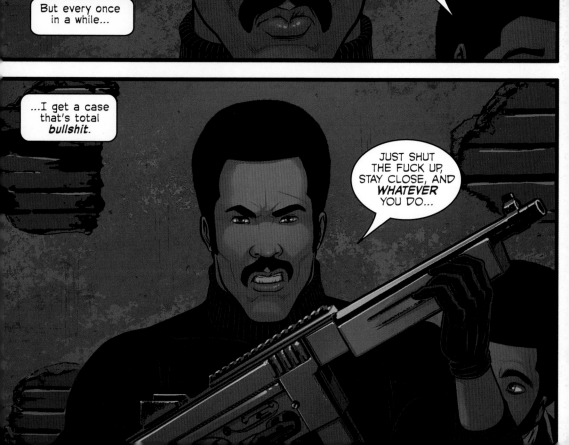

...I get a case that's total *bullshit*.

JUST SHUT THE FUCK UP, STAY CLOSE, AND *WHATEVER* YOU DO...

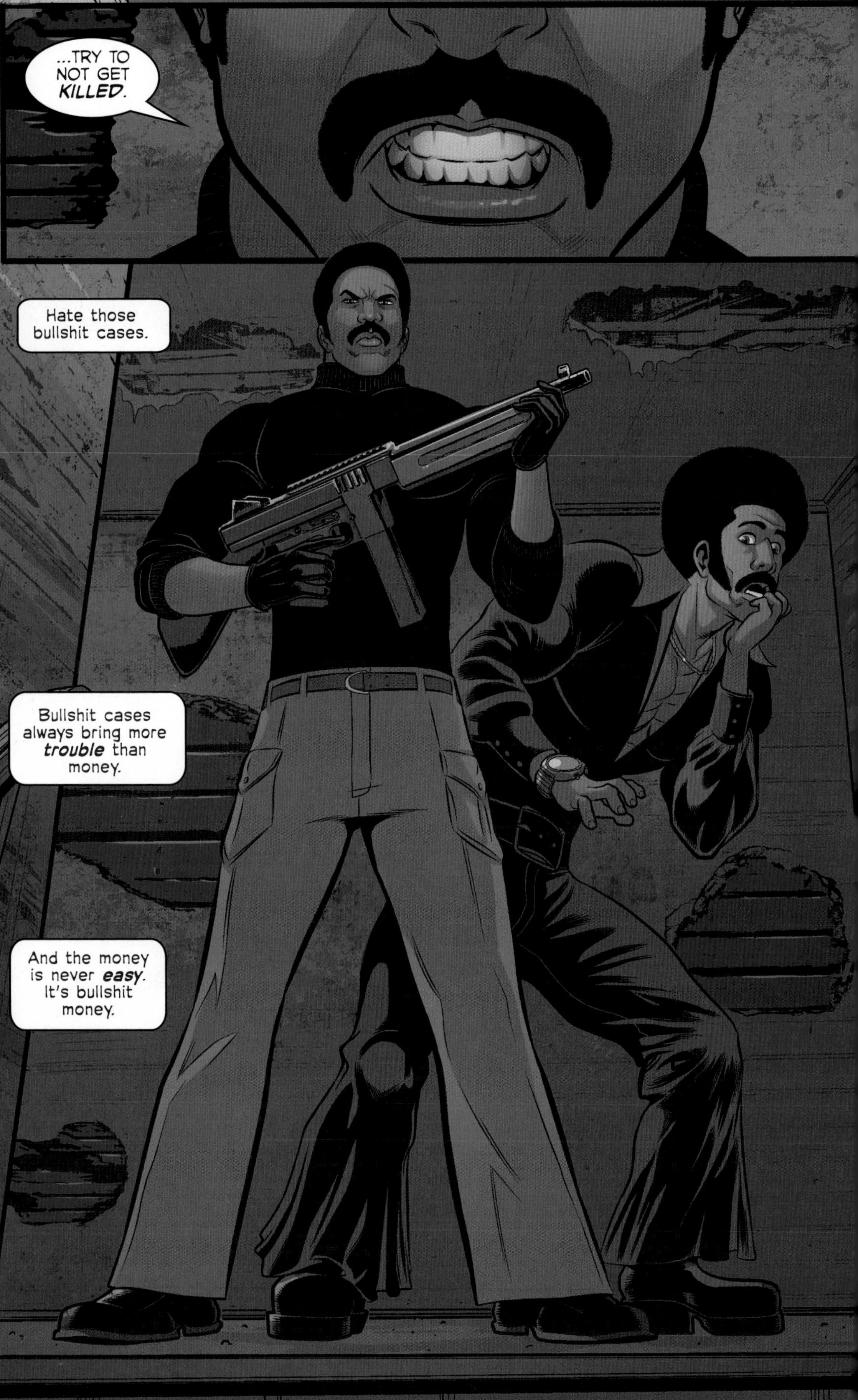
...TRY TO NOT GET *KILLED*.
Hate those bullshit cases.
Bullshit cases always bring more *trouble* than money.
And the money is never *easy*. It's bullshit money.

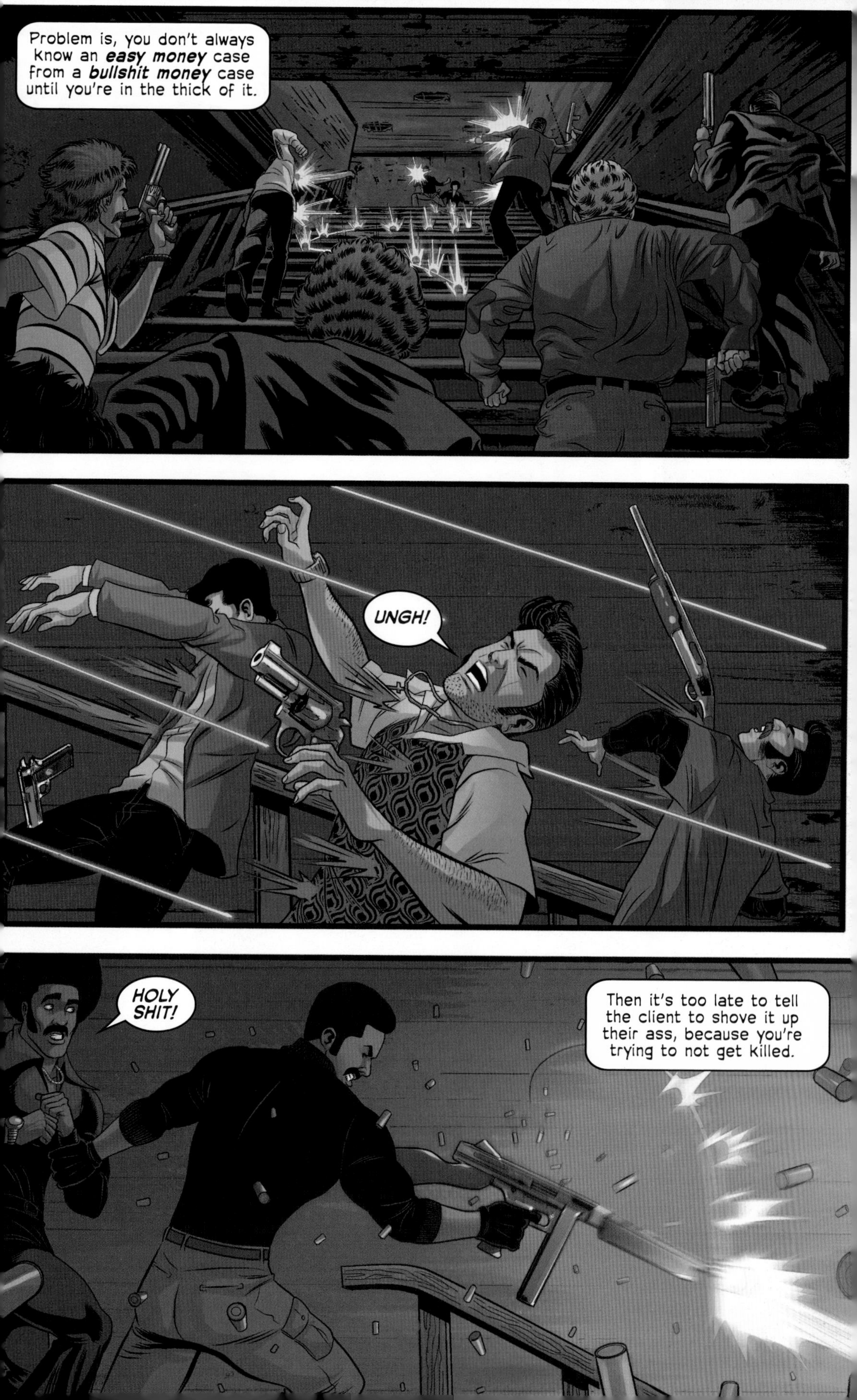
Problem is, you don't always know an ***easy money*** case from a ***bullshit money*** case until you're in the thick of it.
UNGH!
HOLY SHIT!
Then it's too late to tell the client to shove it up their ass, because you're trying to not get killed.

THREE WEEKS EARLIER...

1107

JOHN SHAFT
PRIVATE INVESTIGATOR

"YOU WANT ME TO BE *WHAT*?"

"WE WANT YOU TO BE A *SUPER BAD MOTHER*."

EXACTLY WHAT IS A *SUPER BAD MOTHER*?

C'MON, *BROTHER*. YOU *KNOW* WHAT I MEAN.

HONEE, SHOW HIM, PLEASE.

I *LOVE* THE PICTURES OF YOU INSIDE.

NUBIAN

John Shaft harlem hero

A Nubian Cutie every month

12 Full Color Photographs

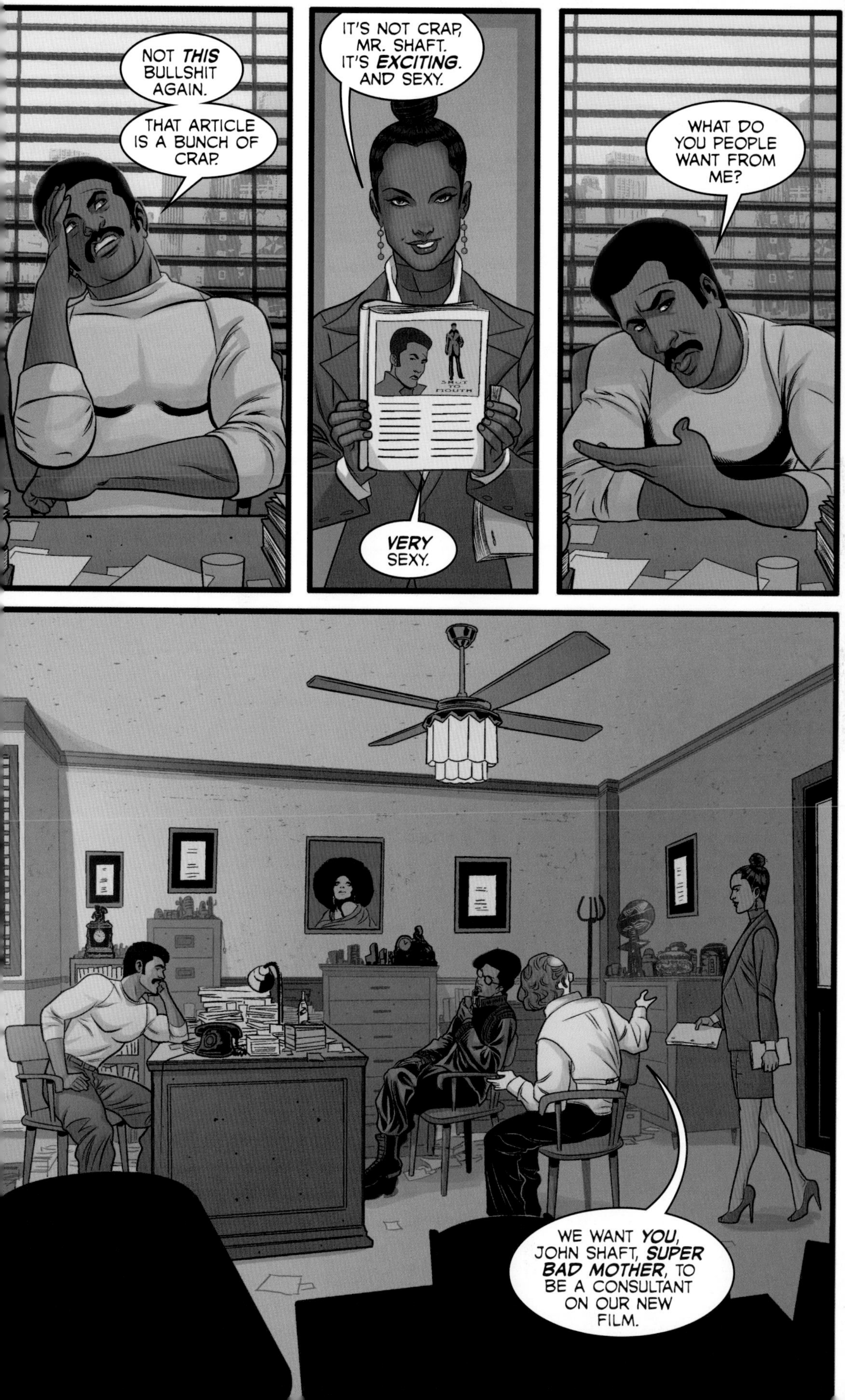

NOT THIS BULLSHIT AGAIN.
THAT ARTICLE IS A BUNCH OF CRAP.
IT'S NOT CRAP, MR. SHAFT. IT'S EXCITING. AND SEXY.
VERY SEXY.
WHAT DO YOU PEOPLE WANT FROM ME?
WE WANT YOU, JOHN SHAFT, SUPER BAD MOTHER, TO BE A CONSULTANT ON OUR NEW FILM.

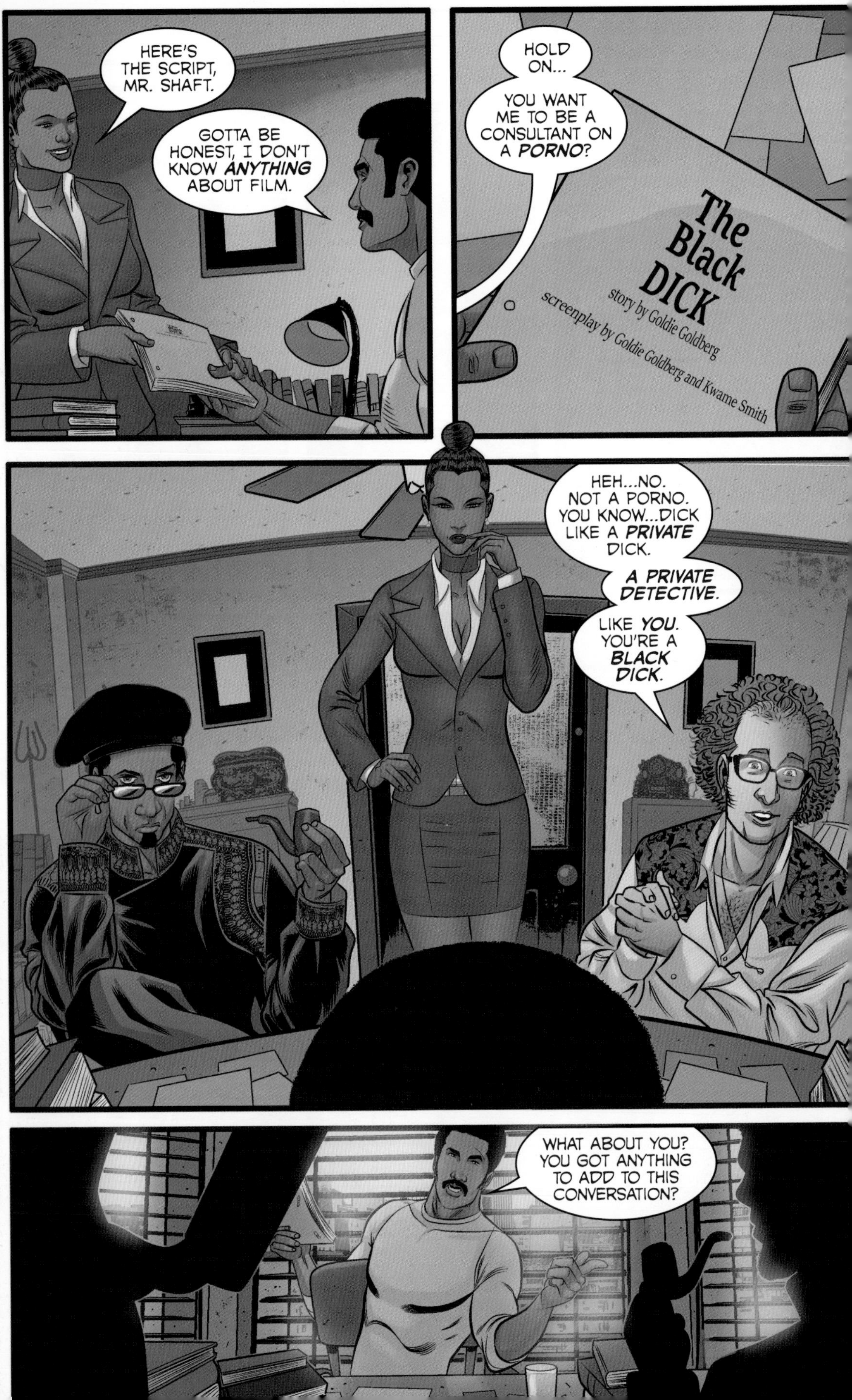
HERE'S THE SCRIPT, MR. SHAFT.
GOTTA BE HONEST, I DON'T KNOW ANYTHING ABOUT FILM.
HOLD ON...
YOU WANT ME TO BE A CONSULTANT ON A PORNO?
The Black DICK
story by Goldie Goldberg
screenplay by Goldie Goldberg and Kwame Smith
HEH...NO. NOT A PORNO. YOU KNOW...DICK LIKE A PRIVATE DICK.
A PRIVATE DETECTIVE.
LIKE YOU. YOU'RE A BLACK DICK.
WHAT ABOUT YOU? YOU GOT ANYTHING TO ADD TO THIS CONVERSATION?

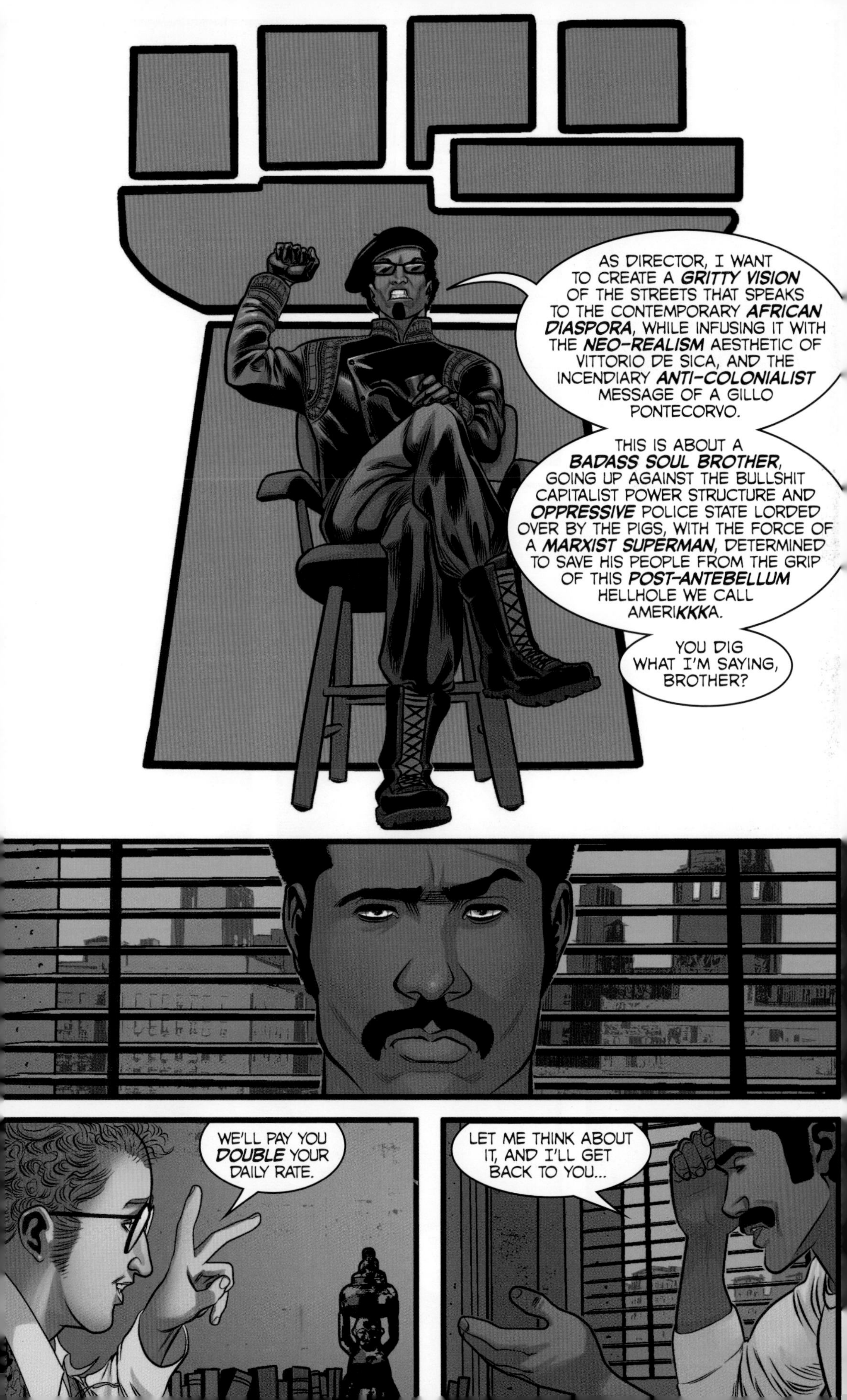
AS DIRECTOR, I WANT TO CREATE A GRITTY VISION OF THE STREETS THAT SPEAKS TO THE CONTEMPORARY AFRICAN DIASPORA, WHILE INFUSING IT WITH THE NEO-REALISM AESTHETIC OF VITTORIO DE SICA, AND THE INCENDIARY ANTI-COLONIALIST MESSAGE OF A GILLO PONTECORVO.
THIS IS ABOUT A BADASS SOUL BROTHER, GOING UP AGAINST THE BULLSHIT CAPITALIST POWER STRUCTURE AND OPPRESSIVE POLICE STATE LORDED OVER BY THE PIGS, WITH THE FORCE OF A MARXIST SUPERMAN, DETERMINED TO SAVE HIS PEOPLE FROM THE GRIP OF THIS POST-ANTEBELLUM HELLHOLE WE CALL AMERIKKKA.
YOU DIG WHAT I'M SAYING, BROTHER?
WE'LL PAY YOU DOUBLE YOUR DAILY RATE.
LET ME THINK ABOUT IT, AND I'LL GET BACK TO YOU...

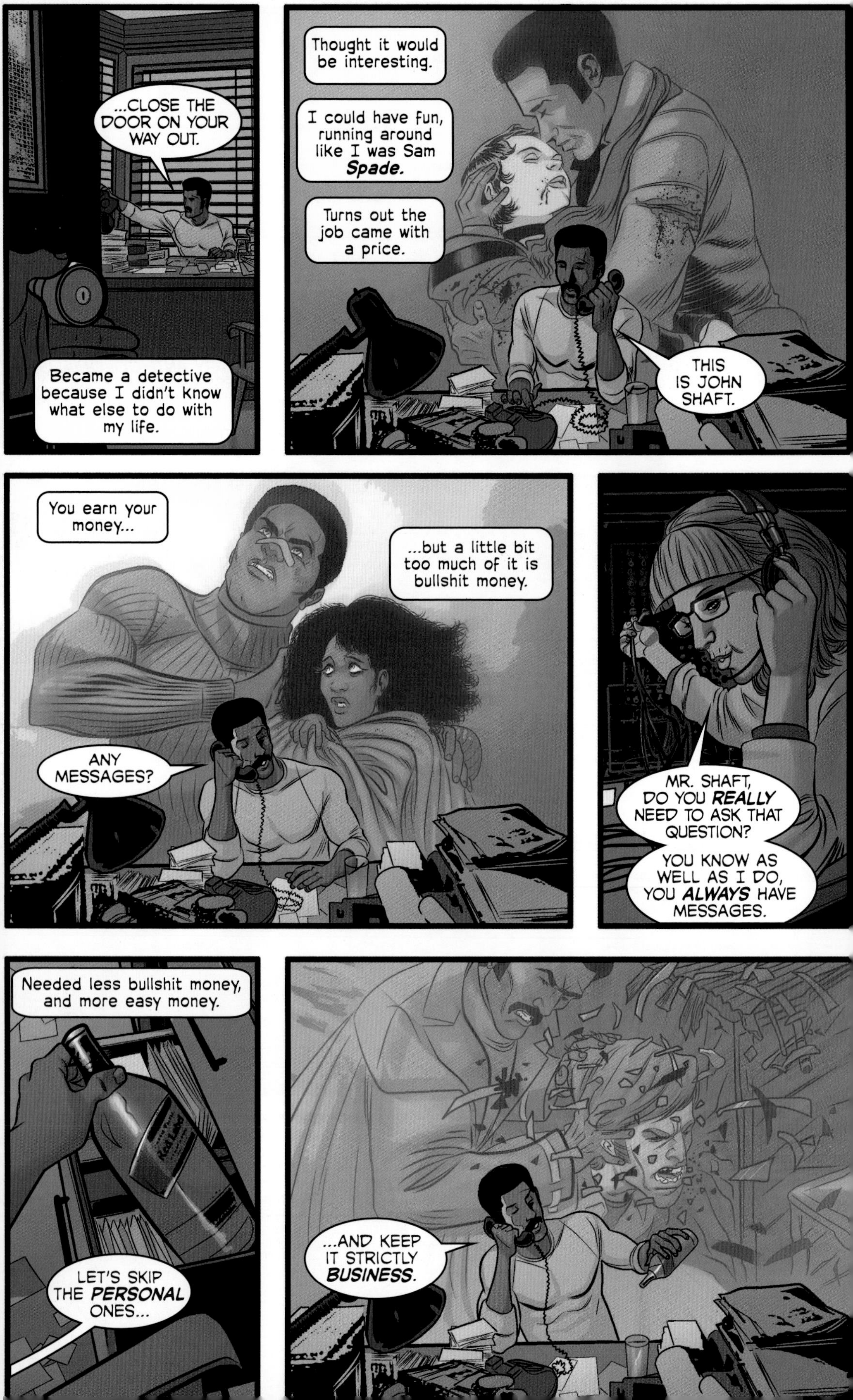
...CLOSE THE DOOR ON YOUR WAY OUT.
Became a detective because I didn't know what else to do with my life.
Thought it would be interesting.
I could have fun, running around like I was Sam *Spade.*
Turns out the job came with a price.
THIS IS JOHN SHAFT.
You earn your money...
...but a little bit too much of it is bullshit money.
ANY MESSAGES?
MR. SHAFT, DO YOU *REALLY* NEED TO ASK THAT QUESTION?
YOU KNOW AS WELL AS I DO, YOU *ALWAYS* HAVE MESSAGES.
Needed less bullshit money, and more easy money.
LET'S SKIP THE *PERSONAL* ONES...
...AND KEEP IT STRICTLY *BUSINESS*.

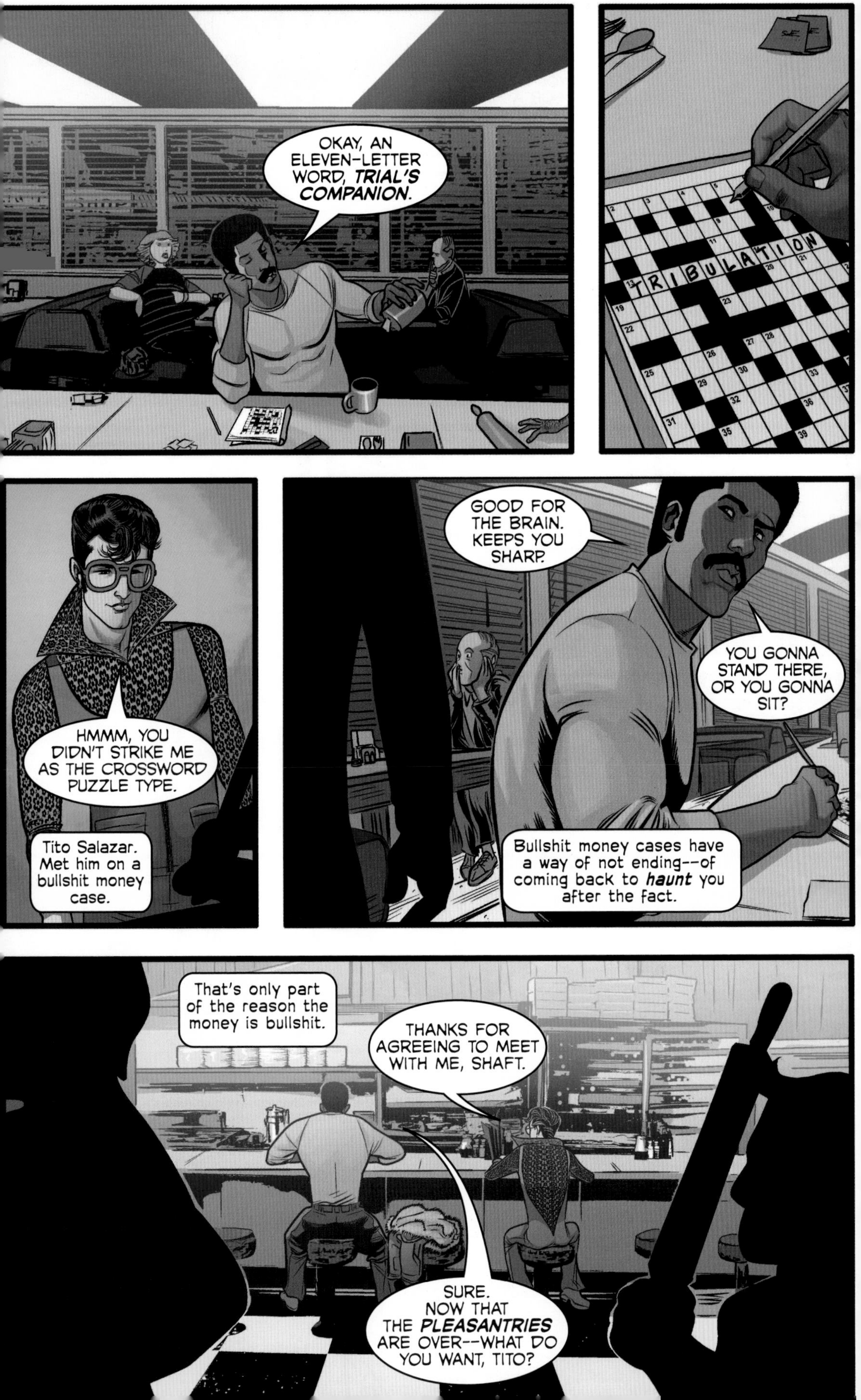
OKAY, AN ELEVEN-LETTER WORD, *TRIAL'S COMPANION*.
TRIBULATION
HMMM, YOU DIDN'T STRIKE ME AS THE CROSSWORD PUZZLE TYPE.
Tito Salazar. Met him on a bullshit money case.
GOOD FOR THE BRAIN. KEEPS YOU SHARP.
YOU GONNA STAND THERE, OR YOU GONNA SIT?
Bullshit money cases have a way of not ending--of coming back to *haunt* you after the fact.
That's only part of the reason the money is bullshit.
THANKS FOR AGREEING TO MEET WITH ME, SHAFT.
SURE. NOW THAT THE *PLEASANTRIES* ARE OVER--WHAT DO YOU WANT, TITO?

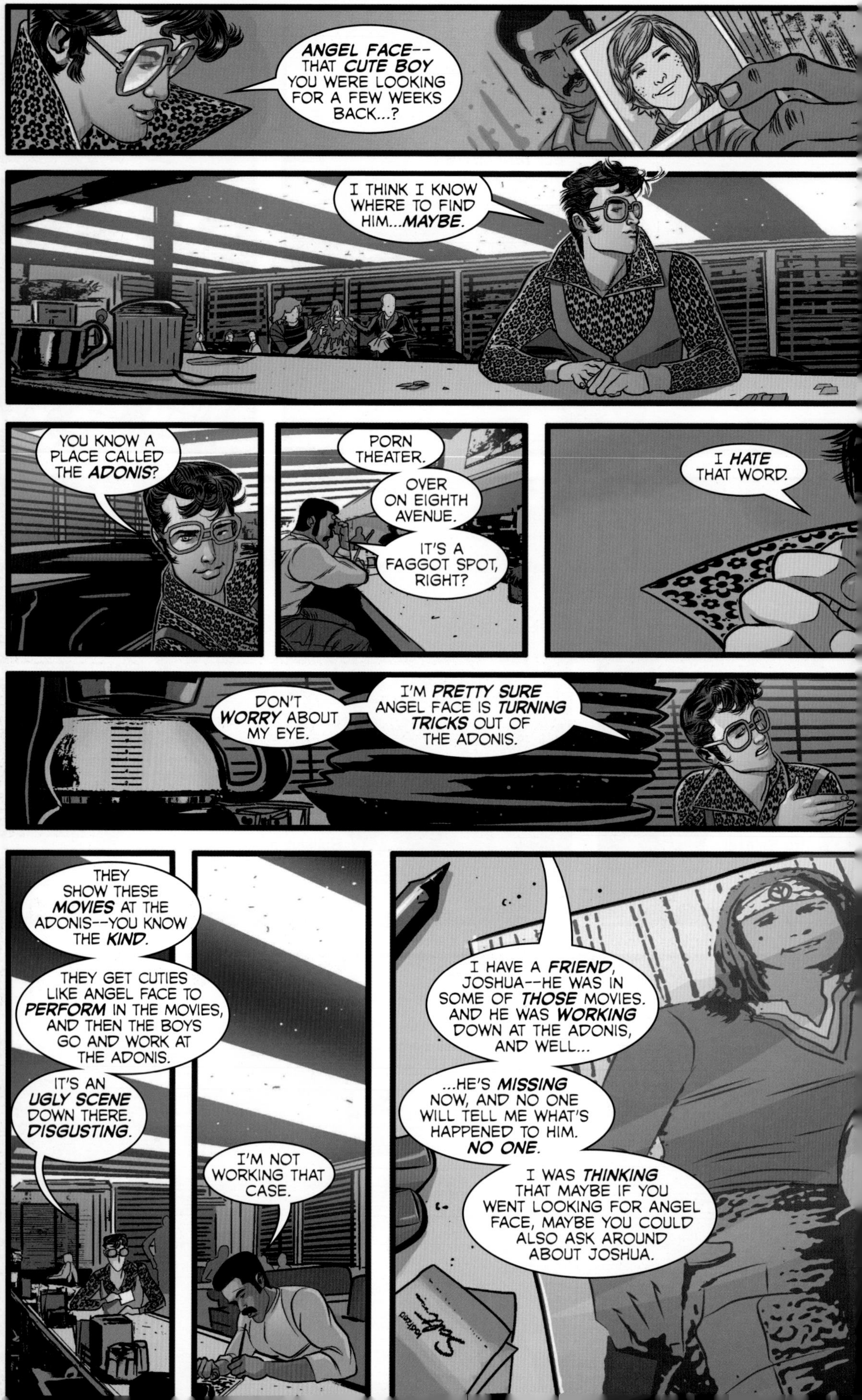
ANGEL FACE-- THAT CUTE BOY YOU WERE LOOKING FOR A FEW WEEKS BACK...?
I THINK I KNOW WHERE TO FIND HIM...MAYBE.
YOU KNOW A PLACE CALLED THE ADONIS?
PORN THEATER.
OVER ON EIGHTH AVENUE.
IT'S A FAGGOT SPOT, RIGHT?
I HATE THAT WORD.
DON'T WORRY ABOUT MY EYE.
I'M PRETTY SURE ANGEL FACE IS TURNING TRICKS OUT OF THE ADONIS.
THEY SHOW THESE MOVIES AT THE ADONIS--YOU KNOW THE KIND.
THEY GET CUTIES LIKE ANGEL FACE TO PERFORM IN THE MOVIES, AND THEN THE BOYS GO AND WORK AT THE ADONIS.
IT'S AN UGLY SCENE DOWN THERE. DISGUSTING.
I'M NOT WORKING THAT CASE.
I HAVE A FRIEND, JOSHUA--HE WAS IN SOME OF THOSE MOVIES. AND HE WAS WORKING DOWN AT THE ADONIS, AND WELL...
...HE'S MISSING NOW, AND NO ONE WILL TELL ME WHAT'S HAPPENED TO HIM. NO ONE.
I WAS THINKING THAT MAYBE IF YOU WENT LOOKING FOR ANGEL FACE, MAYBE YOU COULD ALSO ASK AROUND ABOUT JOSHUA.

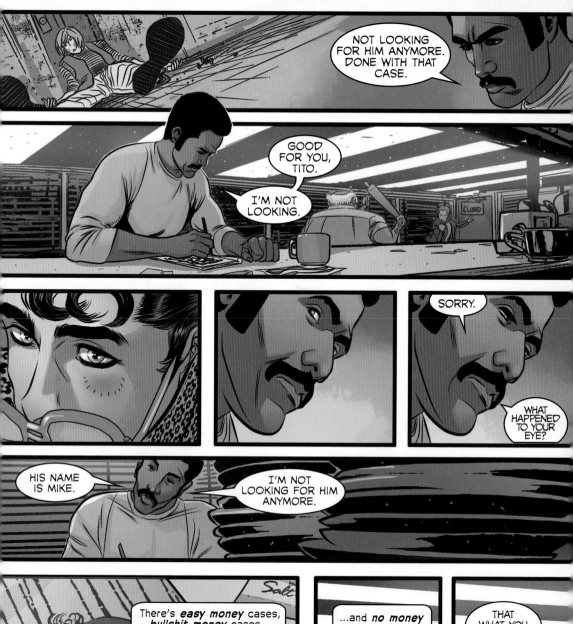

NOT LOOKING FOR HIM ANYMORE. DONE WITH THAT CASE.

GOOD FOR YOU, TITO.

I'M NOT LOOKING.

SORRY.

WHAT HAPPENED TO YOUR EYE?

HIS NAME IS MIKE.

I'M NOT LOOKING FOR HIM ANYMORE.

There's *easy money* cases, *bullshit money* cases...

...and *no money* cases.

THAT WHAT YOU THOUGHT?

Never take a no money case...

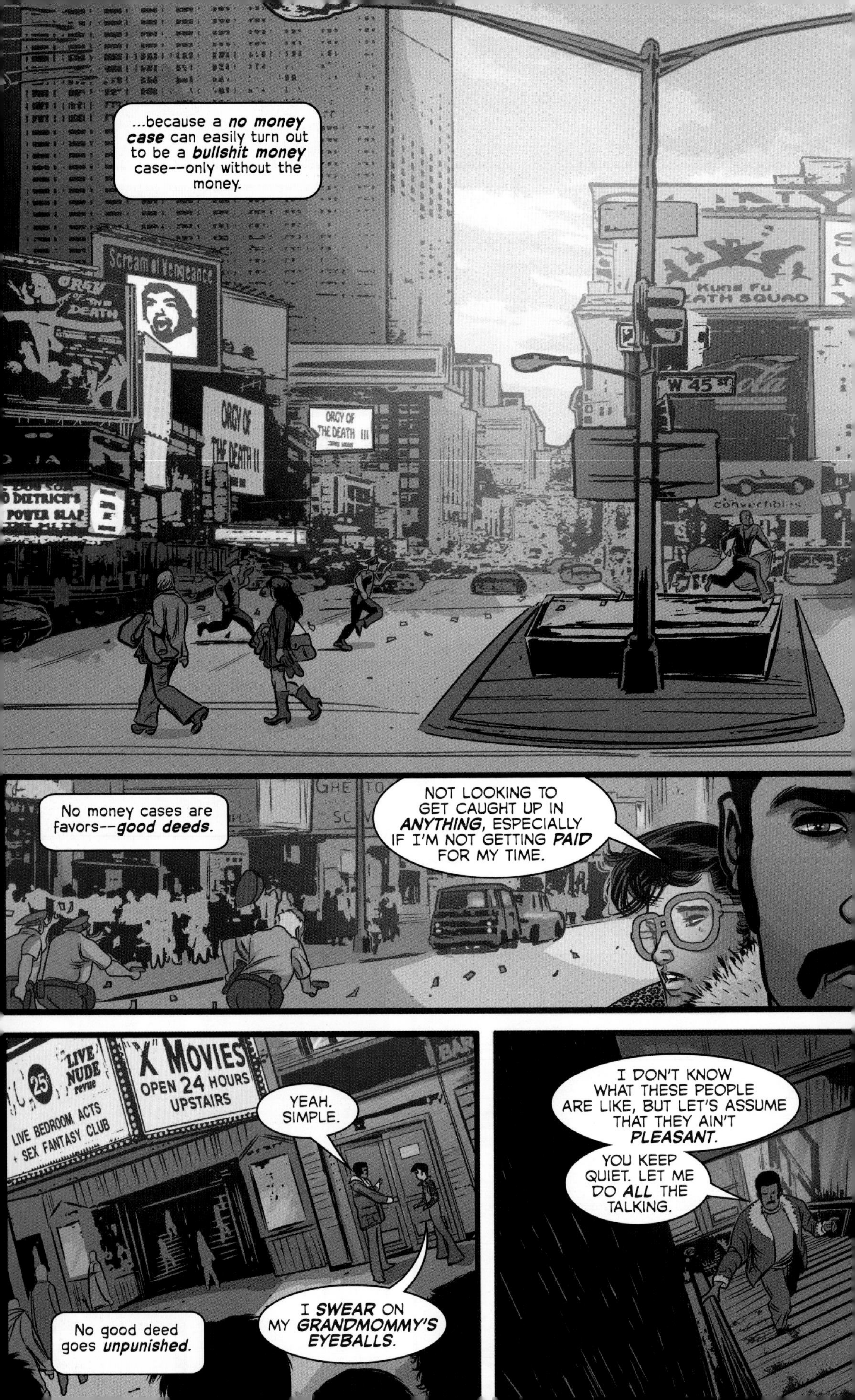
...because a ***no money case*** can easily turn out to be a ***bullshit money*** case--only without the money.
Scream of Vengeance
ORGY OF THE DEATH
ORGY OF THE DEATH II
ORGY OF THE DEATH III
Kung Fu DEATH SQUAD
W 45 St
No money cases are favors--***good deeds.***
NOT LOOKING TO GET CAUGHT UP IN ***ANYTHING***, ESPECIALLY IF I'M NOT GETTING ***PAID*** FOR MY TIME.
25¢
LIVE NUDE revue
LIVE BEDROOM ACTS • SEX FANTASY CLUB
X MOVIES OPEN 24 HOURS UPSTAIRS
YEAH. SIMPLE.
I ***SWEAR*** ON MY ***GRANDMOMMY'S EYEBALLS.***
No good deed goes ***unpunished.***
I DON'T KNOW WHAT THESE PEOPLE ARE LIKE, BUT LET'S ASSUME THAT THEY AIN'T ***PLEASANT***.
YOU KEEP QUIET. LET ME DO ***ALL*** THE TALKING.

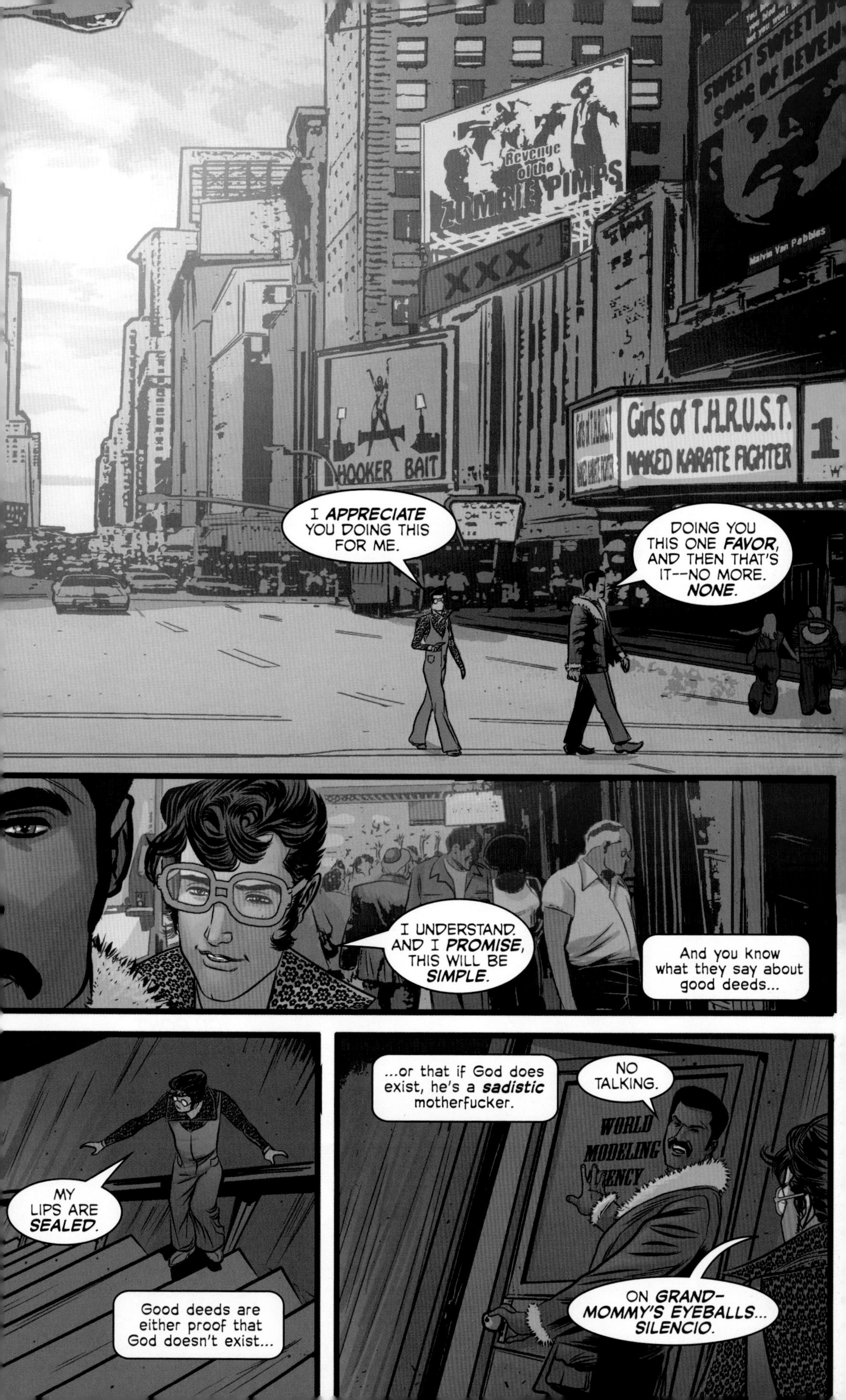
Revenge of the
ZOMBIE PIMPS
XXX
HOOKER BAIT
Girls of T.H.R.U.S.T.
NAKED KARATE FIGHTER
I APPRECIATE YOU DOING THIS FOR ME.
DOING YOU THIS ONE FAVOR, AND THEN THAT'S IT--NO MORE. NONE.
I UNDERSTAND. AND I PROMISE, THIS WILL BE SIMPLE.
And you know what they say about good deeds...
MY LIPS ARE SEALED.
Good deeds are either proof that God doesn't exist...
...or that if God does exist, he's a sadistic motherfucker.
NO TALKING.
WORLD
MODELING
ON GRAND-MOMMY'S EYEBALLS... SILENCIO.

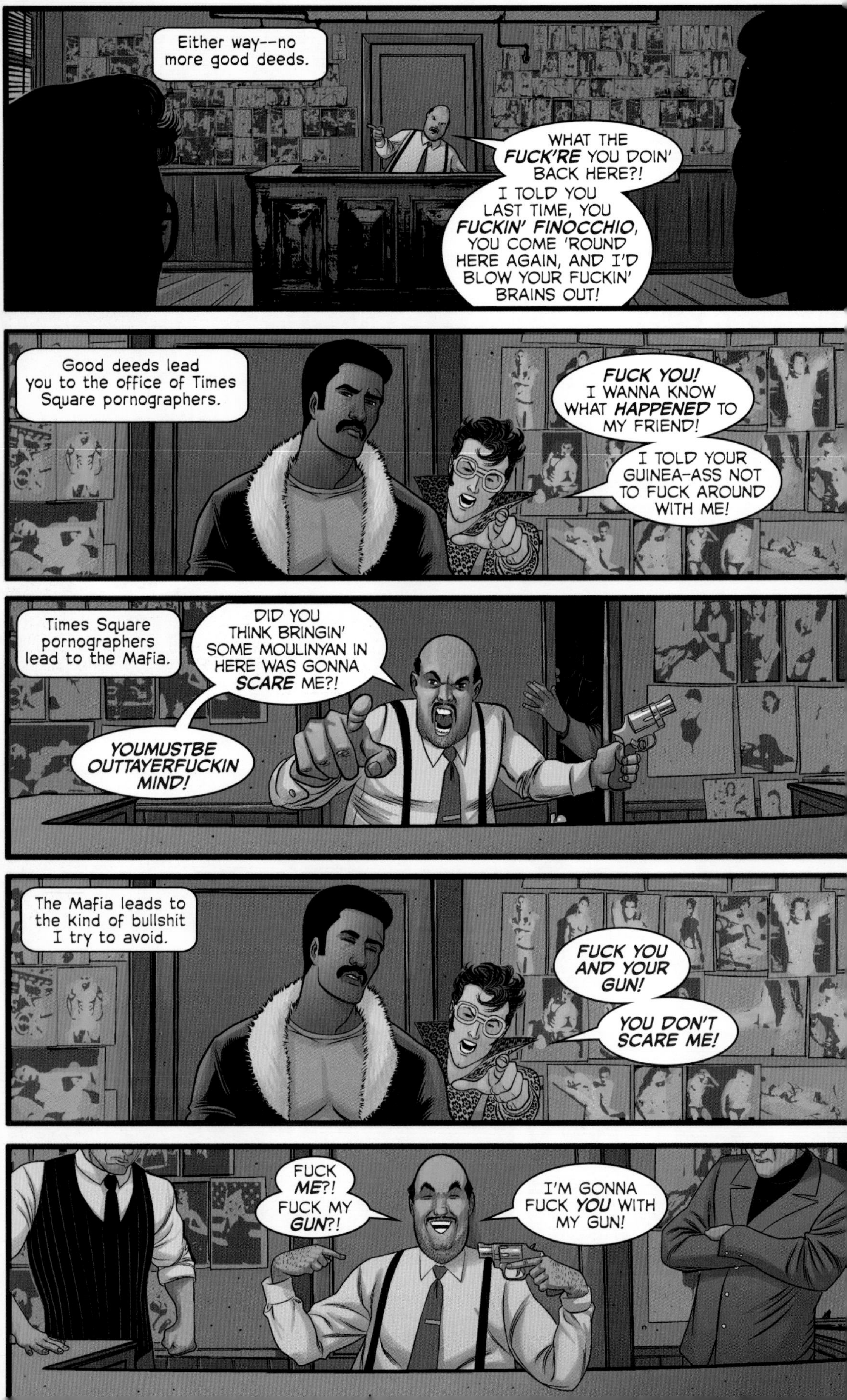

Either way--no more good deeds.
WHAT THE FUCK'RE YOU DOIN' BACK HERE?!
I TOLD YOU LAST TIME, YOU FUCKIN' FINOCCHIO, YOU COME 'ROUND HERE AGAIN, AND I'D BLOW YOUR FUCKIN' BRAINS OUT!
Good deeds lead you to the office of Times Square pornographers.
FUCK YOU! I WANNA KNOW WHAT HAPPENED TO MY FRIEND!
I TOLD YOUR GUINEA-ASS NOT TO FUCK AROUND WITH ME!
Times Square pornographers lead to the Mafia.
DID YOU THINK BRINGIN' SOME MOULINYAN IN HERE WAS GONNA SCARE ME?!
YOUMUSTBE OUTTAYERFUCKIN MIND!
The Mafia leads to the kind of bullshit I try to avoid.
FUCK YOU AND YOUR GUN!
YOU DON'T SCARE ME!
FUCK ME?! FUCK MY GUN?!
I'M GONNA FUCK YOU WITH MY GUN!

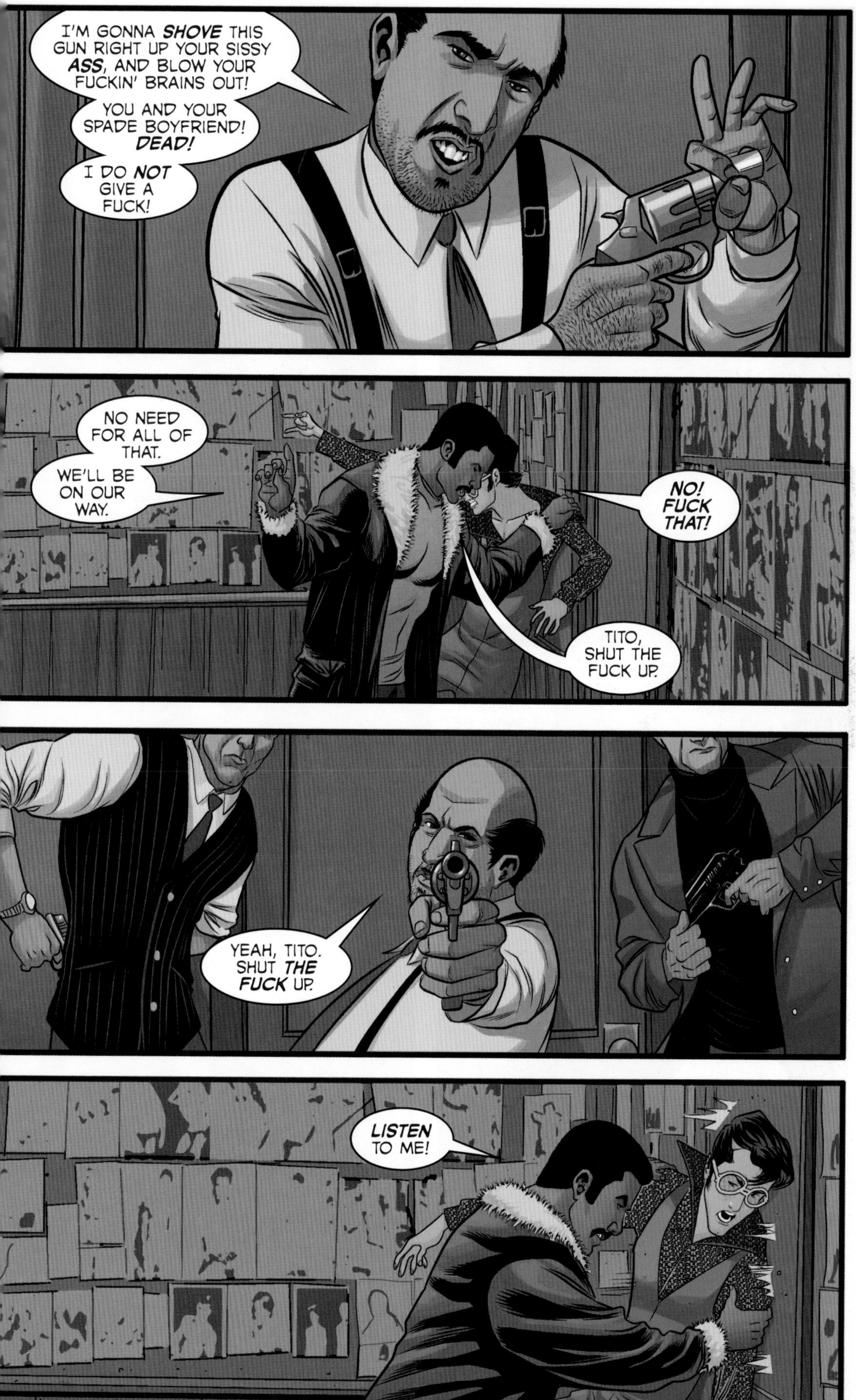
I'M GONNA **SHOVE** THIS GUN RIGHT UP YOUR SISSY **ASS**, AND BLOW YOUR FUCKIN' BRAINS OUT!
YOU AND YOUR SPADE BOYFRIEND! **DEAD!**
I DO **NOT** GIVE A FUCK!
NO NEED FOR ALL OF THAT.
WE'LL BE ON OUR WAY.
NO! FUCK THAT!
TITO, SHUT THE FUCK UP.
YEAH, TITO. SHUT **THE FUCK** UP.
LISTEN TO ME!

I DIDN'T COME HERE TO GET MY ASS KICKED--*OR* GET KILLED.

NOT FOR *YOU*. NOT FOR *ANYONE*.

AND THAT'S WHAT'S ABOUT TO HAPPEN...

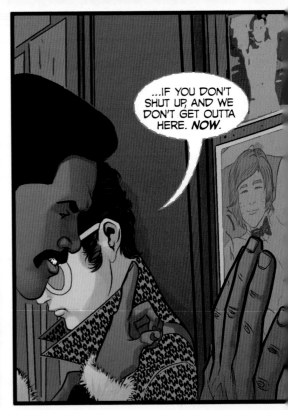

...IF YOU DON'T SHUT UP, AND WE DON'T GET OUTTA HERE. *NOW*.

QUIT WHISPERIN'!

WHAT'S IT *GONNA* BE?

AM I GONNA FUCK YOU'S TWO IN THE ASS WITH MY *GUN*?!

NO NEED FOR THAT. WE'RE OUTTA HERE.

SORRY TO BOTHER YOU.

DON'T SAY A FUCKIN' WORD, AND KEEP MOVING, OR I'LL LEAVE YOU HERE.

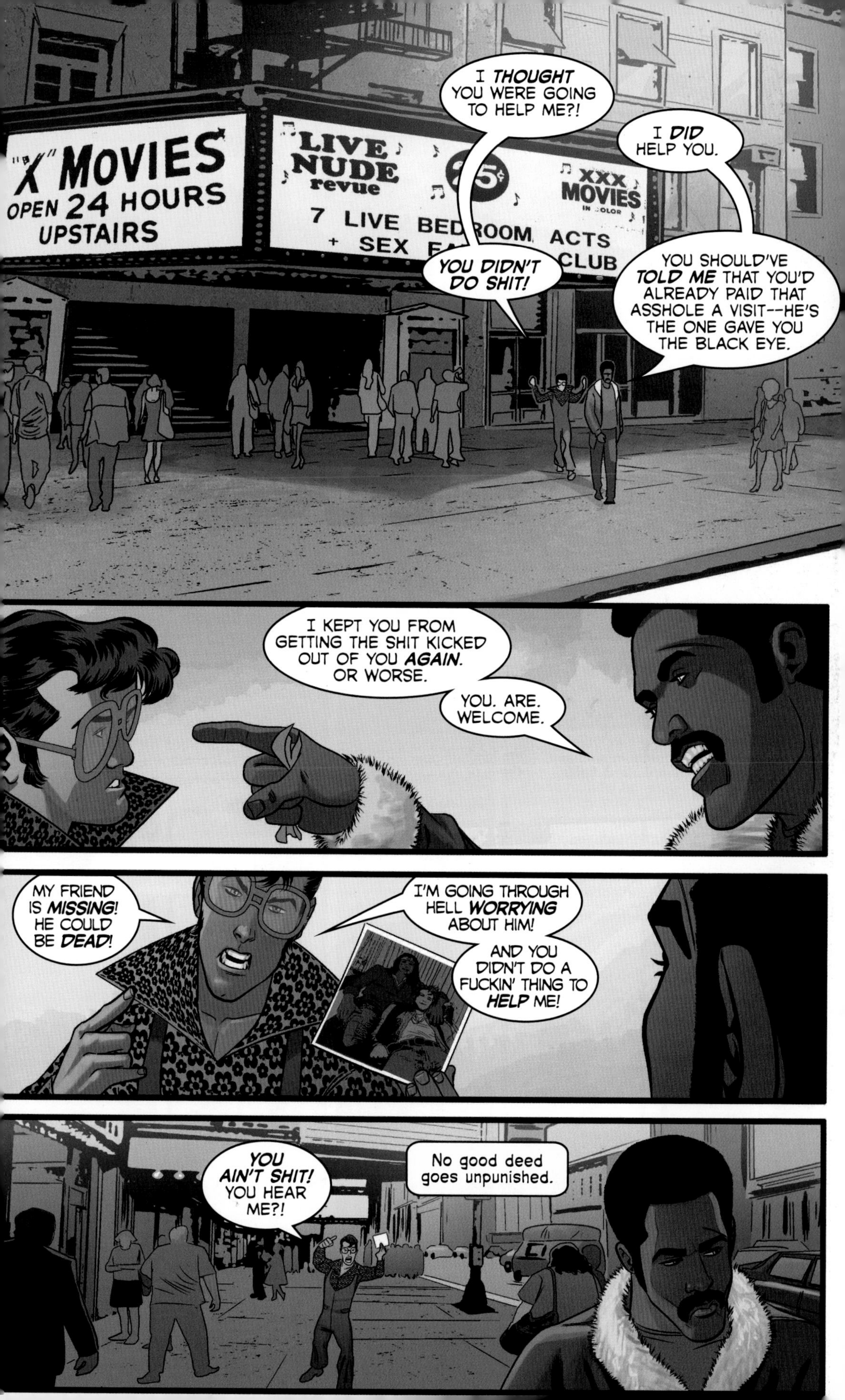
"X" MOVIES
OPEN 24 HOURS
UPSTAIRS
LIVE NUDE revue
25¢
XXX MOVIES IN COLOR
7 LIVE BEDROOM ACTS
+ SEX CLUB
I THOUGHT YOU WERE GOING TO HELP ME?!
YOU DIDN'T DO SHIT!
I DID HELP YOU.
YOU SHOULD'VE TOLD ME THAT YOU'D ALREADY PAID THAT ASSHOLE A VISIT--HE'S THE ONE GAVE YOU THE BLACK EYE.
I KEPT YOU FROM GETTING THE SHIT KICKED OUT OF YOU AGAIN. OR WORSE.
YOU. ARE. WELCOME.
MY FRIEND IS MISSING! HE COULD BE DEAD!
I'M GOING THROUGH HELL WORRYING ABOUT HIM!
AND YOU DIDN'T DO A FUCKIN' THING TO HELP ME!
YOU AIN'T SHIT! YOU HEAR ME?!
No good deed goes unpunished.

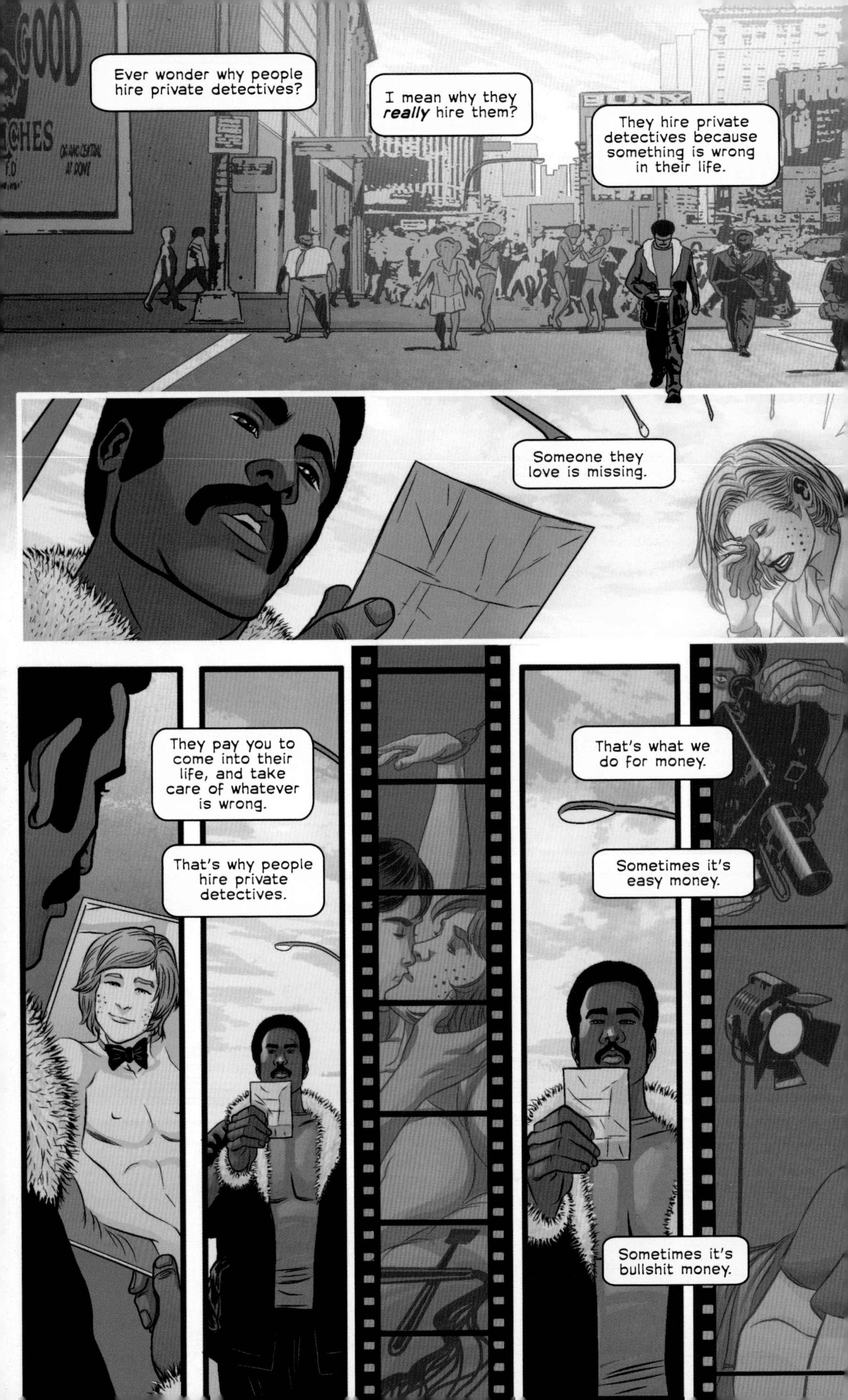
Ever wonder why people hire private detectives?
I mean why they *really* hire them?
They hire private detectives because something is wrong in their life.
Someone they love is missing.
They pay you to come into their life, and take care of whatever is wrong.
That's why people hire private detectives.
That's what we do for money.
Sometimes it's easy money.
Sometimes it's bullshit money.

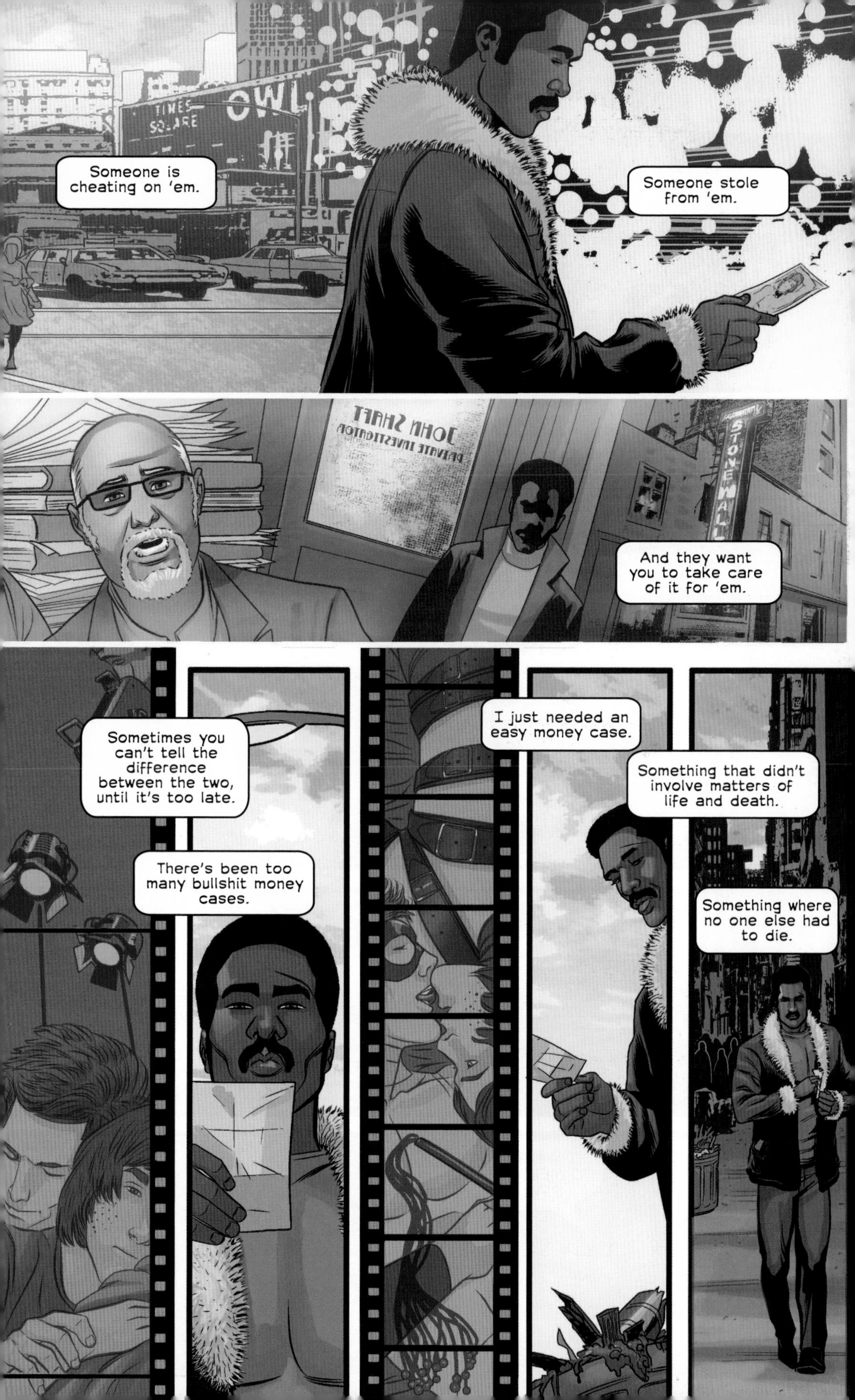
TIMES SQUARE
OWL
Someone is cheating on 'em.
Someone stole from 'em.
JOHN SHAFT PRIVATE INVESTIGATOR
STONEWALL
And they want you to take care of it for 'em.
Sometimes you can't tell the difference between the two, until it's too late.
There's been too many bullshit money cases.
I just needed an easy money case.
Something that didn't involve matters of life and death.
Something where no one else had to die.

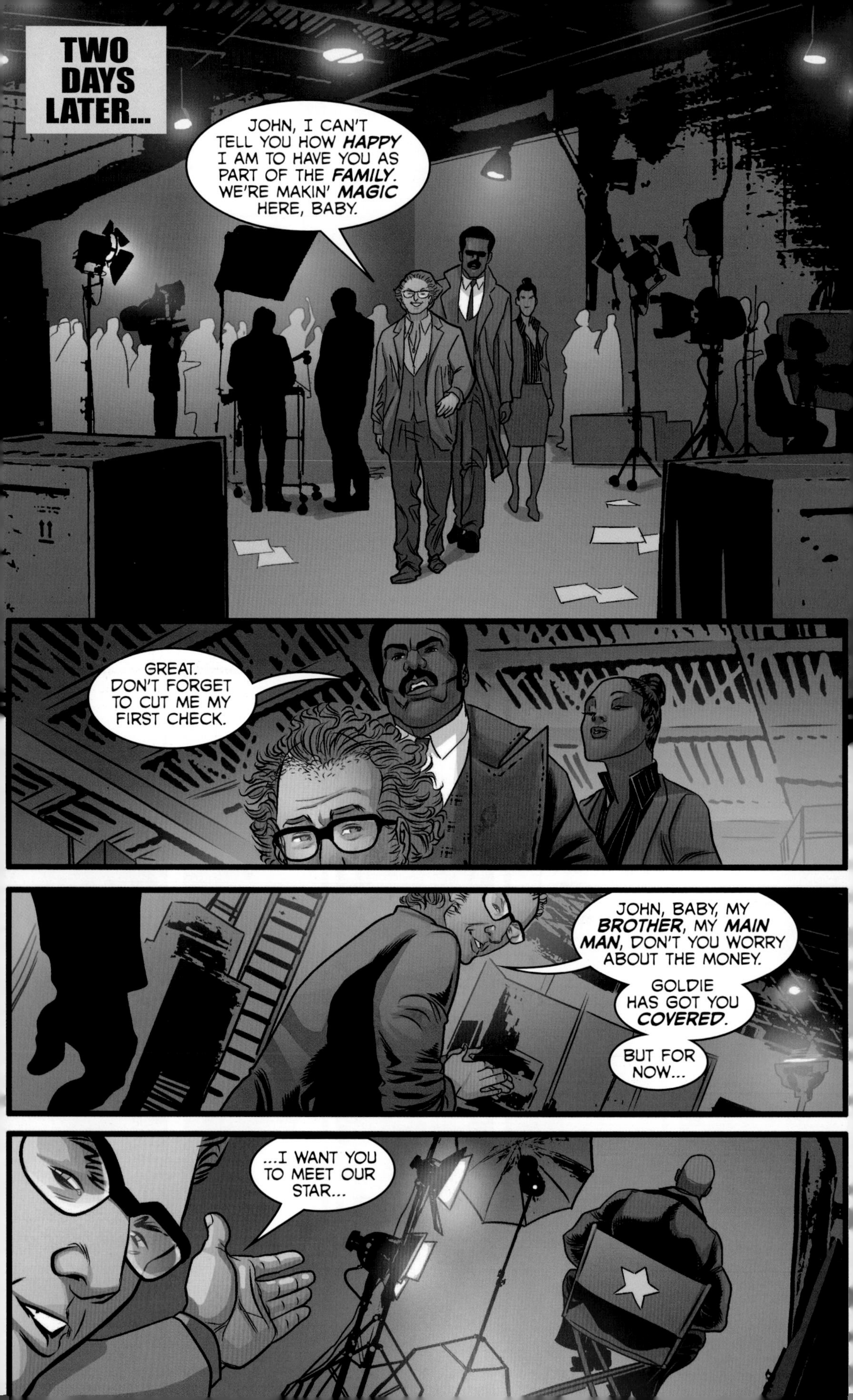
TWO DAYS LATER...
JOHN, I CAN'T TELL YOU HOW HAPPY I AM TO HAVE YOU AS PART OF THE FAMILY. WE'RE MAKIN' MAGIC HERE, BABY.
GREAT. DON'T FORGET TO CUT ME MY FIRST CHECK.
JOHN, BABY, MY BROTHER, MY MAIN MAN, DON'T YOU WORRY ABOUT THE MONEY.
GOLDIE HAS GOT YOU COVERED.
BUT FOR NOW...
...I WANT YOU TO MEET OUR STAR...

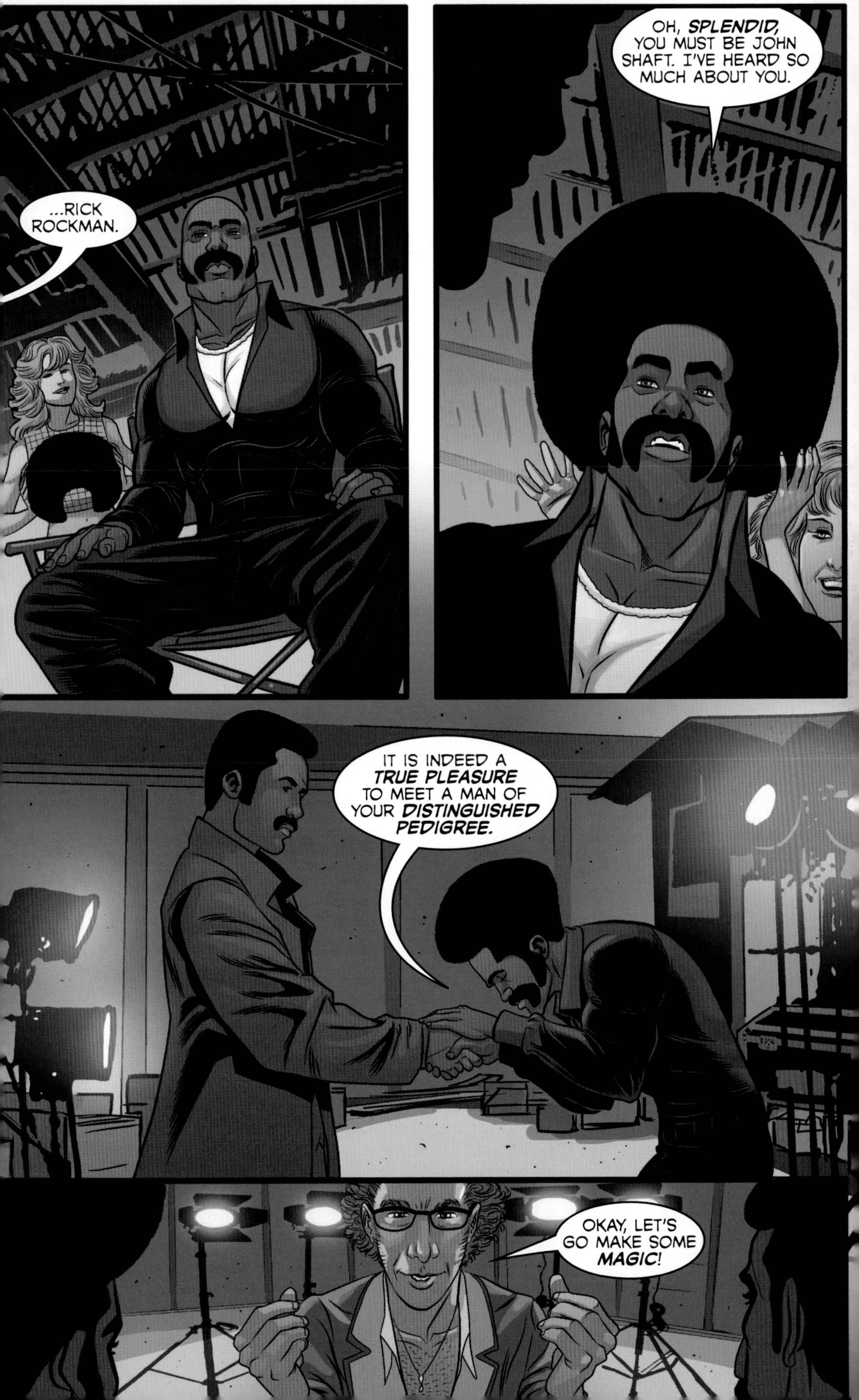
...RICK ROCKMAN.
OH, SPLENDID, YOU MUST BE JOHN SHAFT. I'VE HEARD SO MUCH ABOUT YOU.
IT IS INDEED A TRUE PLEASURE TO MEET A MAN OF YOUR DISTINGUISHED PEDIGREE.
OKAY, LET'S GO MAKE SOME MAGIC!

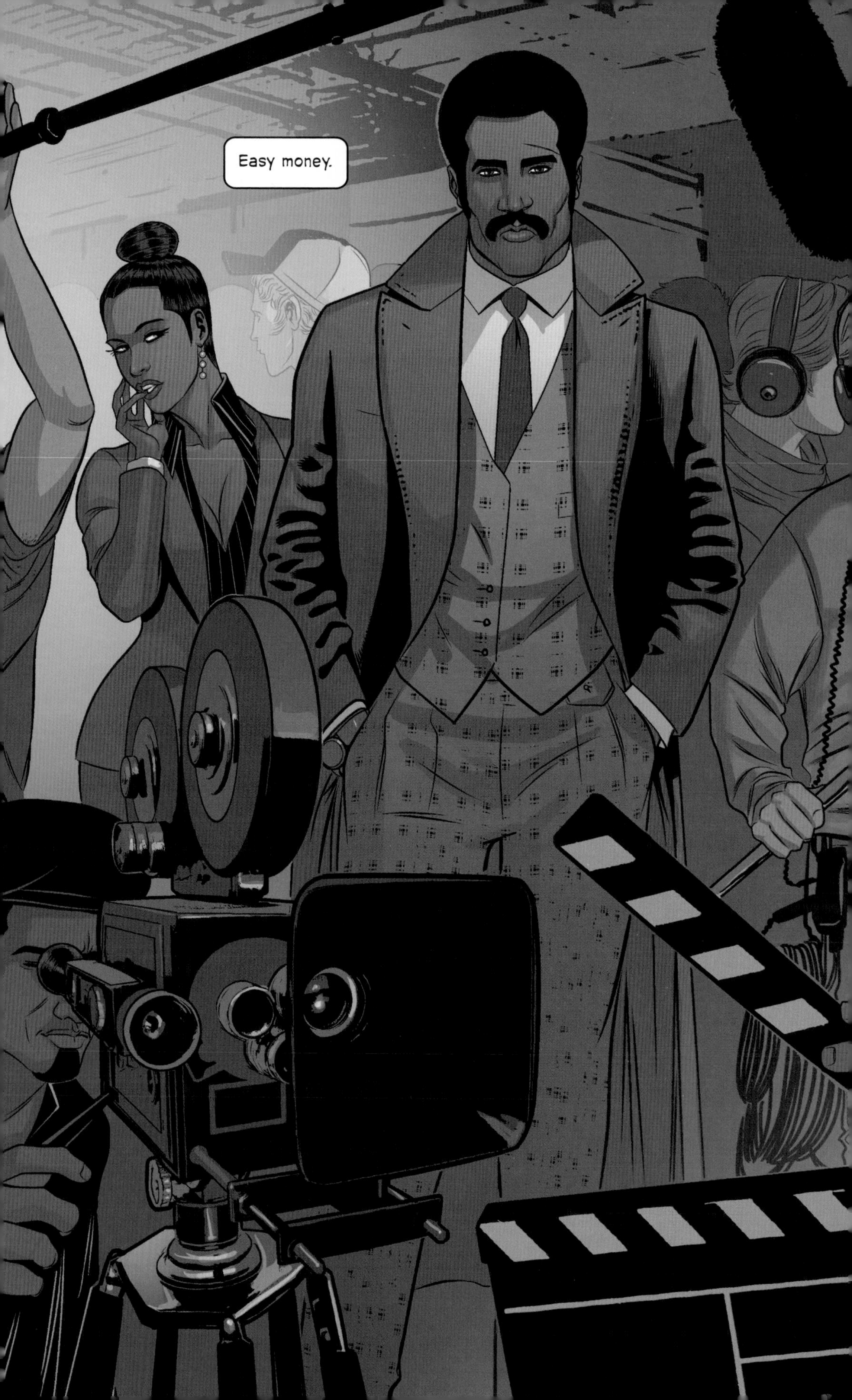
Easy money.

DAVID F. WALKER • DIETRICH SMITH

SHAFT

IMITATION OF LIFE

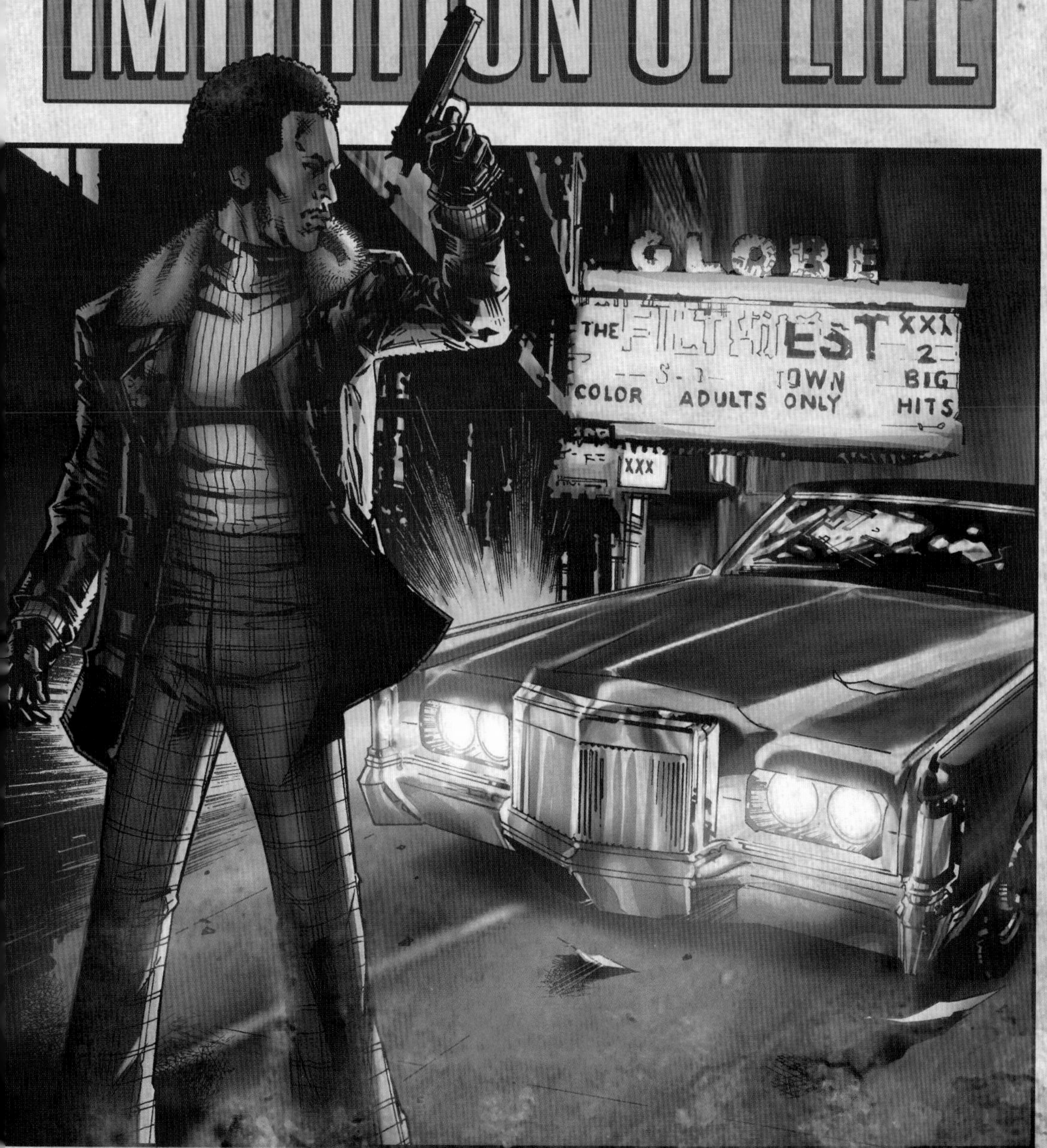
GLOBE
THE FILTHIEST
XXX 2 BIG HITS
TOWN
COLOR ADULTS ONLY
XXX

Part Three: LOVE AND LOSS

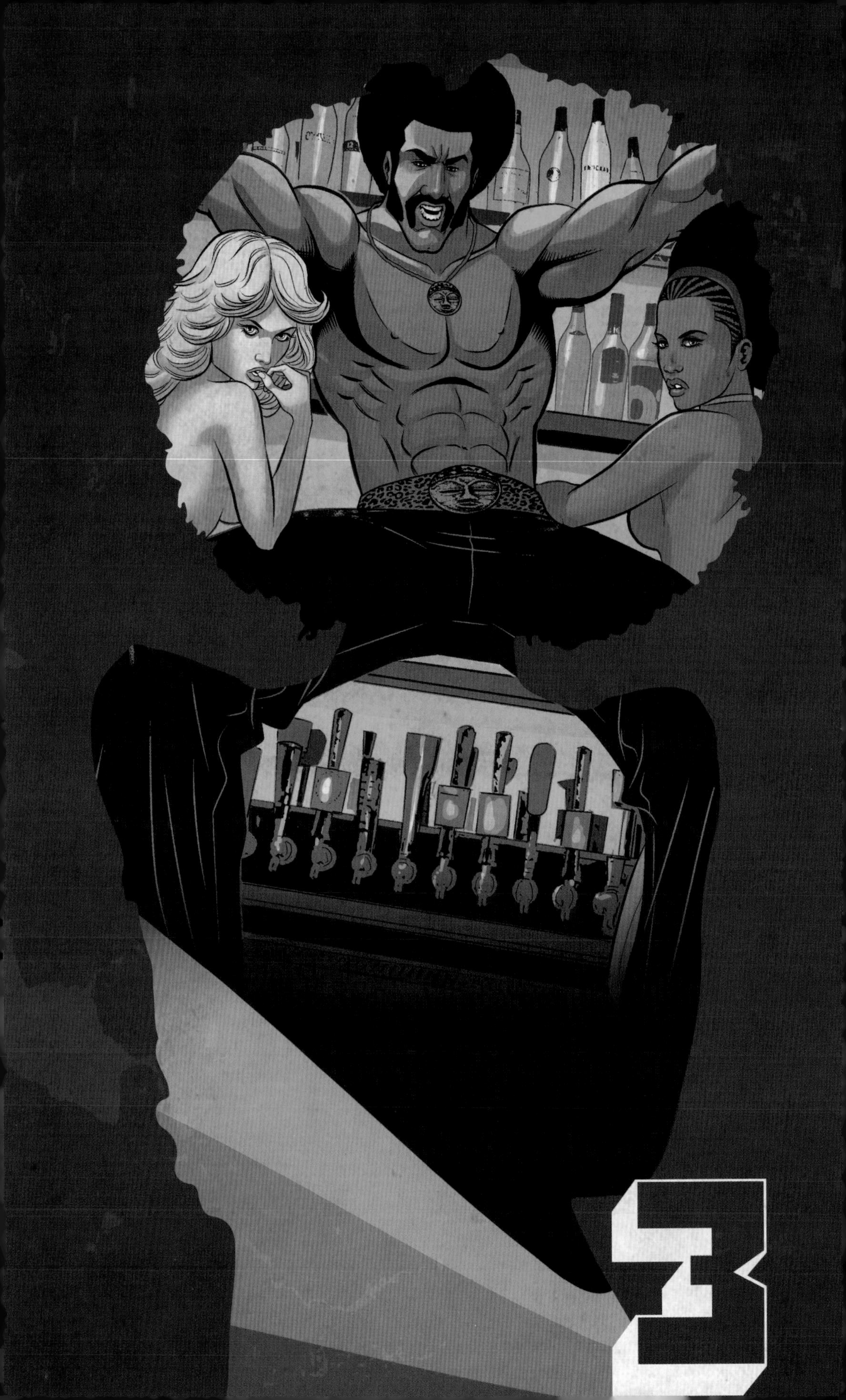
3

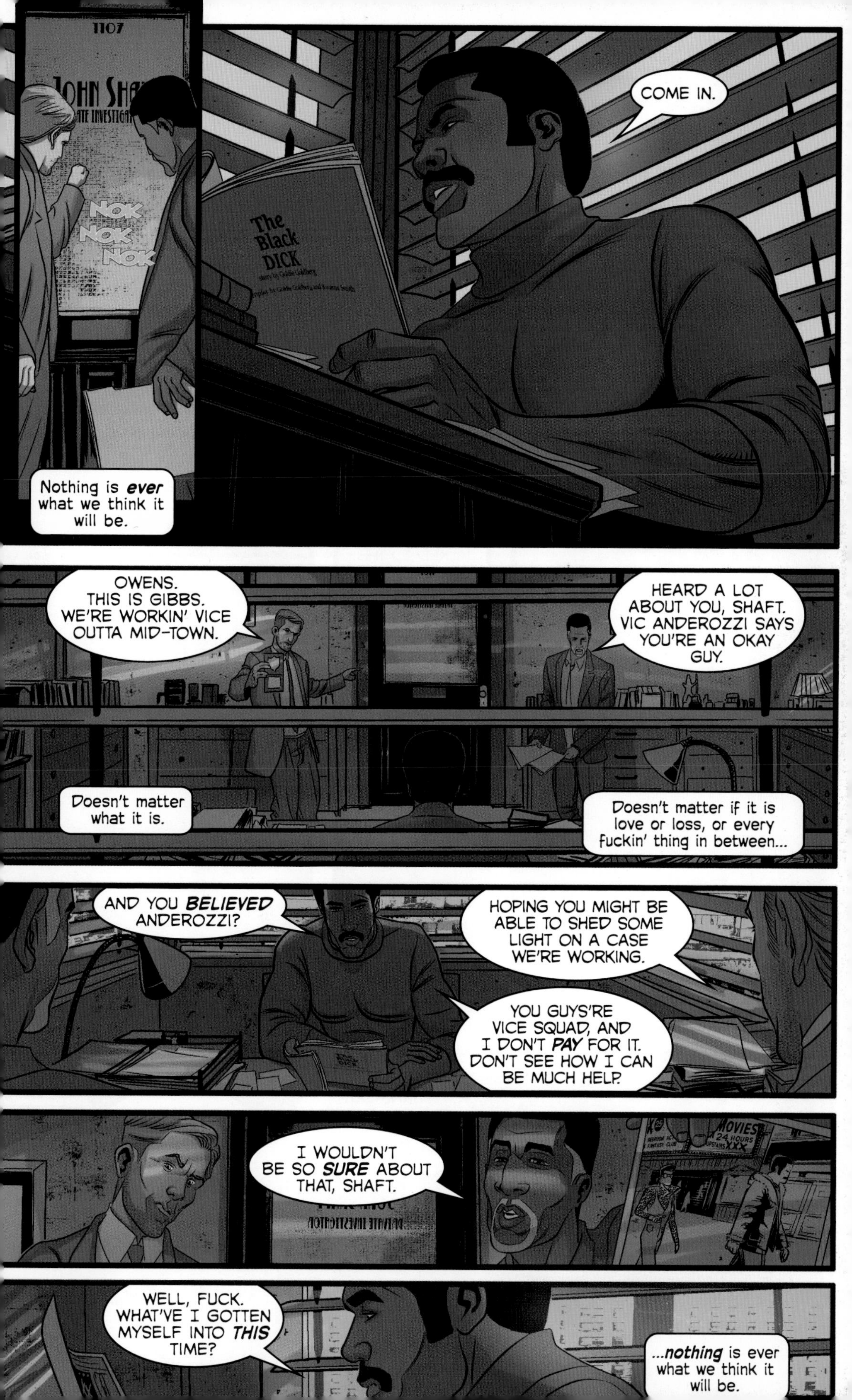
1107
NOK NOK NOK
Nothing is *ever* what we think it will be.
The Black DICK
COME IN.
OWENS. THIS IS GIBBS. WE'RE WORKIN' VICE OUTTA MID-TOWN.
HEARD A LOT ABOUT YOU, SHAFT. VIC ANDEROZZI SAYS YOU'RE AN OKAY GUY.
Doesn't matter what it is.
Doesn't matter if it is love or loss, or every fuckin' thing in between...
AND YOU *BELIEVED* ANDEROZZI?
HOPING YOU MIGHT BE ABLE TO SHED SOME LIGHT ON A CASE WE'RE WORKING.
YOU GUYS'RE VICE SQUAD, AND I DON'T *PAY* FOR IT. DON'T SEE HOW I CAN BE MUCH HELP.
I WOULDN'T BE SO *SURE* ABOUT THAT, SHAFT.
MOVIES
24 HOURS
XXX
WELL, FUCK. WHAT'VE I GOTTEN MYSELF INTO *THIS* TIME?
...*nothing* is ever what we think it will be.

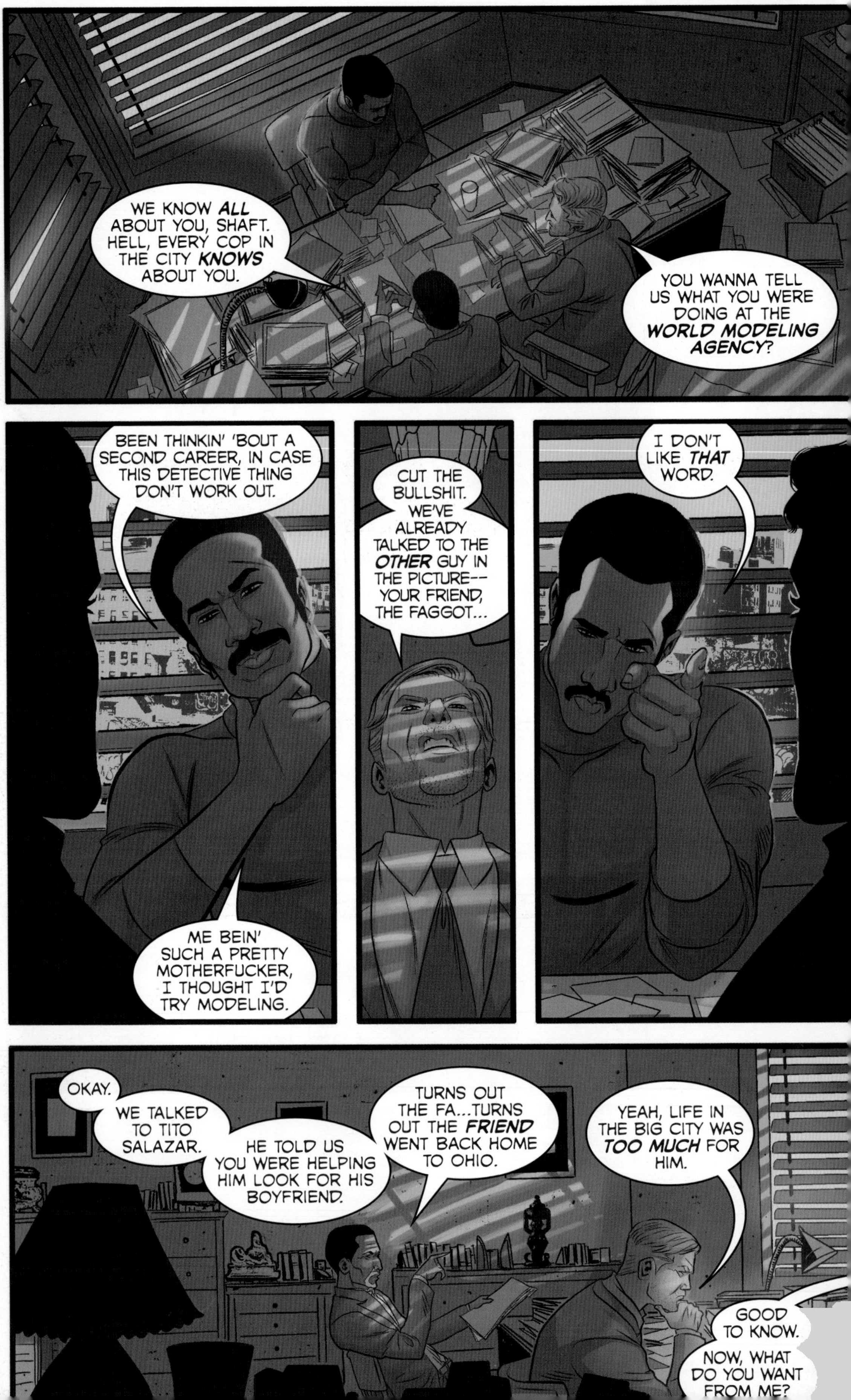
WE KNOW ALL ABOUT YOU, SHAFT. HELL, EVERY COP IN THE CITY KNOWS ABOUT YOU.
YOU WANNA TELL US WHAT YOU WERE DOING AT THE WORLD MODELING AGENCY?
BEEN THINKIN' 'BOUT A SECOND CAREER, IN CASE THIS DETECTIVE THING DON'T WORK OUT.
ME BEIN' SUCH A PRETTY MOTHERFUCKER, I THOUGHT I'D TRY MODELING.
CUT THE BULLSHIT. WE'VE ALREADY TALKED TO THE OTHER GUY IN THE PICTURE-- YOUR FRIEND, THE FAGGOT...
I DON'T LIKE THAT WORD.
OKAY.
WE TALKED TO TITO SALAZAR.
HE TOLD US YOU WERE HELPING HIM LOOK FOR HIS BOYFRIEND.
TURNS OUT THE FA...TURNS OUT THE FRIEND WENT BACK HOME TO OHIO.
YEAH, LIFE IN THE BIG CITY WAS TOO MUCH FOR HIM.
GOOD TO KNOW.
NOW, WHAT DO YOU WANT FROM ME?

WE'RE WONDERING IF YOU DID ANY *SNOOPING* AROUND--TRIED TO DIG UP ANY DIRT ON WORLD MODELING AGENCY.

NO. WENT WITH TITO, AND GOT HIM OUTTA THERE BEFORE WE BOTH GOT INTO TROUBLE.

TROUBLE?

PLACE HAD A DISTINCTLY ITALIAN SMELL, IF YOU CATCH MY *MEANING*.

WORLD MODELING AGENCY IS RUN BY SAMMY RIZZO...

...RIZZO WORKS FOR LOU PERIANO--*LOLLIPOP LOU*. THE GUY'S A REAL PIECE OF SHIT. KIDNAPPING. EXTORTION. MURDER.

PERIANO'S ALSO INTO PORN--AND NOT THE WHOLESOME STUFF, LIKE *DEEP THROAT*. WE'RE TALKIN' THE KIND OF STUFF THAT LED GOD TO DESTROY SODOM AND GOMORRAH.

WE'RE PRETTY SURE HE'S MADE SOME *SNUFF FILMS*, USING *TALENT* FROM WORLD MODELING, BUT WE HAVEN'T BEEN ABLE TO PROVE A DAMN THING.

I'D LOVE TO HELP YOU GUYS...

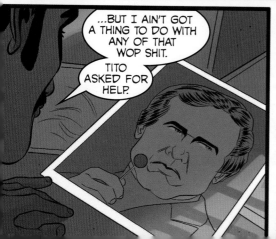

...BUT I AIN'T GOT A THING TO DO WITH ANY OF THAT WOP SHIT.

TITO ASKED FOR HELP.

THE MOMENT I *REALIZED* THE KIND OF PEOPLE INVOLVED, I GOT THE HELL OUTTA THERE.

THE DAYS OF RISKING MY NECK ARE OVER. NOW IT'S NOTHING BUT *SIMPLE* CASES...

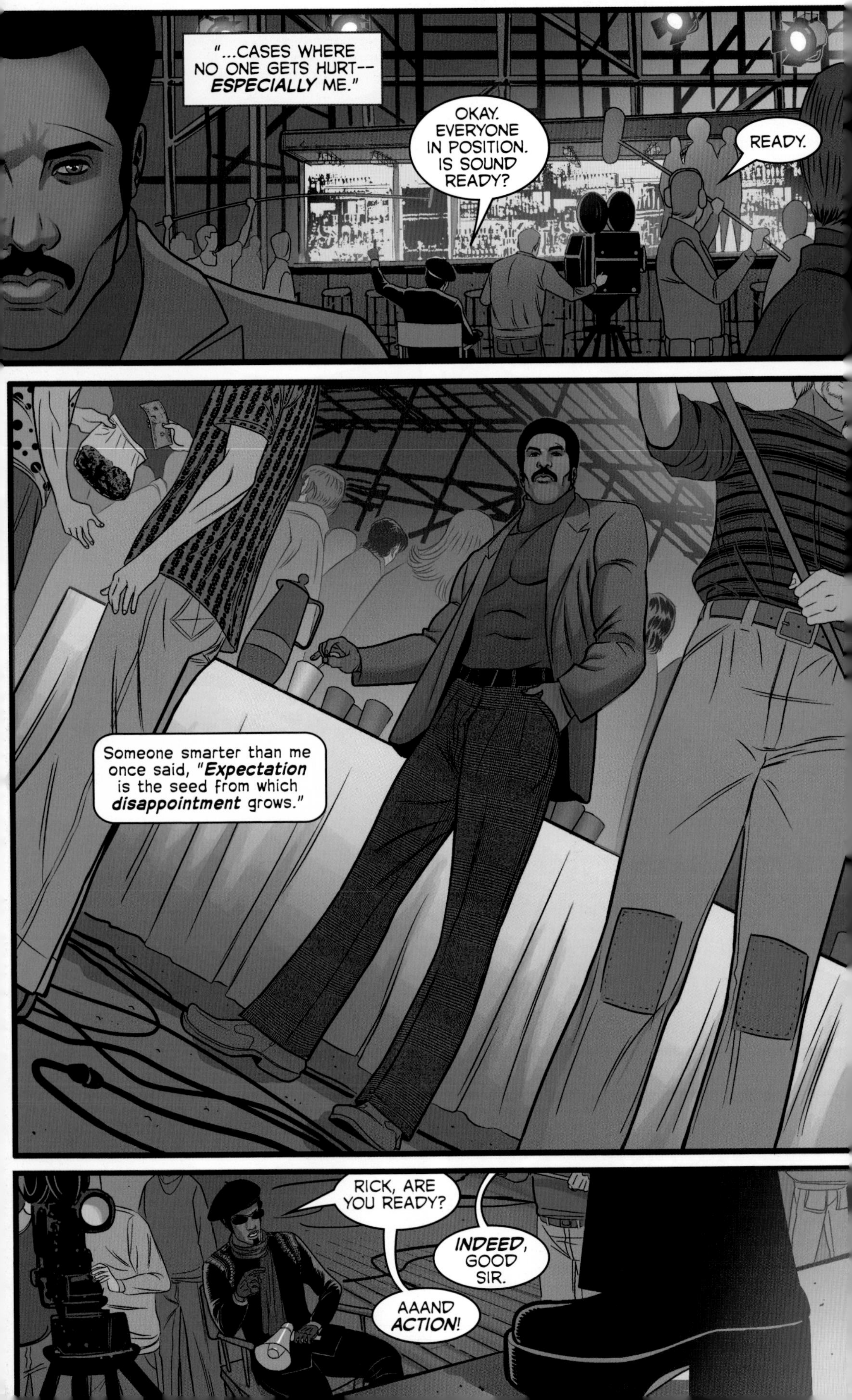
"...CASES WHERE NO ONE GETS HURT-- ESPECIALLY ME."
OKAY. EVERYONE IN POSITION. IS SOUND READY?
READY.
Someone smarter than me once said, "Expectation is the seed from which disappointment grows."
RICK, ARE YOU READY?
INDEED, GOOD SIR.
AAAND ACTION!

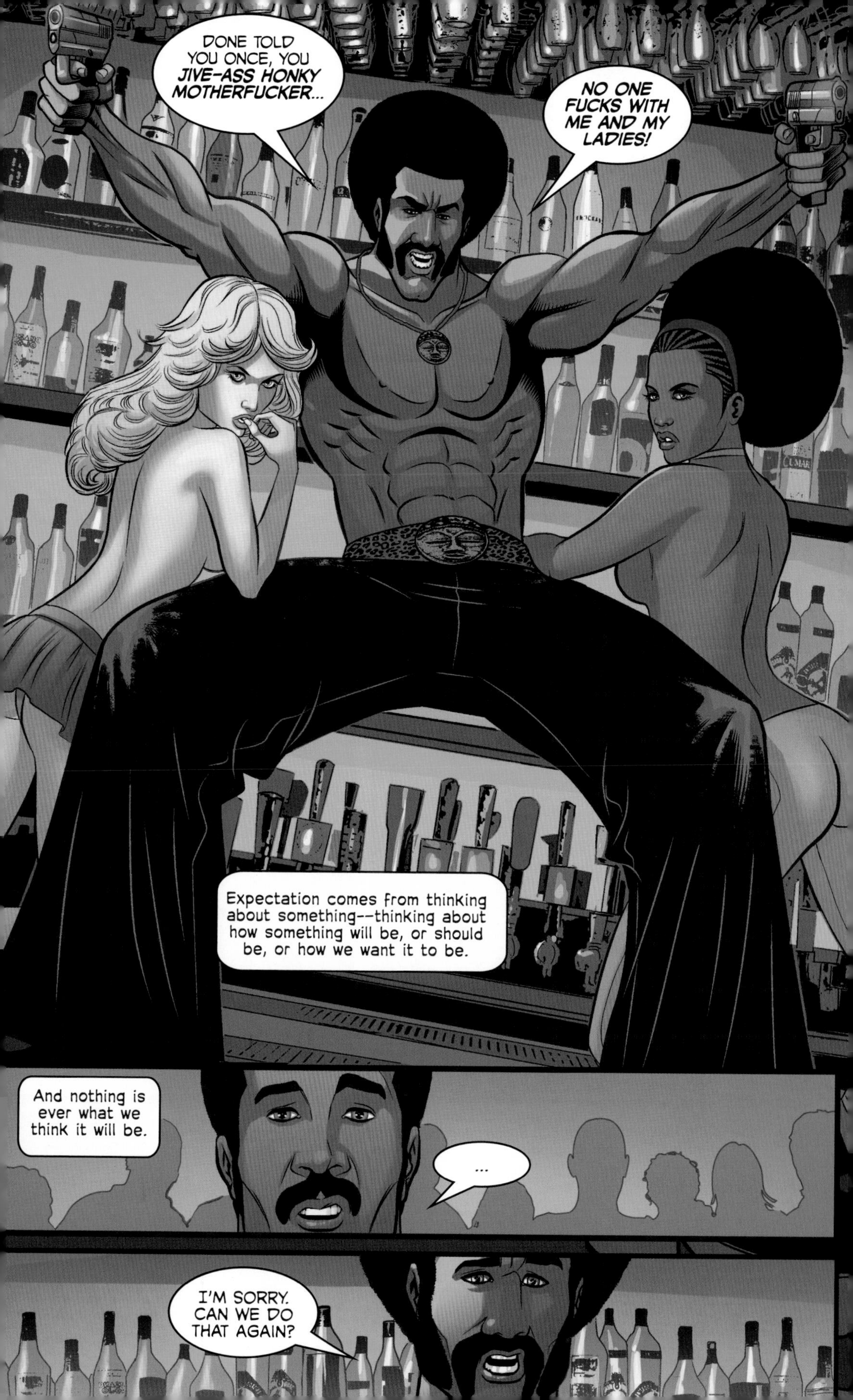
DONE TOLD YOU ONCE, YOU *JIVE-ASS HONKY MOTHERFUCKER...*
NO ONE FUCKS WITH ME AND MY LADIES!
Expectation comes from thinking about something--thinking about how something will be, or should be, or how we want it to be.
And nothing is ever what we think it will be.
...
I'M SORRY. CAN WE DO THAT AGAIN?

SOMETHING DIDN'T *FEEL* RIGHT.

CUT!

RICK... WHAT'S THE PROBLEM *THIS TIME*?

WOULDN'T IT MAKE MORE SENSE IF I CALLED HIM A *JIVE-ASS MOTHERFUCKING HONKY*, AS OPPOSED TO CALLING HIM A *JIVE-ASS HONKY MOTHERFUCKER*?

THE FORMER ROLLS OF THE TONGUE WITH MUCH MORE *GRACE* THAN THE LATTER. DO YOU NOT CONCUR?

YOU KNOW... I DON'T KNOW.

WHAT DO *YOU* THINK, JOHN?

WHAT DO I THINK ABOUT *WHAT*?

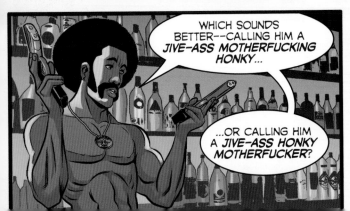

WHICH SOUNDS BETTER--CALLING HIM A *JIVE-ASS MOTHERFUCKING HONKY*...

...OR CALLING HIM A *JIVE-ASS HONKY MOTHERFUCKER*?

UM...HOW 'BOUT *MOTHERFUCKIN' JIVE-ASS*? HONKY?

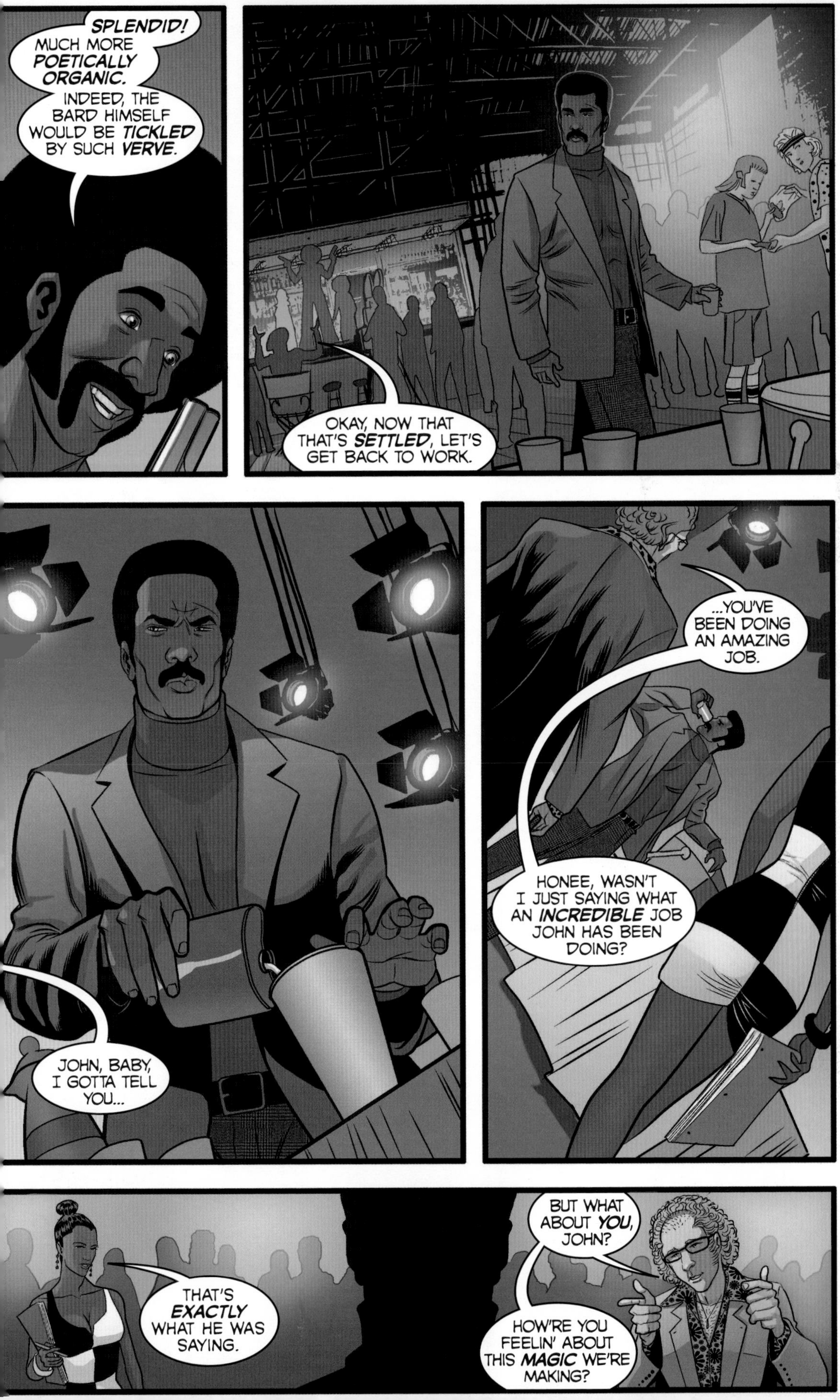
SPLENDID! MUCH MORE POETICALLY ORGANIC.
INDEED, THE BARD HIMSELF WOULD BE TICKLED BY SUCH VERVE.
OKAY, NOW THAT THAT'S SETTLED, LET'S GET BACK TO WORK.
JOHN, BABY, I GOTTA TELL YOU...
...YOU'VE BEEN DOING AN AMAZING JOB.
HONEE, WASN'T I JUST SAYING WHAT AN INCREDIBLE JOB JOHN HAS BEEN DOING?
THAT'S EXACTLY WHAT HE WAS SAYING.
BUT WHAT ABOUT YOU, JOHN?
HOW'RE YOU FEELIN' ABOUT THIS MAGIC WE'RE MAKING?

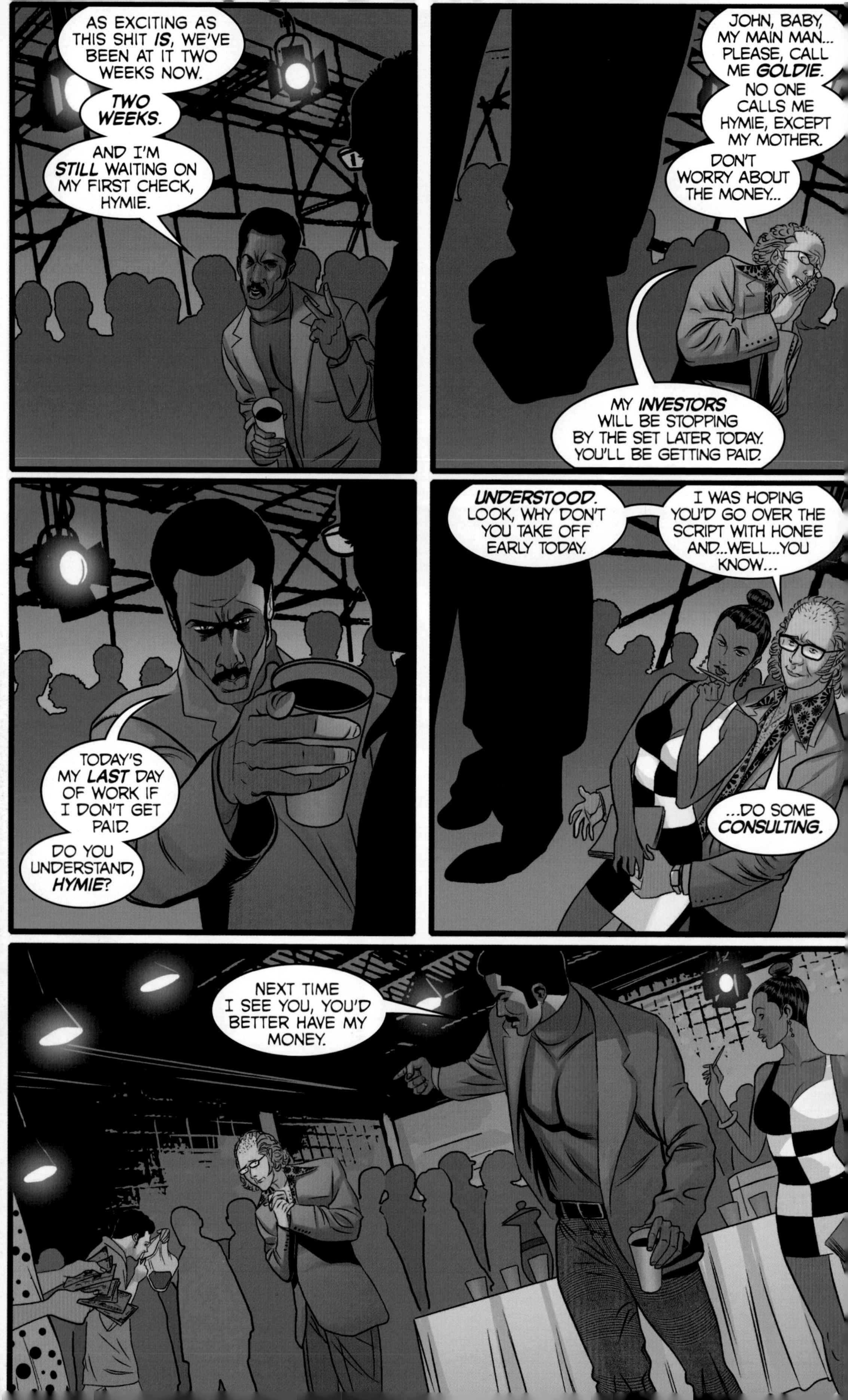
AS EXCITING AS THIS SHIT *IS*, WE'VE BEEN AT IT TWO WEEKS NOW.
TWO WEEKS.
AND I'M *STILL* WAITING ON MY FIRST CHECK, HYMIE.
JOHN, BABY, MY MAIN MAN... PLEASE, CALL ME *GOLDIE*.
NO ONE CALLS ME HYMIE, EXCEPT MY MOTHER.
DON'T WORRY ABOUT THE MONEY...
MY *INVESTORS* WILL BE STOPPING BY THE SET LATER TODAY. YOU'LL BE GETTING PAID.
TODAY'S MY *LAST* DAY OF WORK IF I DON'T GET PAID.
DO YOU UNDERSTAND, *HYMIE*?
UNDERSTOOD. LOOK, WHY DON'T YOU TAKE OFF EARLY TODAY.
I WAS HOPING YOU'D GO OVER THE SCRIPT WITH HONEE AND...WELL...YOU KNOW...
...DO SOME *CONSULTING*.
NEXT TIME I SEE YOU, YOU'D BETTER HAVE MY MONEY.

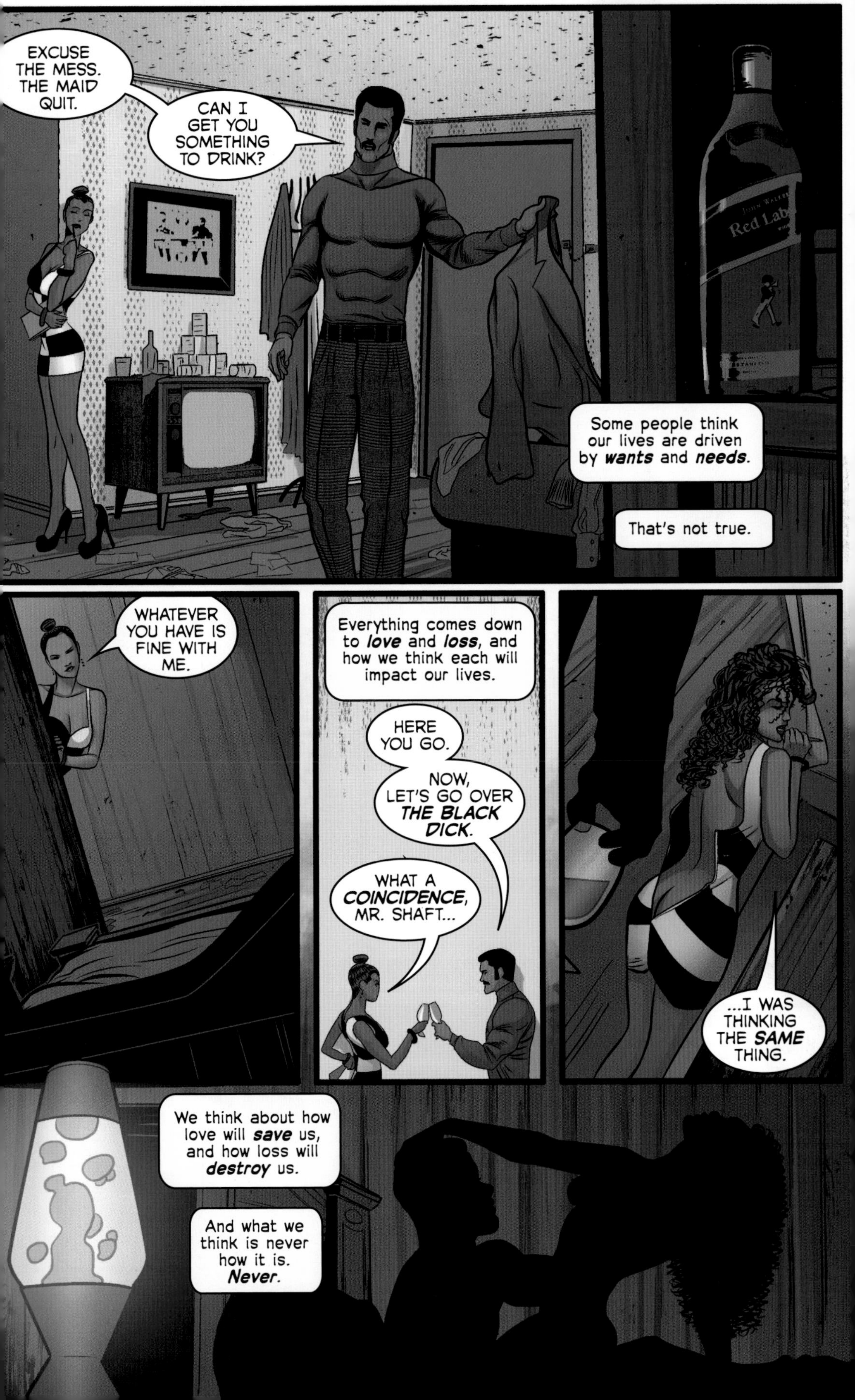
EXCUSE THE MESS. THE MAID QUIT.
CAN I GET YOU SOMETHING TO DRINK?
Some people think our lives are driven by ***wants*** and ***needs***.
That's not true.
WHATEVER YOU HAVE IS FINE WITH ME.
Everything comes down to ***love*** and ***loss***, and how we think each will impact our lives.
HERE YOU GO.
NOW, LET'S GO OVER ***THE BLACK DICK***.
WHAT A ***COINCIDENCE***, MR. SHAFT...
...I WAS THINKING THE ***SAME*** THING.
We think about how love will ***save*** us, and how loss will ***destroy*** us.
And what we think is never how it is. ***Never***.

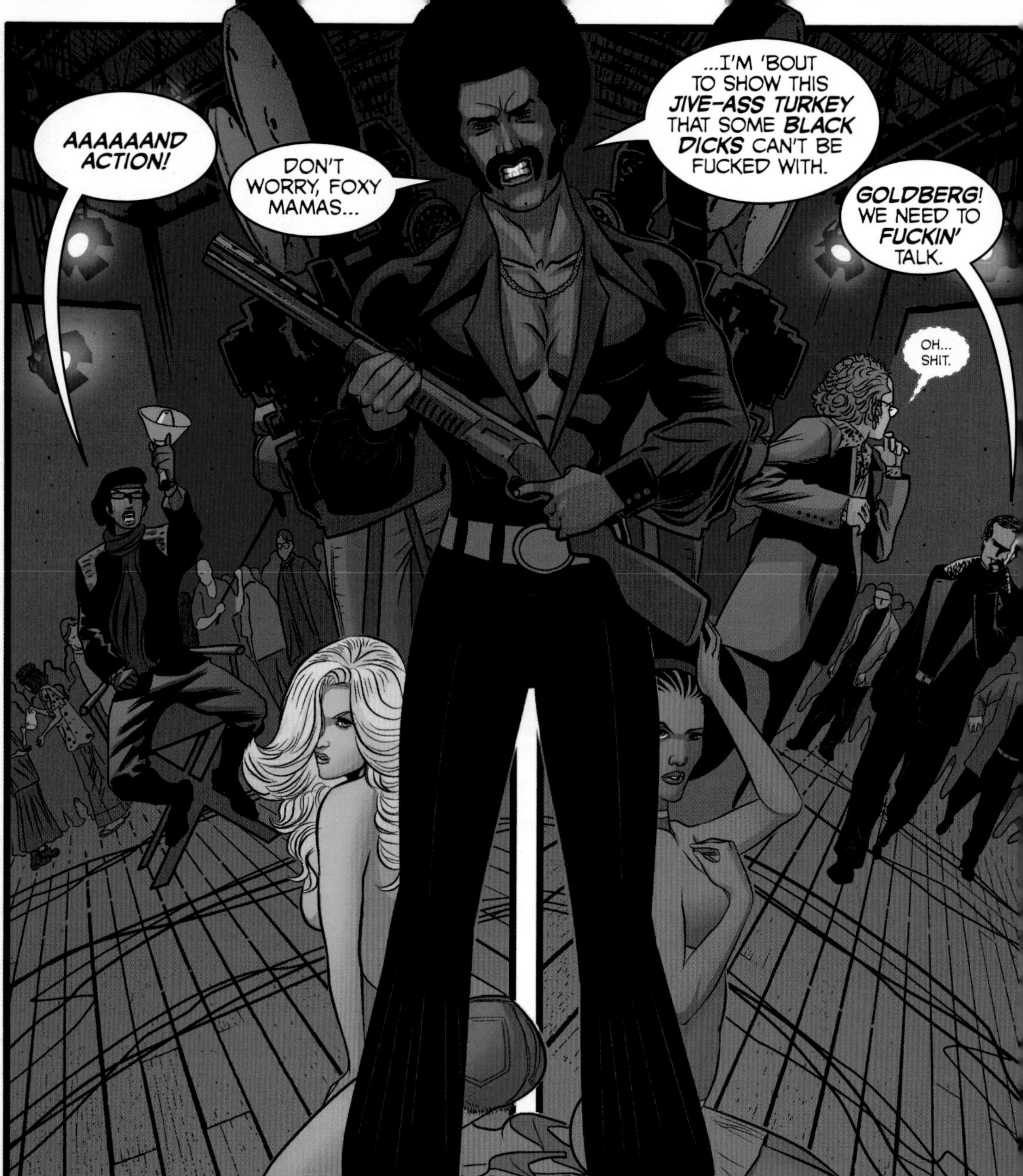
AAAAAAND ACTION!
DON'T WORRY, FOXY MAMAS...
...I'M 'BOUT TO SHOW THIS JIVE-ASS TURKEY THAT SOME BLACK DICKS CAN'T BE FUCKED WITH.
GOLDBERG! WE NEED TO FUCKIN' TALK.
OH... SHIT.

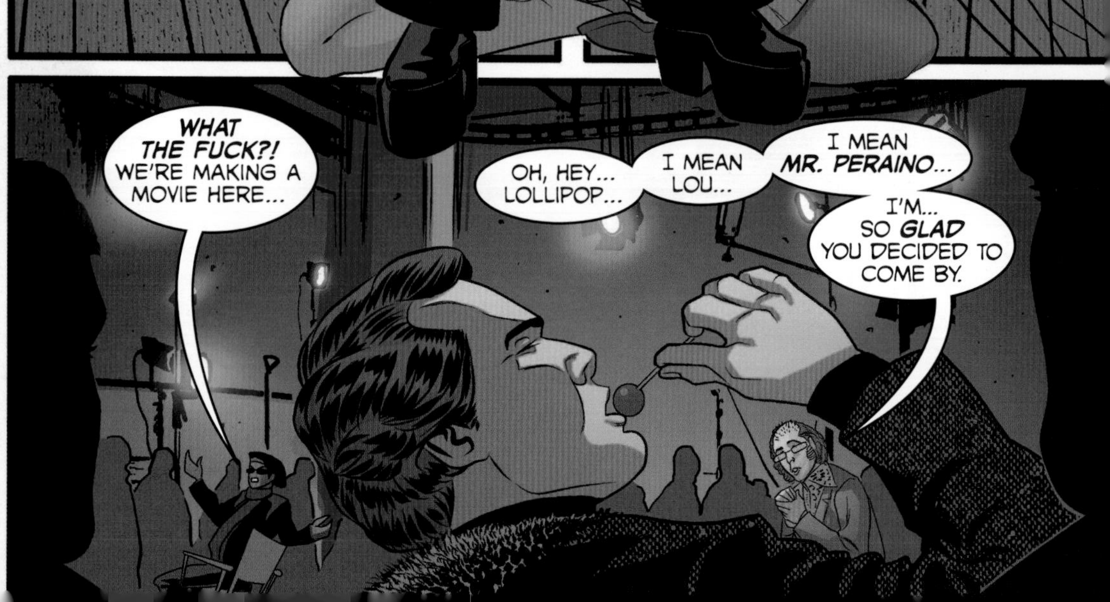
WHAT THE FUCK?! WE'RE MAKING A MOVIE HERE...
OH, HEY... LOLLIPOP...
I MEAN LOU...
I MEAN MR. PERAINO...
I'M... SO GLAD YOU DECIDED TO COME BY.

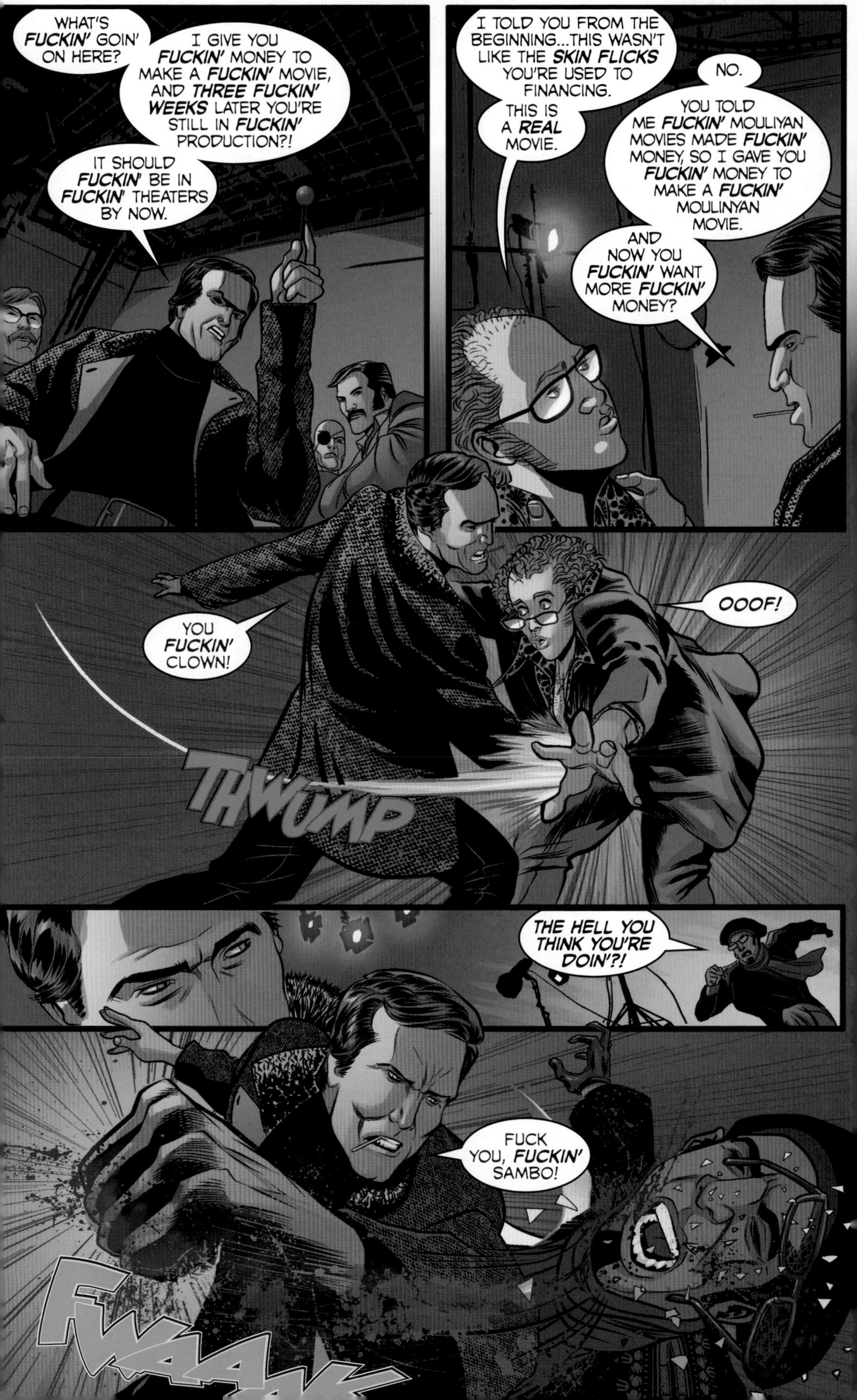
WHAT'S FUCKIN' GOIN' ON HERE?
I GIVE YOU FUCKIN' MONEY TO MAKE A FUCKIN' MOVIE, AND THREE FUCKIN' WEEKS LATER YOU'RE STILL IN FUCKIN' PRODUCTION?!
IT SHOULD FUCKIN' BE IN FUCKIN' THEATERS BY NOW.
I TOLD YOU FROM THE BEGINNING...THIS WASN'T LIKE THE SKIN FLICKS YOU'RE USED TO FINANCING.
THIS IS A REAL MOVIE.
NO.
YOU TOLD ME FUCKIN' MOULIYAN MOVIES MADE FUCKIN' MONEY, SO I GAVE YOU FUCKIN' MONEY TO MAKE A FUCKIN' MOULINYAN MOVIE.
AND NOW YOU FUCKIN' WANT MORE FUCKIN' MONEY?
YOU FUCKIN' CLOWN!
OOOF!
THWUMP
THE HELL YOU THINK YOU'RE DOIN'?!
FUCK YOU, FUCKIN' SAMBO!
FWAAK

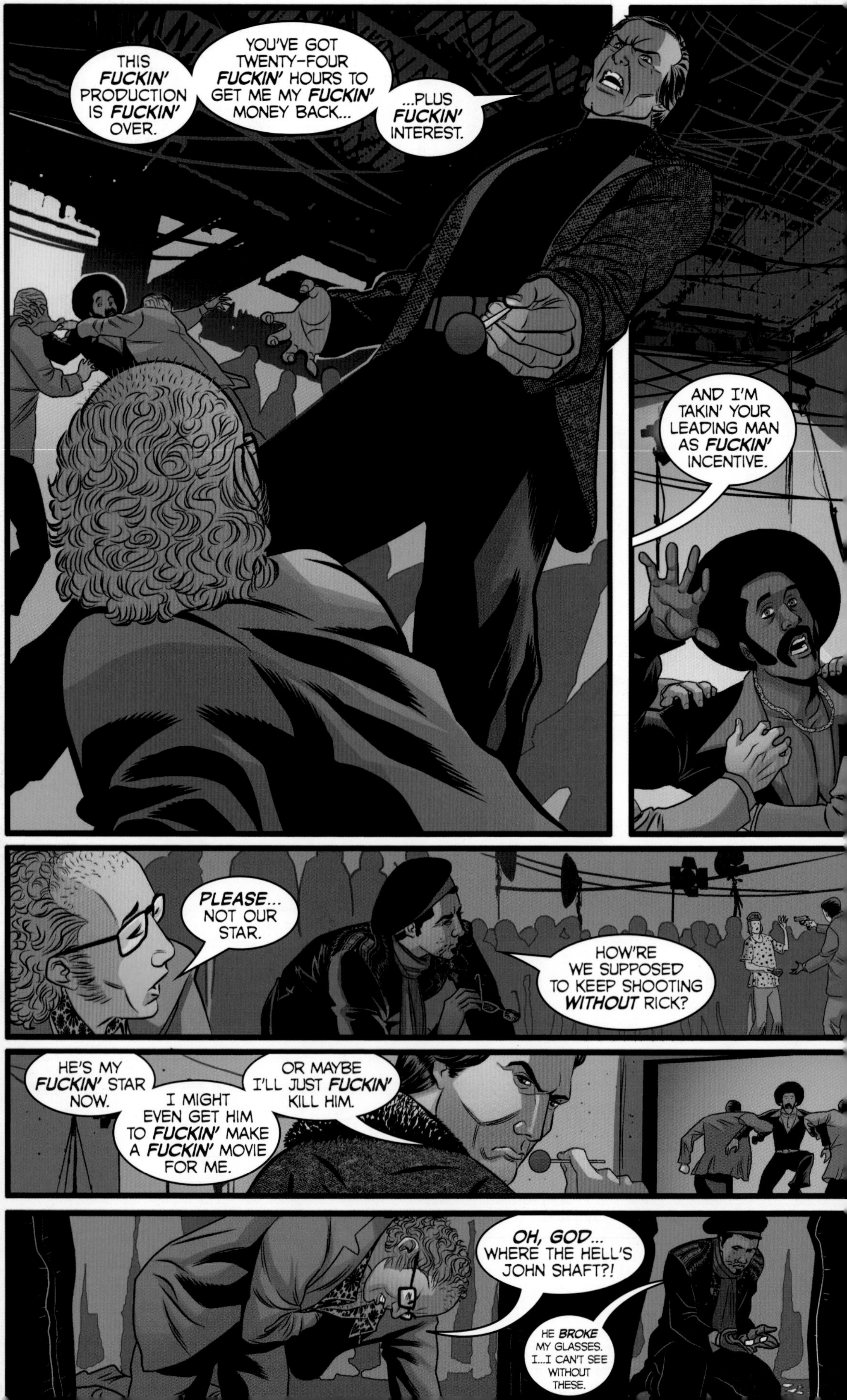
THIS FUCKIN' PRODUCTION IS FUCKIN' OVER.
YOU'VE GOT TWENTY-FOUR FUCKIN' HOURS TO GET ME MY FUCKIN' MONEY BACK...
...PLUS FUCKIN' INTEREST.
AND I'M TAKIN' YOUR LEADING MAN AS FUCKIN' INCENTIVE.
PLEASE... NOT OUR STAR.
HOW'RE WE SUPPOSED TO KEEP SHOOTING WITHOUT RICK?
HE'S MY FUCKIN' STAR NOW.
I MIGHT EVEN GET HIM TO FUCKIN' MAKE A FUCKIN' MOVIE FOR ME.
OR MAYBE I'LL JUST FUCKIN' KILL HIM.
OH, GOD... WHERE THE HELL'S JOHN SHAFT?!
HE BROKE MY GLASSES. I...I CAN'T SEE WITHOUT THESE.

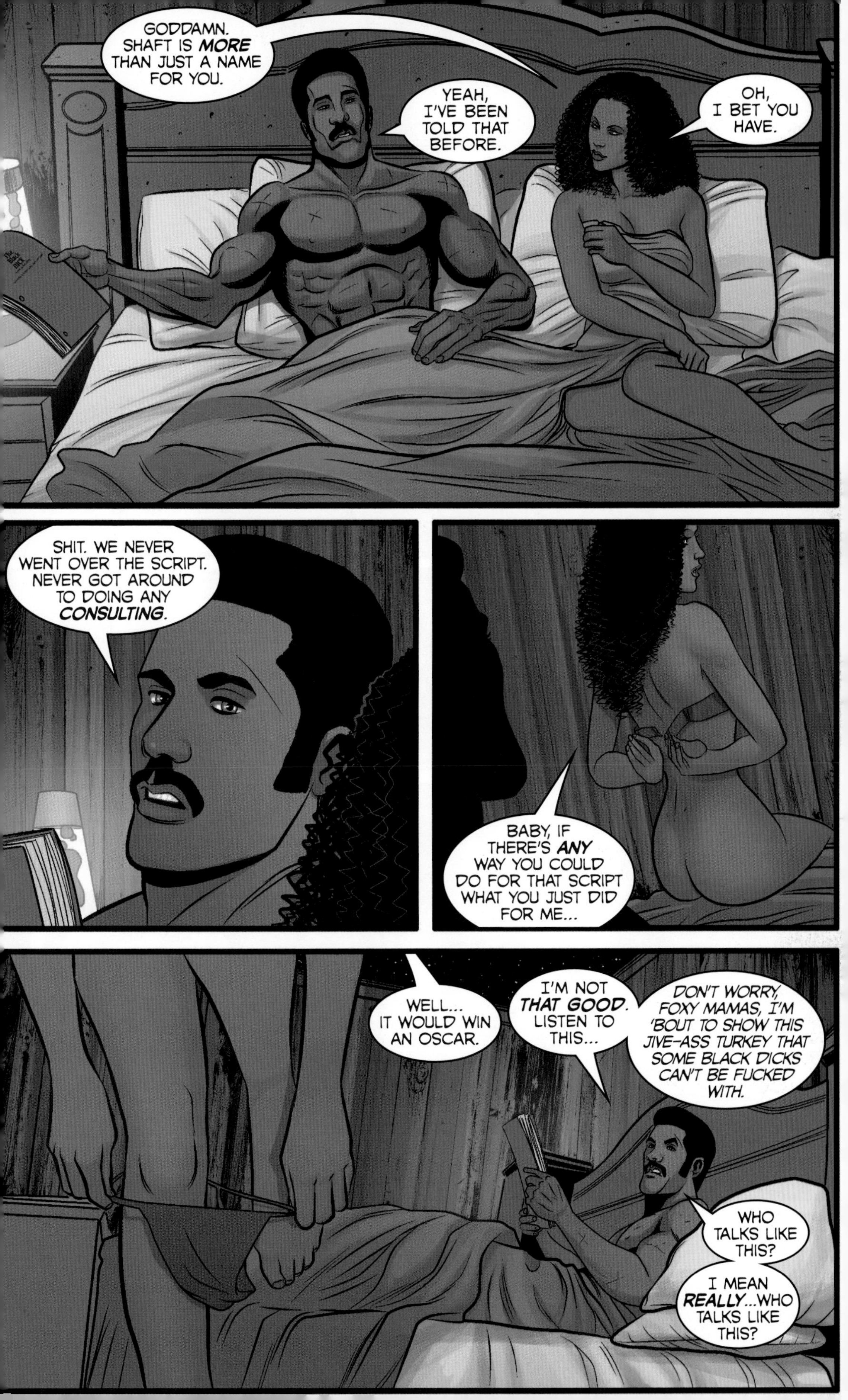
GODDAMN. SHAFT IS MORE THAN JUST A NAME FOR YOU.
YEAH, I'VE BEEN TOLD THAT BEFORE.
OH, I BET YOU HAVE.
SHIT. WE NEVER WENT OVER THE SCRIPT. NEVER GOT AROUND TO DOING ANY CONSULTING.
BABY, IF THERE'S ANY WAY YOU COULD DO FOR THAT SCRIPT WHAT YOU JUST DID FOR ME...
WELL... IT WOULD WIN AN OSCAR.
I'M NOT THAT GOOD. LISTEN TO THIS...
DON'T WORRY, FOXY MAMAS, I'M 'BOUT TO SHOW THIS JIVE-ASS TURKEY THAT SOME BLACK DICKS CAN'T BE FUCKED WITH.
WHO TALKS LIKE THIS?
I MEAN REALLY...WHO TALKS LIKE THIS?

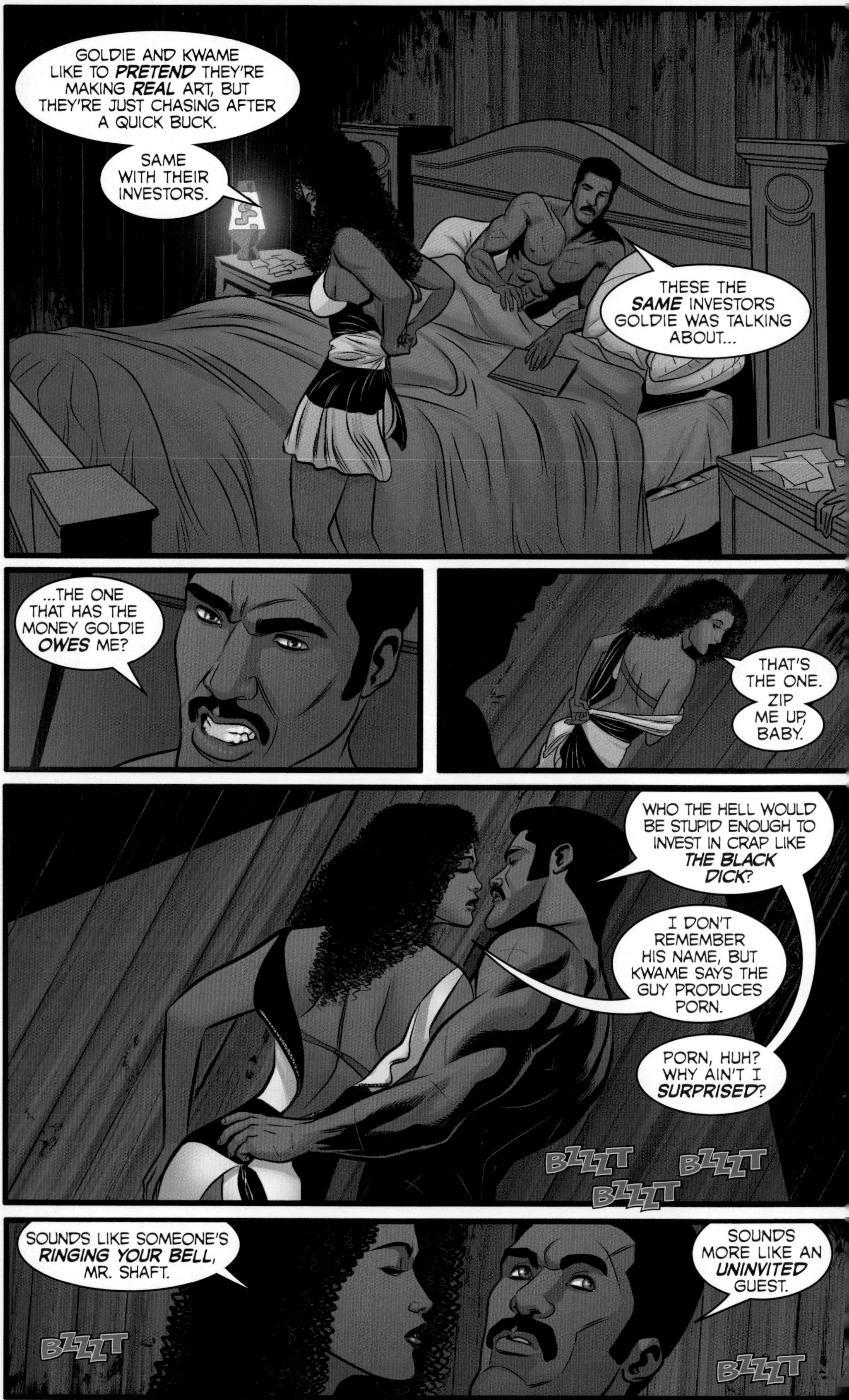
GOLDIE AND KWAME LIKE TO PRETEND THEY'RE MAKING REAL ART, BUT THEY'RE JUST CHASING AFTER A QUICK BUCK.
SAME WITH THEIR INVESTORS.
THESE THE SAME INVESTORS GOLDIE WAS TALKING ABOUT...
...THE ONE THAT HAS THE MONEY GOLDIE OWES ME?
THAT'S THE ONE. ZIP ME UP, BABY.
WHO THE HELL WOULD BE STUPID ENOUGH TO INVEST IN CRAP LIKE THE BLACK DICK?
I DON'T REMEMBER HIS NAME, BUT KWAME SAYS THE GUY PRODUCES PORN.
PORN, HUH? WHY AIN'T I SURPRISED?
BZZZT BZZZT BZZZT
SOUNDS LIKE SOMEONE'S RINGING YOUR BELL, MR. SHAFT.
SOUNDS MORE LIKE AN UNINVITED GUEST.
BZZZT BZZZT

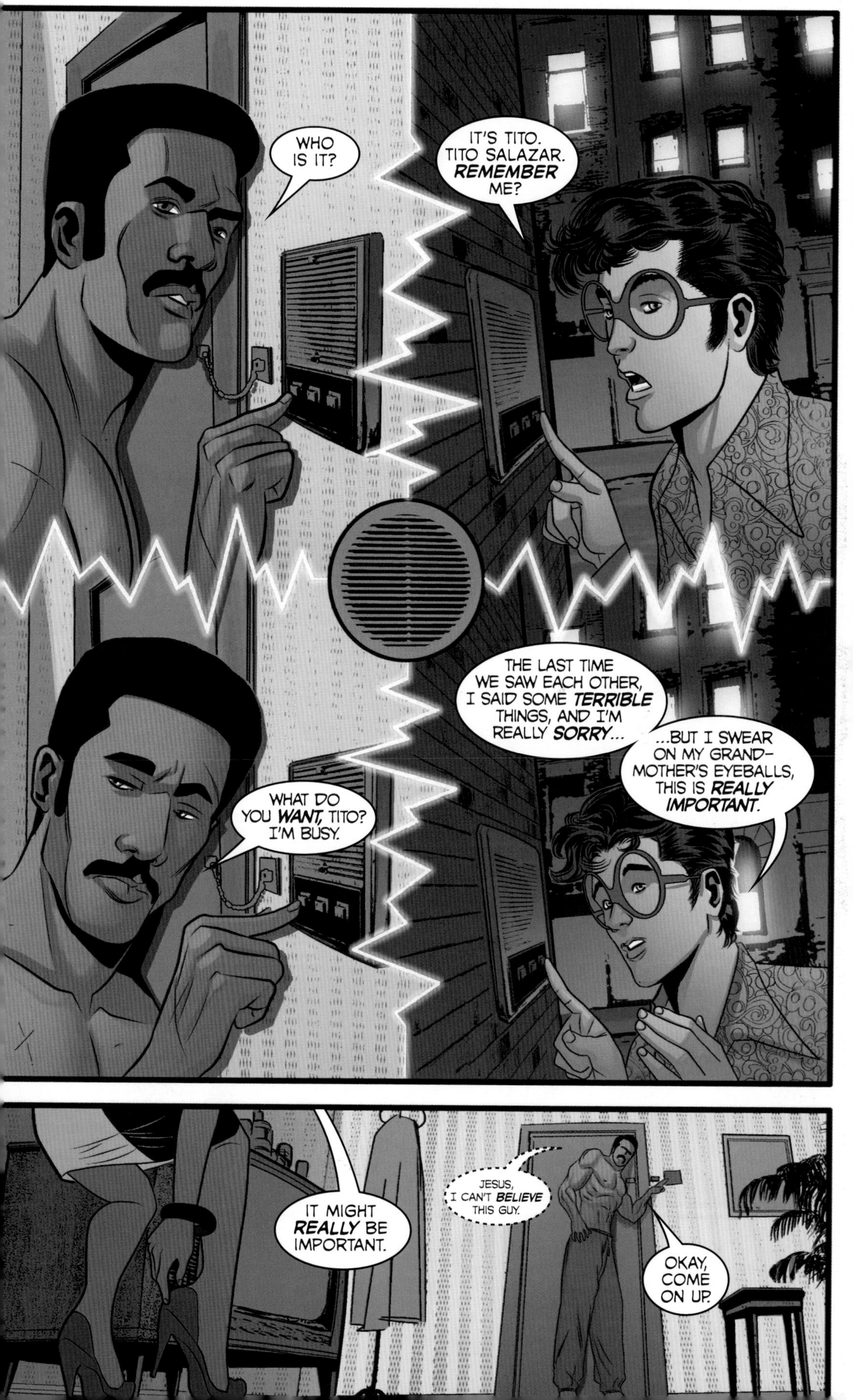
WHO IS IT?
IT'S TITO. TITO SALAZAR. REMEMBER ME?
THE LAST TIME WE SAW EACH OTHER, I SAID SOME TERRIBLE THINGS, AND I'M REALLY SORRY...
...BUT I SWEAR ON MY GRAND-MOTHER'S EYEBALLS, THIS IS REALLY IMPORTANT.
WHAT DO YOU WANT, TITO? I'M BUSY.
IT MIGHT REALLY BE IMPORTANT.
JESUS, I CAN'T BELIEVE THIS GUY.
OKAY, COME ON UP.

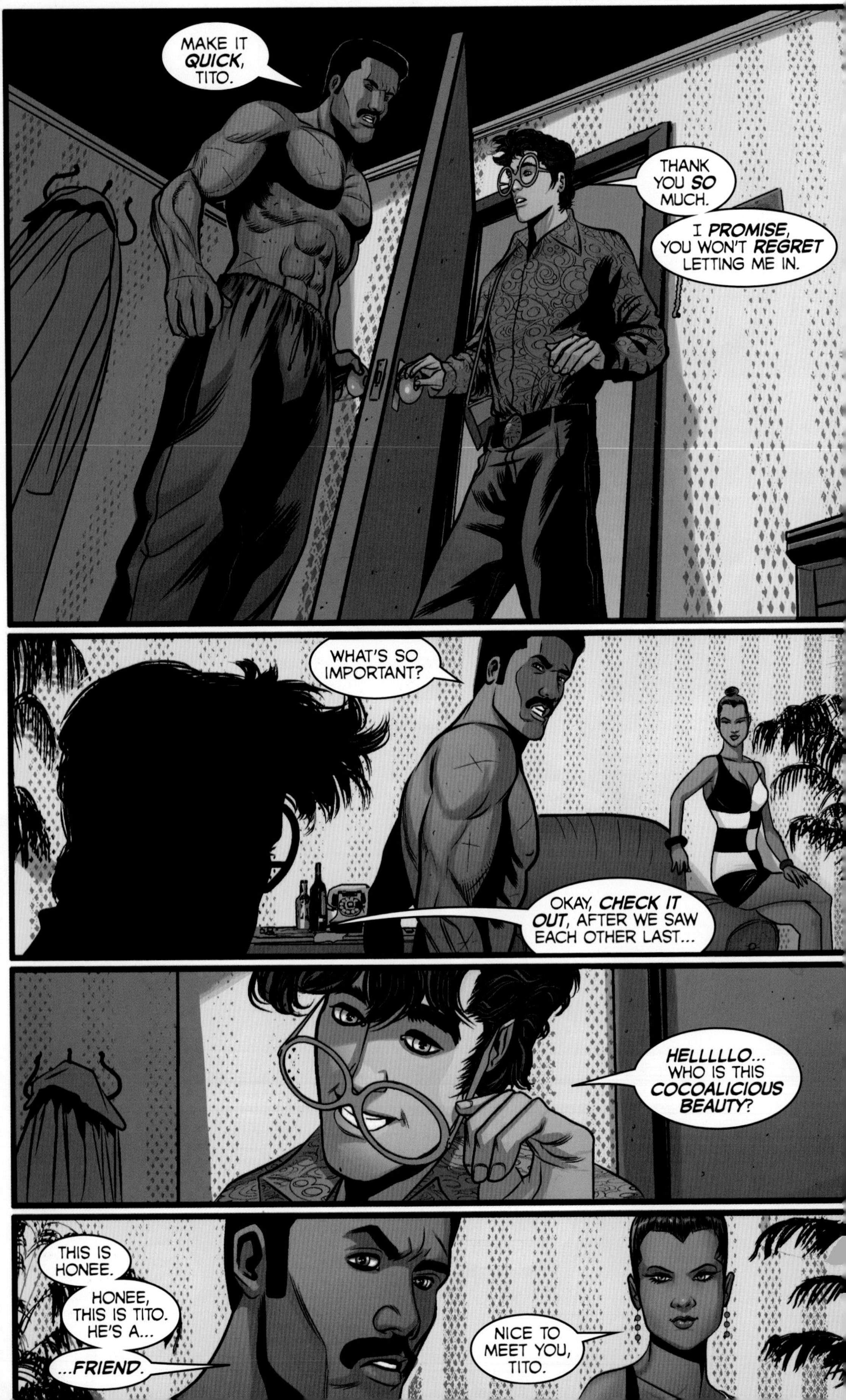

MAKE IT QUICK, TITO.
THANK YOU SO MUCH.
I PROMISE, YOU WON'T REGRET LETTING ME IN.
WHAT'S SO IMPORTANT?
OKAY, CHECK IT OUT, AFTER WE SAW EACH OTHER LAST...
HELLLLLO... WHO IS THIS COCOALICIOUS BEAUTY?
THIS IS HONEE.
HONEE, THIS IS TITO. HE'S A...
...FRIEND.
NICE TO MEET YOU, TITO.

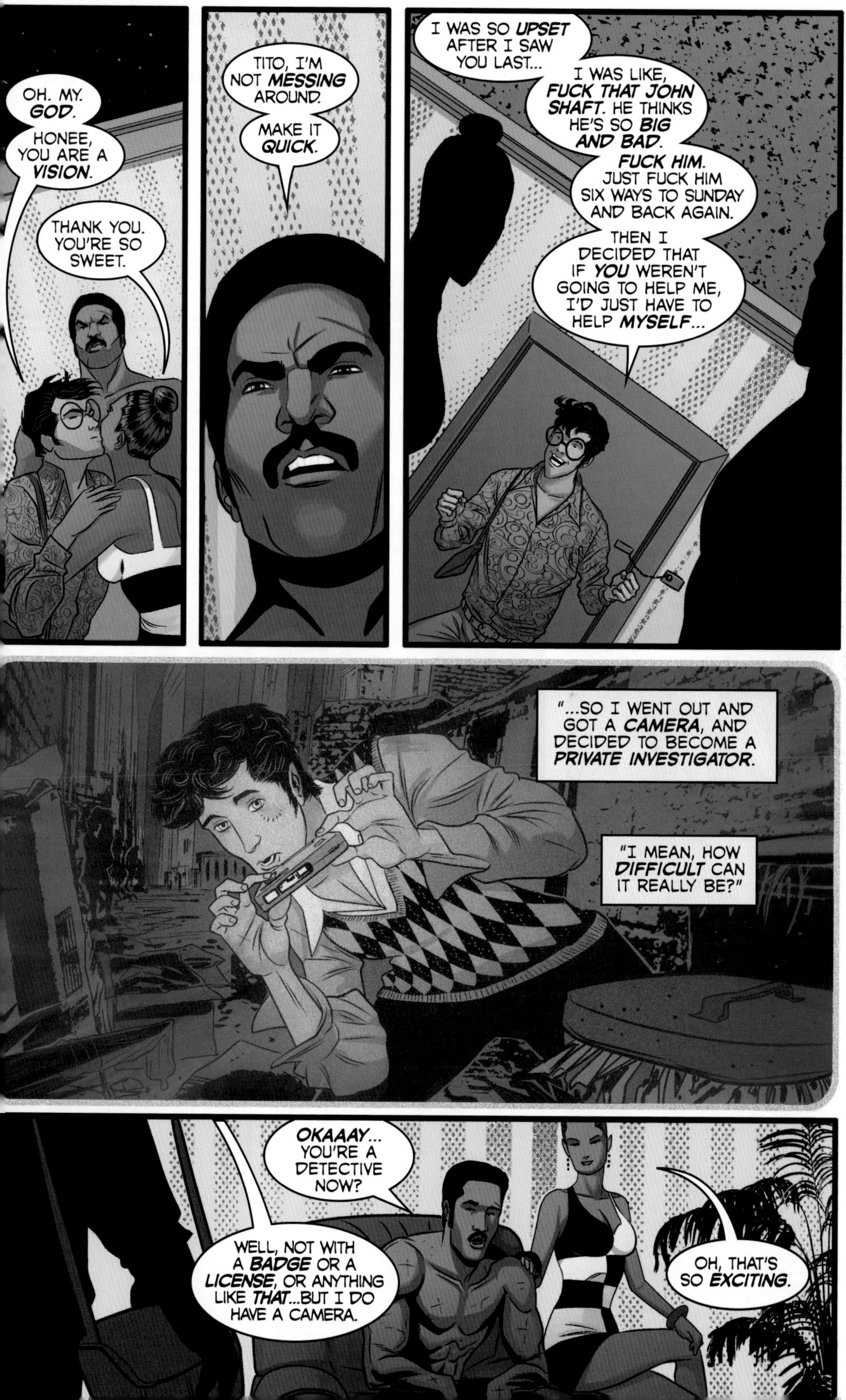
OH. MY. GOD.
HONEE, YOU ARE A VISION.
THANK YOU. YOU'RE SO SWEET.
TITO, I'M NOT MESSING AROUND.
MAKE IT QUICK.
I WAS SO UPSET AFTER I SAW YOU LAST...
I WAS LIKE, FUCK THAT JOHN SHAFT. HE THINKS HE'S SO BIG AND BAD.
FUCK HIM. JUST FUCK HIM SIX WAYS TO SUNDAY AND BACK AGAIN.
THEN I DECIDED THAT IF YOU WEREN'T GOING TO HELP ME, I'D JUST HAVE TO HELP MYSELF...
"...SO I WENT OUT AND GOT A CAMERA, AND DECIDED TO BECOME A PRIVATE INVESTIGATOR.
"I MEAN, HOW DIFFICULT CAN IT REALLY BE?"
OKAAAY... YOU'RE A DETECTIVE NOW?
WELL, NOT WITH A BADGE OR A LICENSE, OR ANYTHING LIKE THAT...BUT I DO HAVE A CAMERA.
OH, THAT'S SO EXCITING.

YOU DON'T EVEN KNOW THE *HALF* OF IT.

I STARTED FOLLOWING AROUND THAT *NASTY* SAMMY RIZZO, BECAUSE I THOUGHT HE COULD LEAD ME TO MY *MISSING FRIEND*, JOSHUA.

TURNS OUT JOSHUA WENT BACK TO OHIO...SO MUCH FOR *BEING IN LOVE.*

BUT YOU KNOW WHAT? THAT DOESN'T *MATTER...*

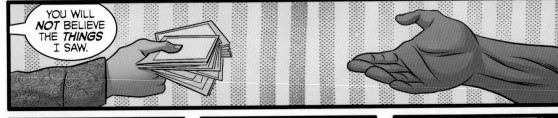

YOU WILL *NOT* BELIEVE THE *THINGS* I SAW.

UM...

...THESE ARE ALL *BLURRY.*

TITO, I THINK YOU GOT YOUR FINGER IN FRONT OF THE LENS ON A FEW OF THESE.

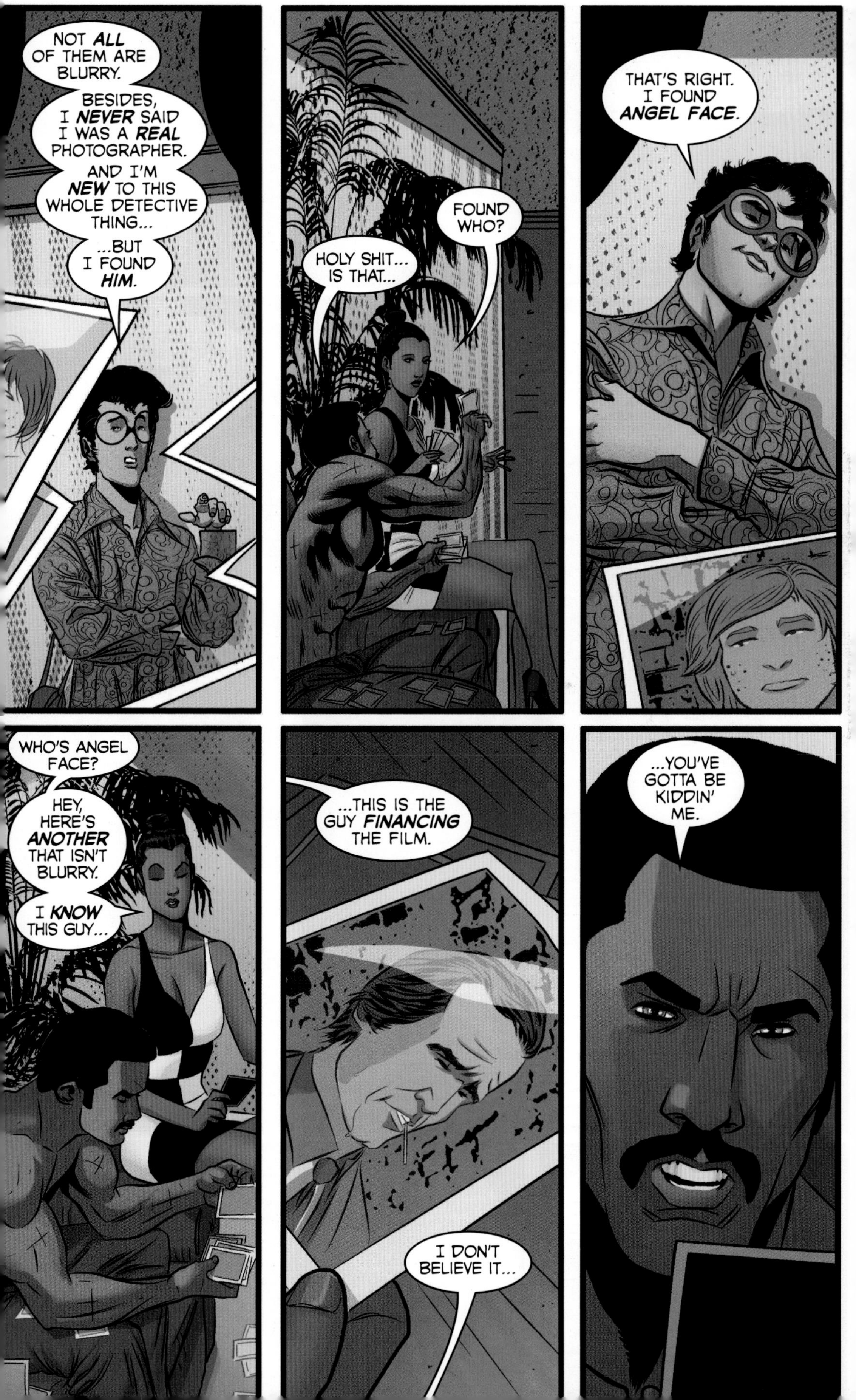
NOT ALL OF THEM ARE BLURRY.
BESIDES, I NEVER SAID I WAS A REAL PHOTOGRAPHER.
AND I'M NEW TO THIS WHOLE DETECTIVE THING...
...BUT I FOUND HIM.
HOLY SHIT... IS THAT...
FOUND WHO?
THAT'S RIGHT. I FOUND ANGEL FACE.
WHO'S ANGEL FACE?
HEY, HERE'S ANOTHER THAT ISN'T BLURRY.
I KNOW THIS GUY...
...THIS IS THE GUY FINANCING THE FILM.
I DON'T BELIEVE IT...
...YOU'VE GOTTA BE KIDDIN' ME.

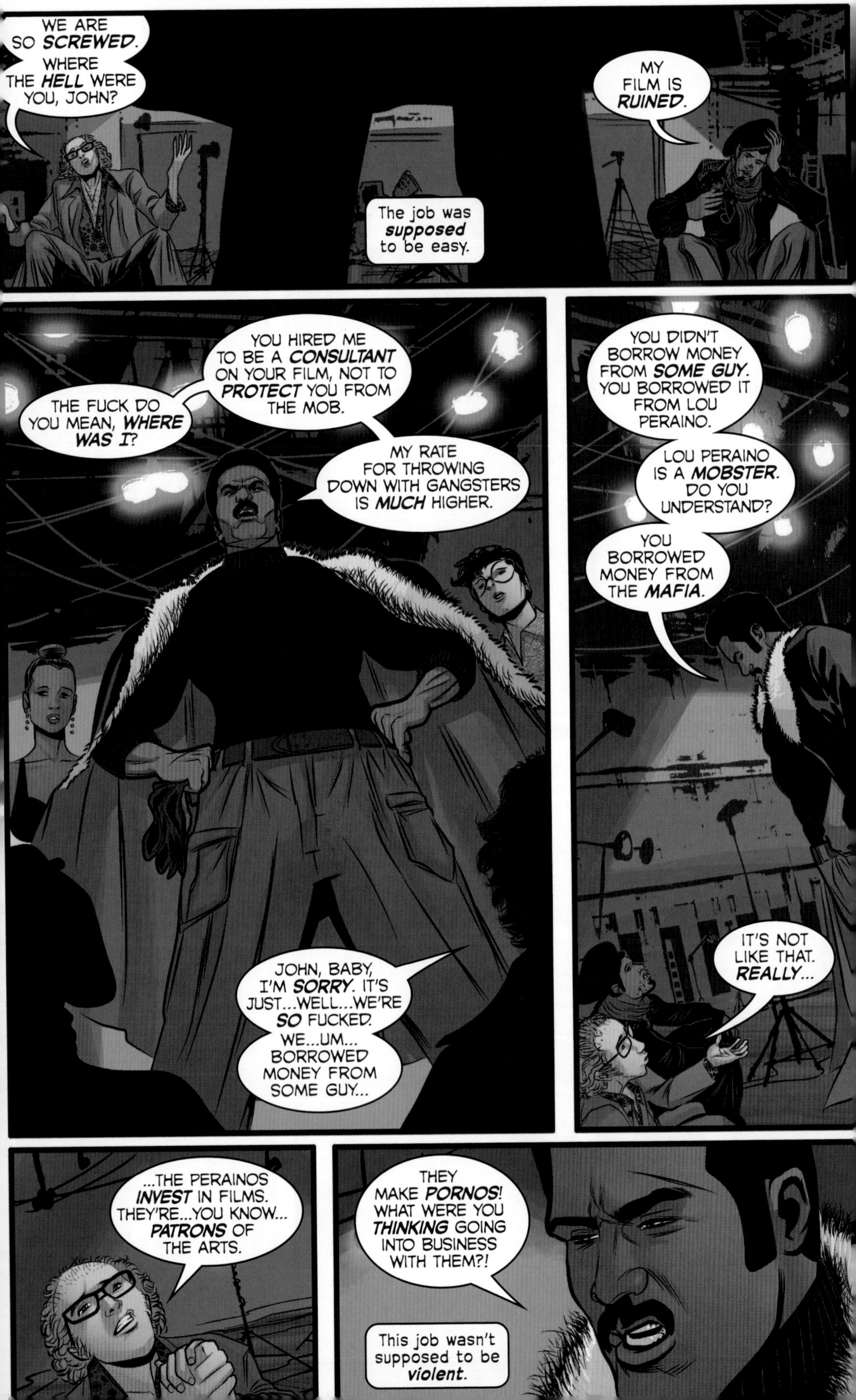
WE ARE SO SCREWED. WHERE THE HELL WERE YOU, JOHN?
The job was supposed to be easy.
MY FILM IS RUINED.
THE FUCK DO YOU MEAN, WHERE WAS I?
YOU HIRED ME TO BE A CONSULTANT ON YOUR FILM, NOT TO PROTECT YOU FROM THE MOB.
MY RATE FOR THROWING DOWN WITH GANGSTERS IS MUCH HIGHER.
JOHN, BABY, I'M SORRY. IT'S JUST...WELL...WE'RE SO FUCKED. WE...UM... BORROWED MONEY FROM SOME GUY...
YOU DIDN'T BORROW MONEY FROM SOME GUY. YOU BORROWED IT FROM LOU PERAINO.
LOU PERAINO IS A MOBSTER. DO YOU UNDERSTAND?
YOU BORROWED MONEY FROM THE MAFIA.
IT'S NOT LIKE THAT. REALLY...
...THE PERAINOS INVEST IN FILMS. THEY'RE...YOU KNOW... PATRONS OF THE ARTS.
THEY MAKE PORNOS! WHAT WERE YOU THINKING GOING INTO BUSINESS WITH THEM?!
This job wasn't supposed to be violent.

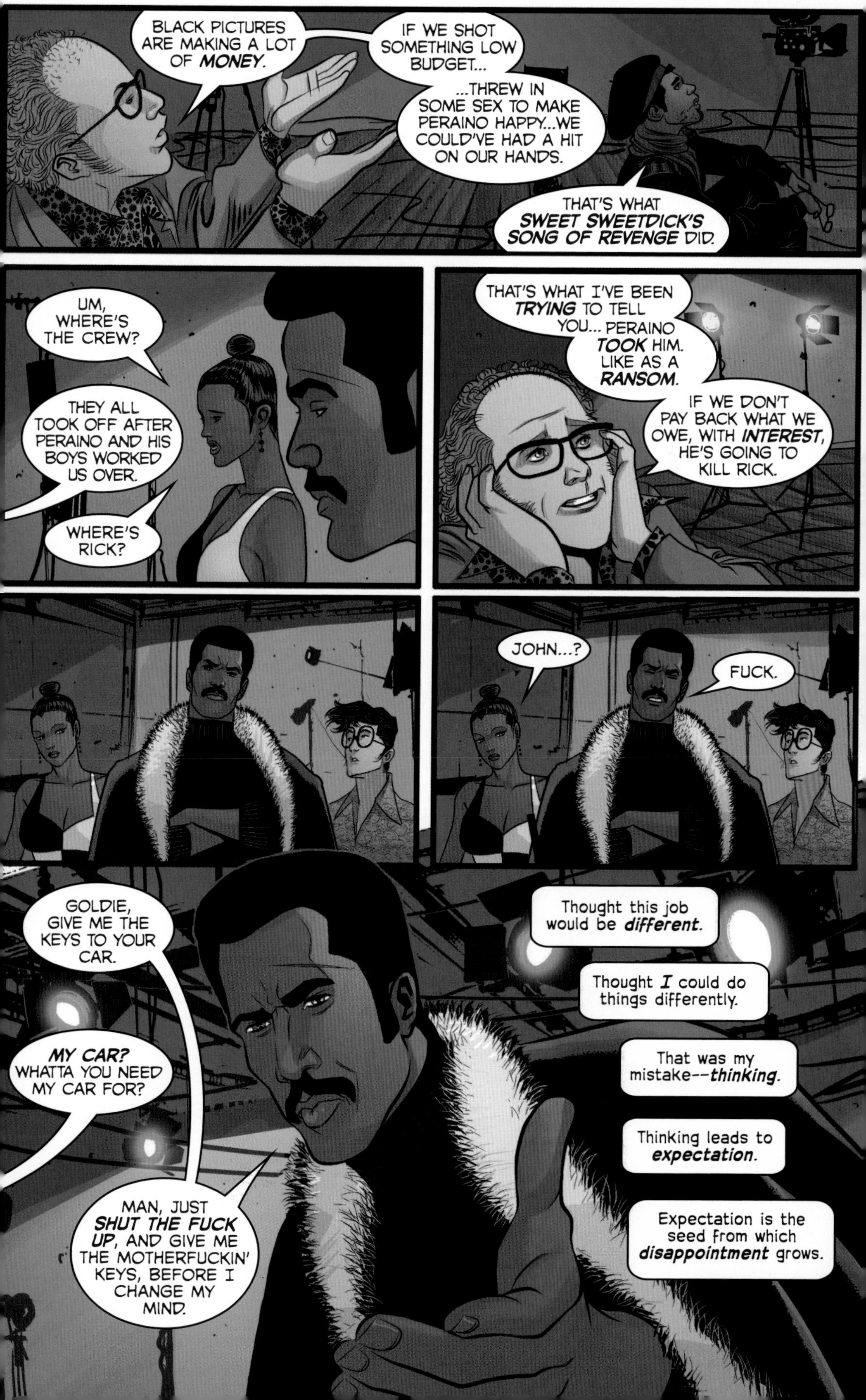
BLACK PICTURES ARE MAKING A LOT OF *MONEY*.
IF WE SHOT SOMETHING LOW BUDGET...
...THREW IN SOME SEX TO MAKE PERAINO HAPPY...WE COULD'VE HAD A HIT ON OUR HANDS.
THAT'S WHAT ***SWEET SWEETDICK'S SONG OF REVENGE*** DID.
UM, WHERE'S THE CREW?
THEY ALL TOOK OFF AFTER PERAINO AND HIS BOYS WORKED US OVER.
WHERE'S RICK?
THAT'S WHAT I'VE BEEN *TRYING* TO TELL YOU... PERAINO *TOOK* HIM. LIKE AS A *RANSOM*.
IF WE DON'T PAY BACK WHAT WE OWE, WITH *INTEREST*, HE'S GOING TO KILL RICK.
JOHN...?
FUCK.
GOLDIE, GIVE ME THE KEYS TO YOUR CAR.
MY CAR? WHATTA YOU NEED MY CAR FOR?
MAN, JUST ***SHUT THE FUCK UP***, AND GIVE ME THE MOTHERFUCKIN' KEYS, BEFORE I CHANGE MY MIND.
Thought this job would be *different*.
Thought *I* could do things differently.
That was my mistake--*thinking*.
Thinking leads to *expectation*.
Expectation is the seed from which *disappointment* grows.

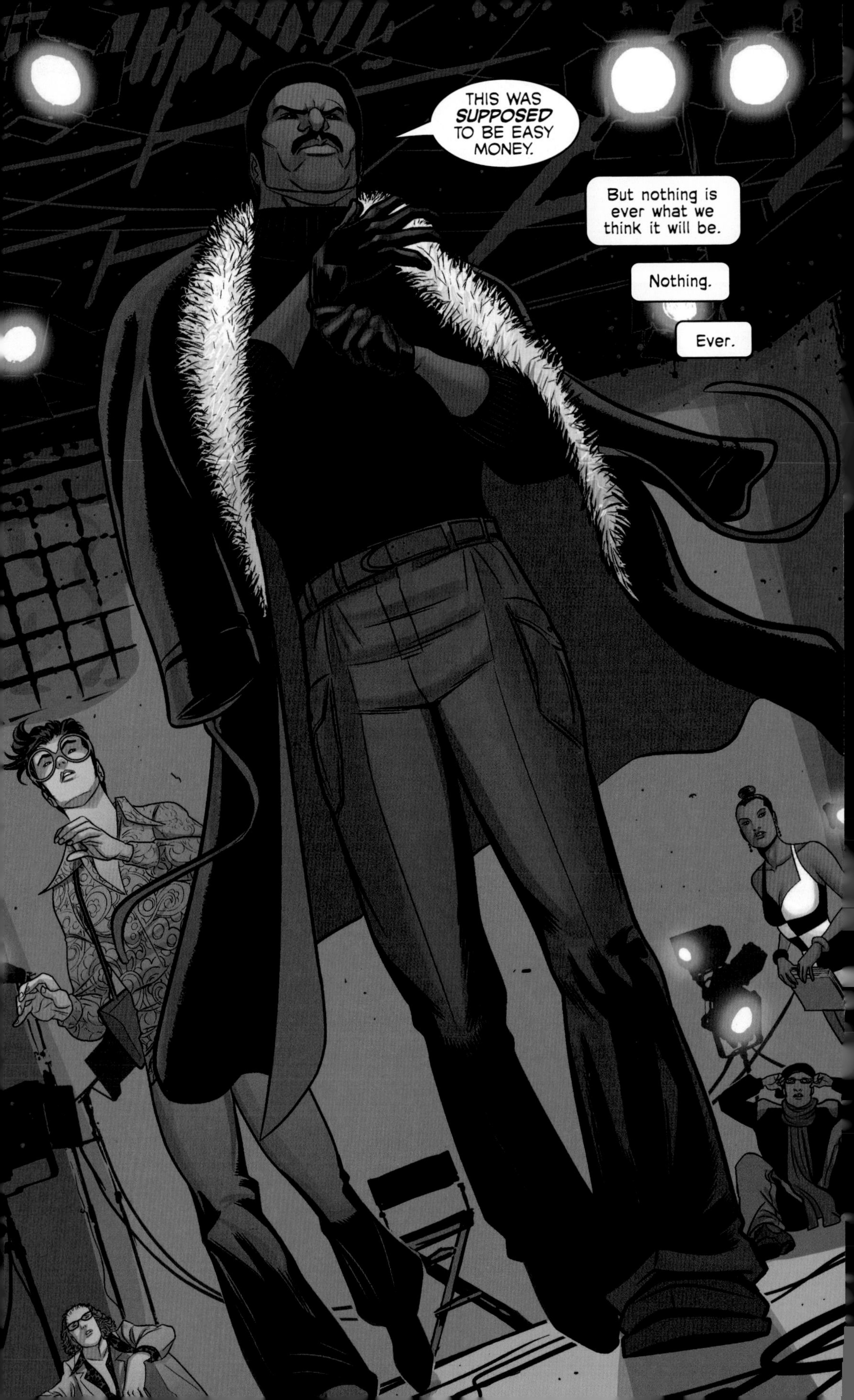
THIS WAS SUPPOSED TO BE EASY MONEY.
But nothing is ever what we think it will be.
Nothing.
Ever.

DAVID F. WALKER • DIETRICH SMITH

SHAFT

IMITATION OF LIFE

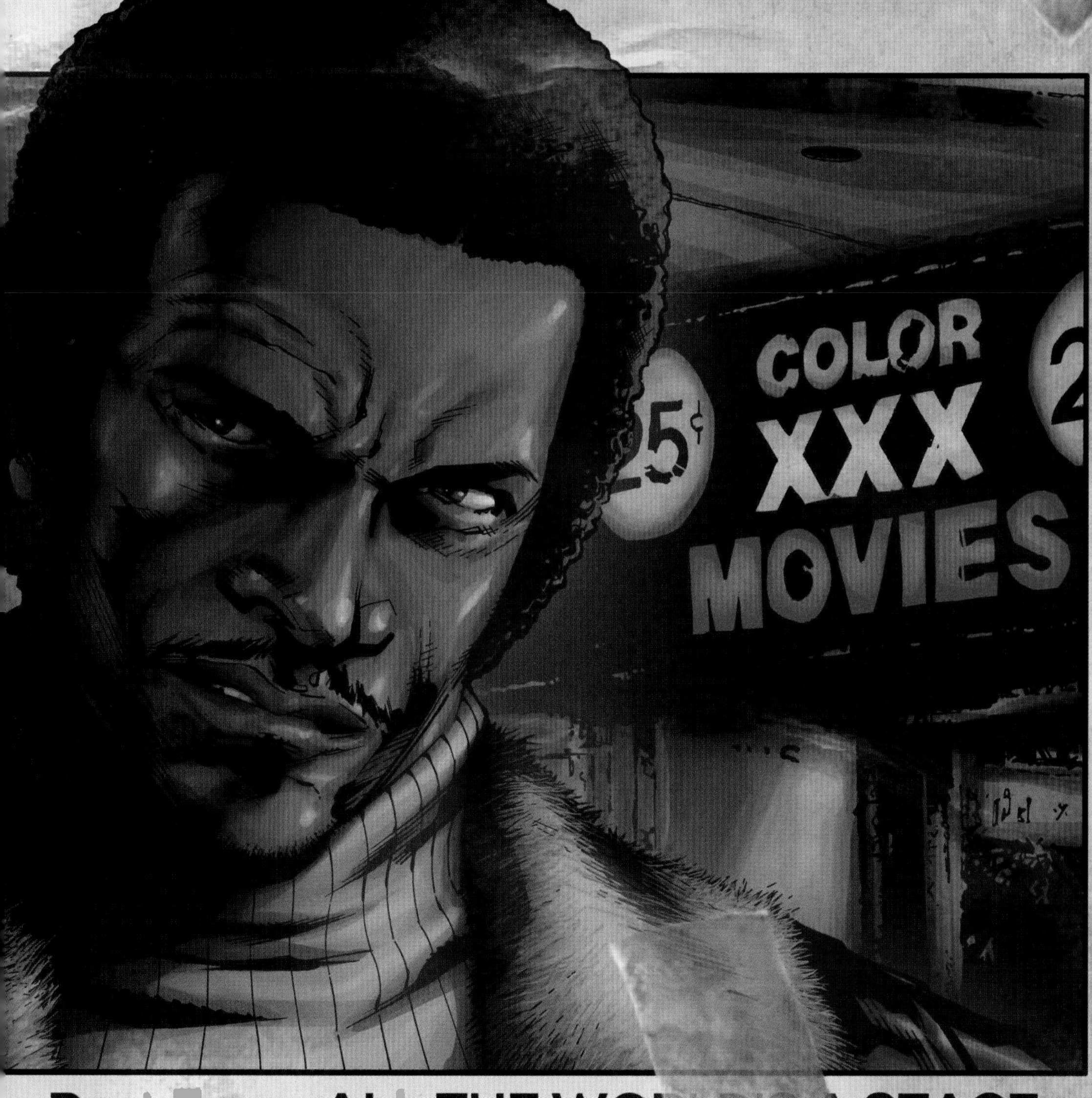
COLOR
25¢
XXX
MOVIES

Part Four: ALL THE WORLD'S A STAGE

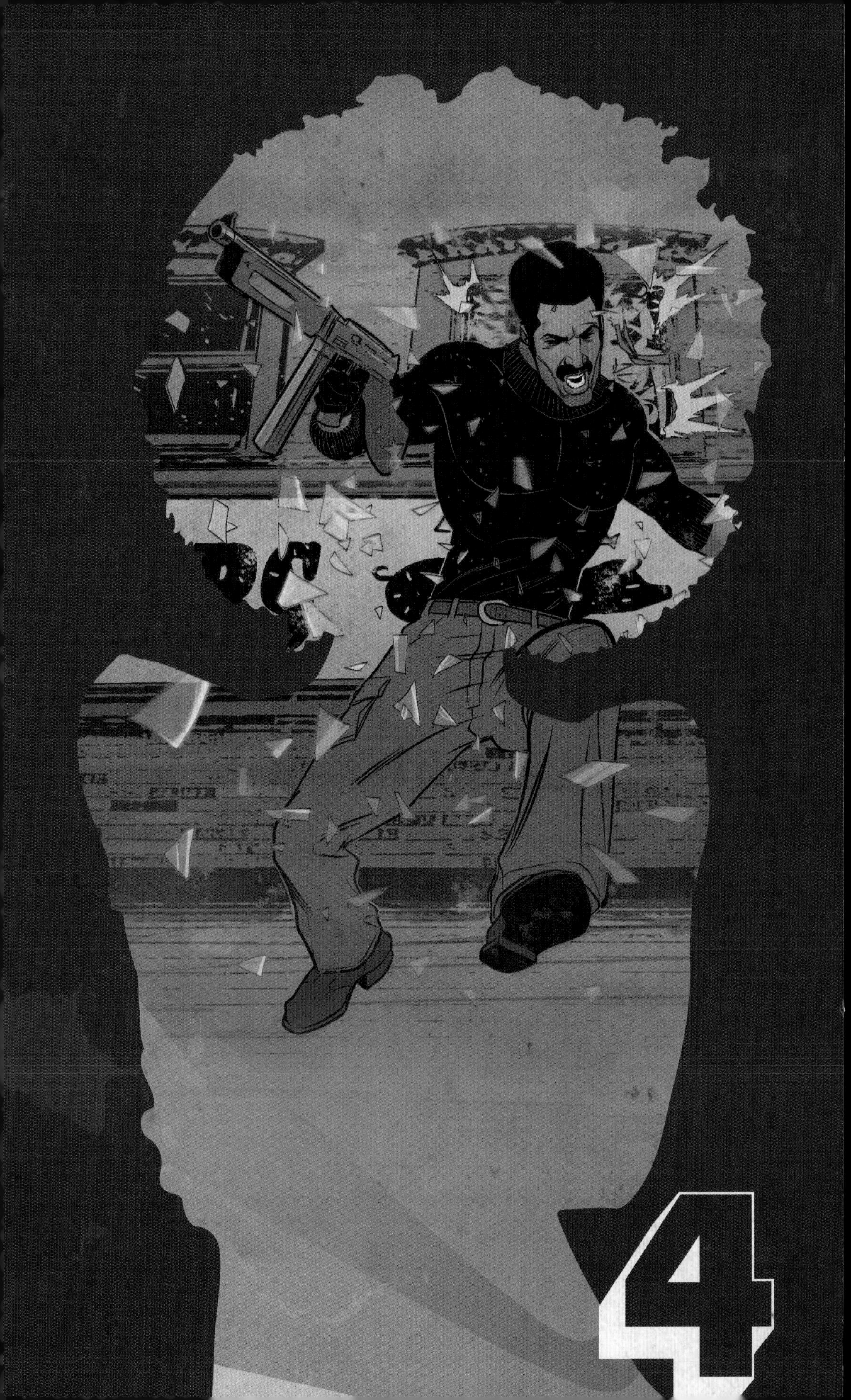
4

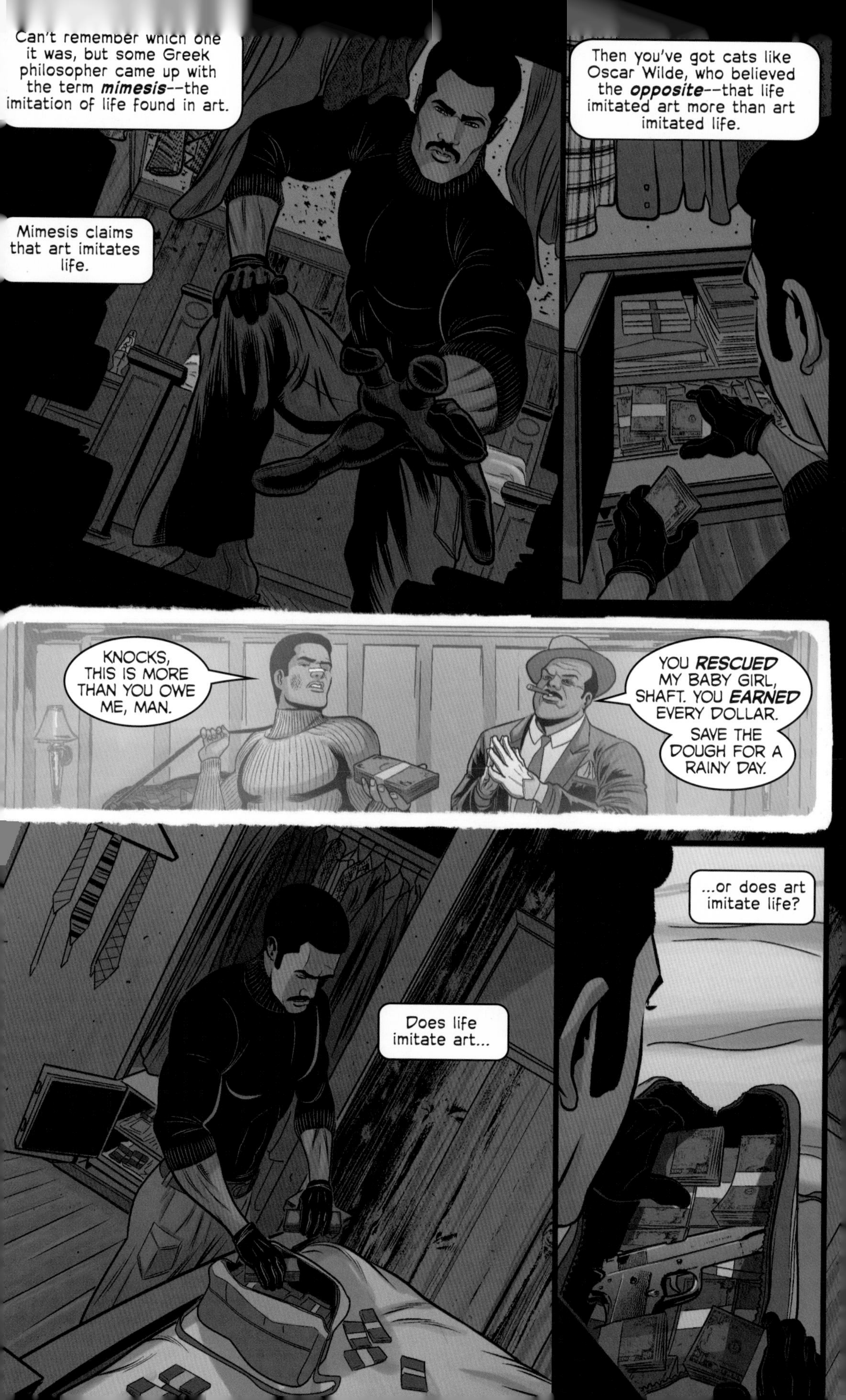
Can't remember which one it was, but some Greek philosopher came up with the term ***mimesis***--the imitation of life found in art.
Mimesis claims that art imitates life.
Then you've got cats like Oscar Wilde, who believed the ***opposite***--that life imitated art more than art imitated life.
KNOCKS, THIS IS MORE THAN YOU OWE ME, MAN.
YOU ***RESCUED*** MY BABY GIRL, SHAFT. YOU ***EARNED*** EVERY DOLLAR.
SAVE THE DOUGH FOR A RAINY DAY.
Does life imitate art...
...or does art imitate life?

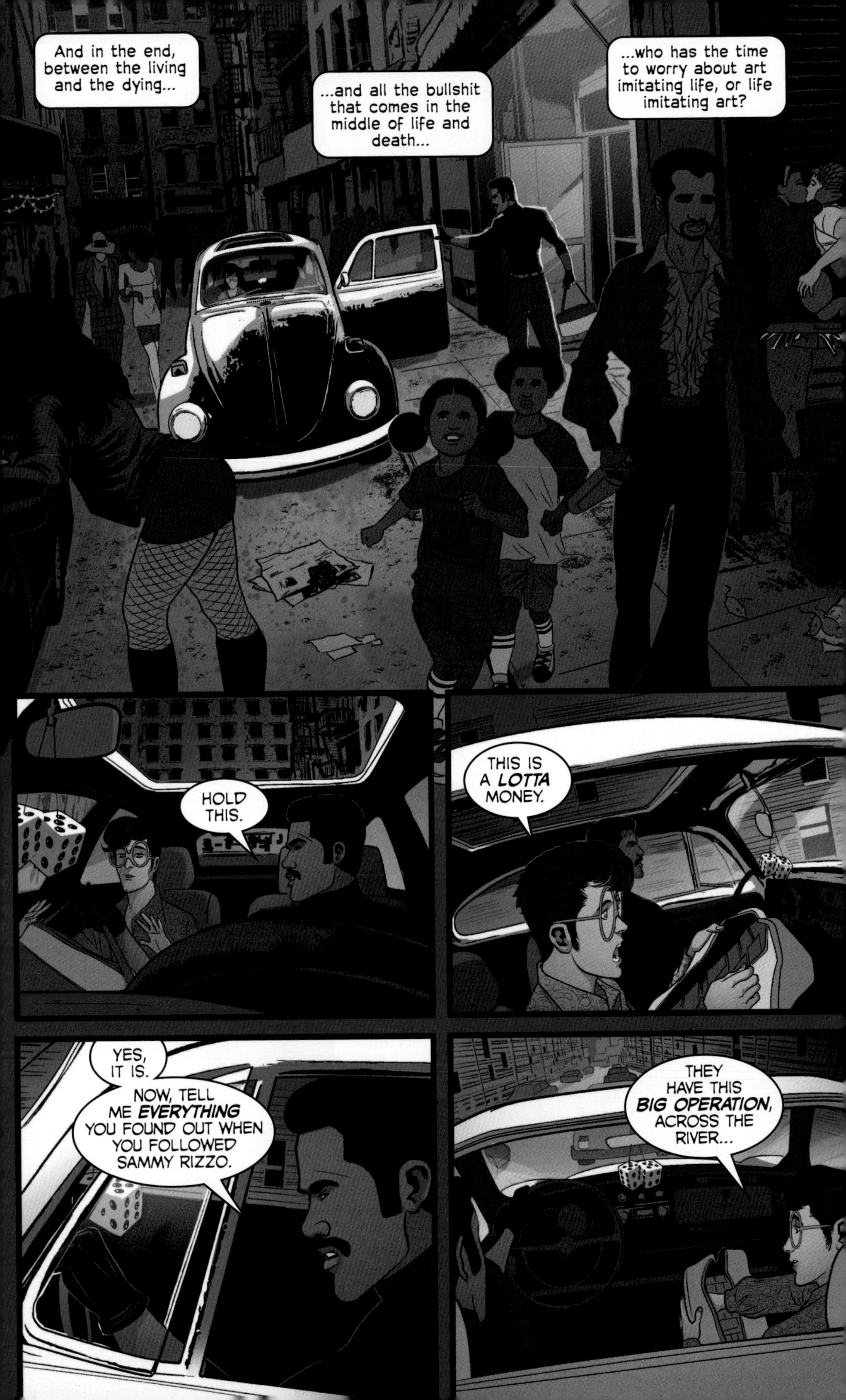
And in the end, between the living and the dying...
...and all the bullshit that comes in the middle of life and death...
...who has the time to worry about art imitating life, or life imitating art?
HOLD THIS.
THIS IS A *LOTTA* MONEY.
YES, IT IS.
NOW, TELL ME ***EVERYTHING*** YOU FOUND OUT WHEN YOU FOLLOWED SAMMY RIZZO.
THEY HAVE THIS ***BIG OPERATION***, ACROSS THE RIVER...

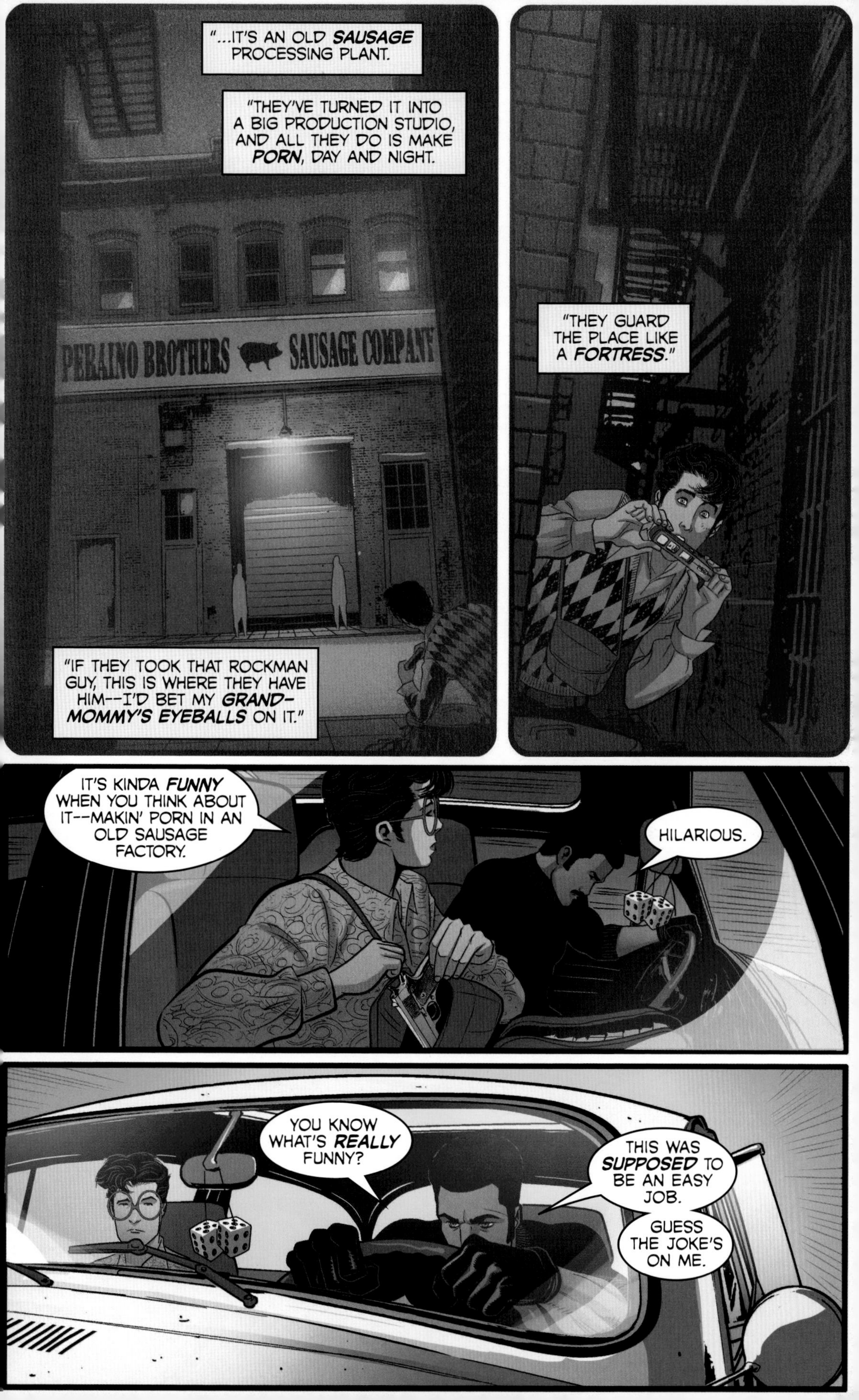
"...IT'S AN OLD SAUSAGE PROCESSING PLANT.
"THEY'VE TURNED IT INTO A BIG PRODUCTION STUDIO, AND ALL THEY DO IS MAKE PORN, DAY AND NIGHT.
PERAINO BROTHERS SAUSAGE COMPANY
"IF THEY TOOK THAT ROCKMAN GUY, THIS IS WHERE THEY HAVE HIM--I'D BET MY GRAND-MOMMY'S EYEBALLS ON IT."
"THEY GUARD THE PLACE LIKE A FORTRESS."
IT'S KINDA FUNNY WHEN YOU THINK ABOUT IT--MAKIN' PORN IN AN OLD SAUSAGE FACTORY.
HILARIOUS.
YOU KNOW WHAT'S REALLY FUNNY?
THIS WAS SUPPOSED TO BE AN EASY JOB.
GUESS THE JOKE'S ON ME.

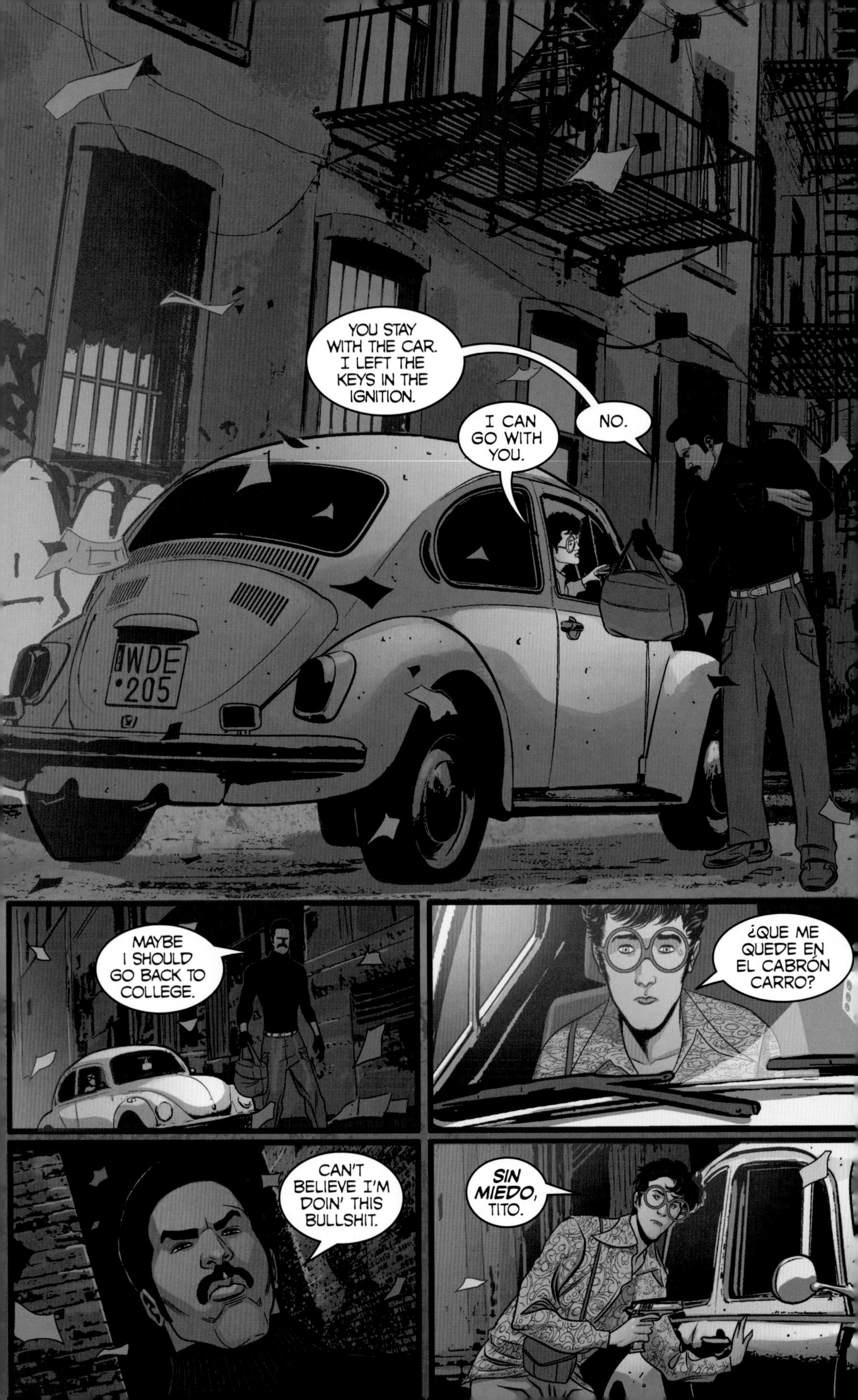
YOU STAY WITH THE CAR. I LEFT THE KEYS IN THE IGNITION.
I CAN GO WITH YOU.
NO.
WDE 205
MAYBE I SHOULD GO BACK TO COLLEGE.
¿QUE ME QUEDE EN EL CABRÓN CARRO?
CAN'T BELIEVE I'M DOIN' THIS BULLSHIT.
SIN MIEDO, TITO.

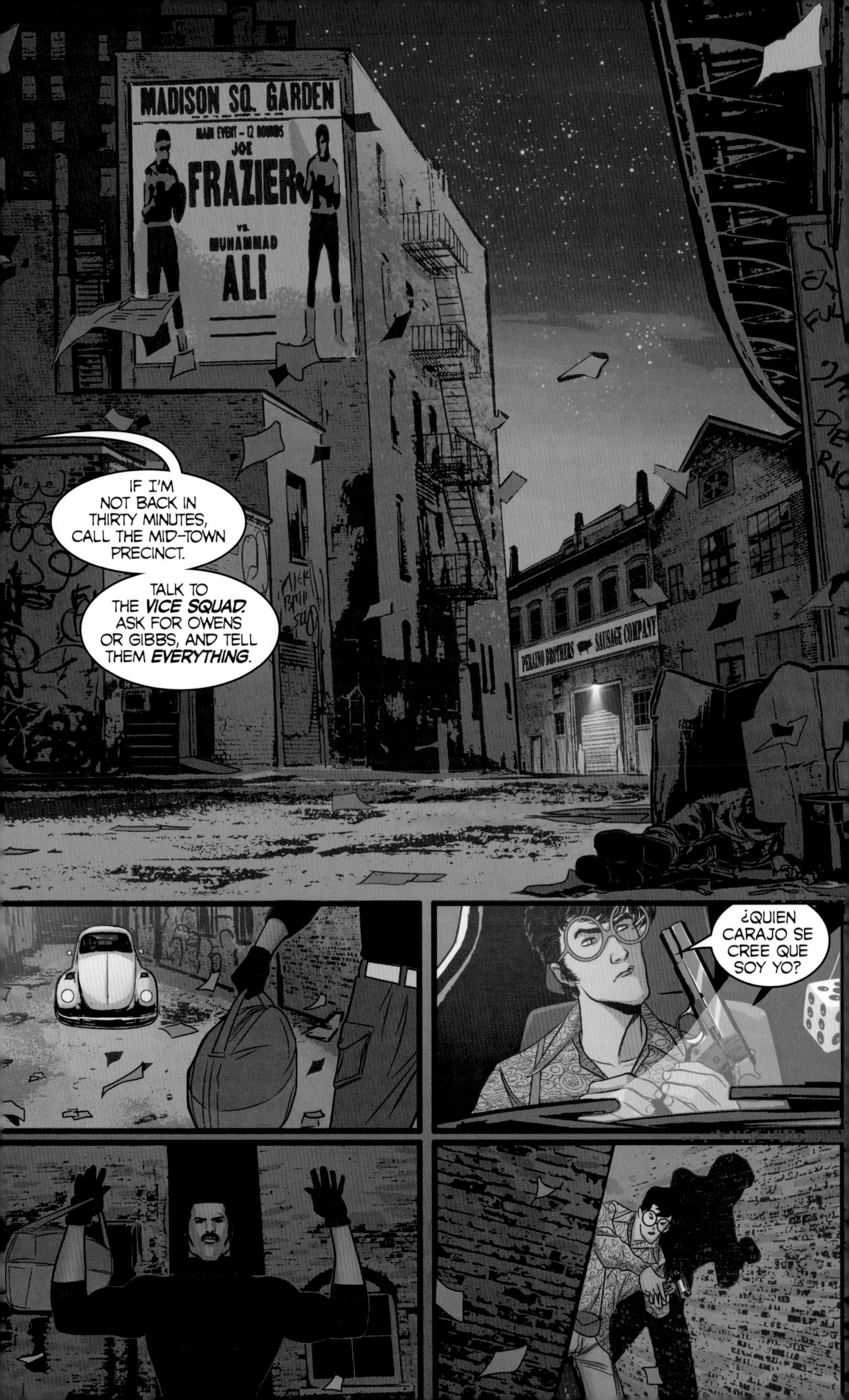
MADISON SQ. GARDEN
MAIN EVENT – 12 ROUNDS
JOE
FRAZIER
VS.
MUHAMMAD
ALI
IF I'M NOT BACK IN THIRTY MINUTES, CALL THE MID-TOWN PRECINCT.
TALK TO THE *VICE SQUAD.* ASK FOR OWENS OR GIBBS, AND TELL THEM *EVERYTHING*.
PERAINO BROTHERS SAUSAGE COMPANY
¿QUIEN CARAJO SE CREE QUE SOY YO?

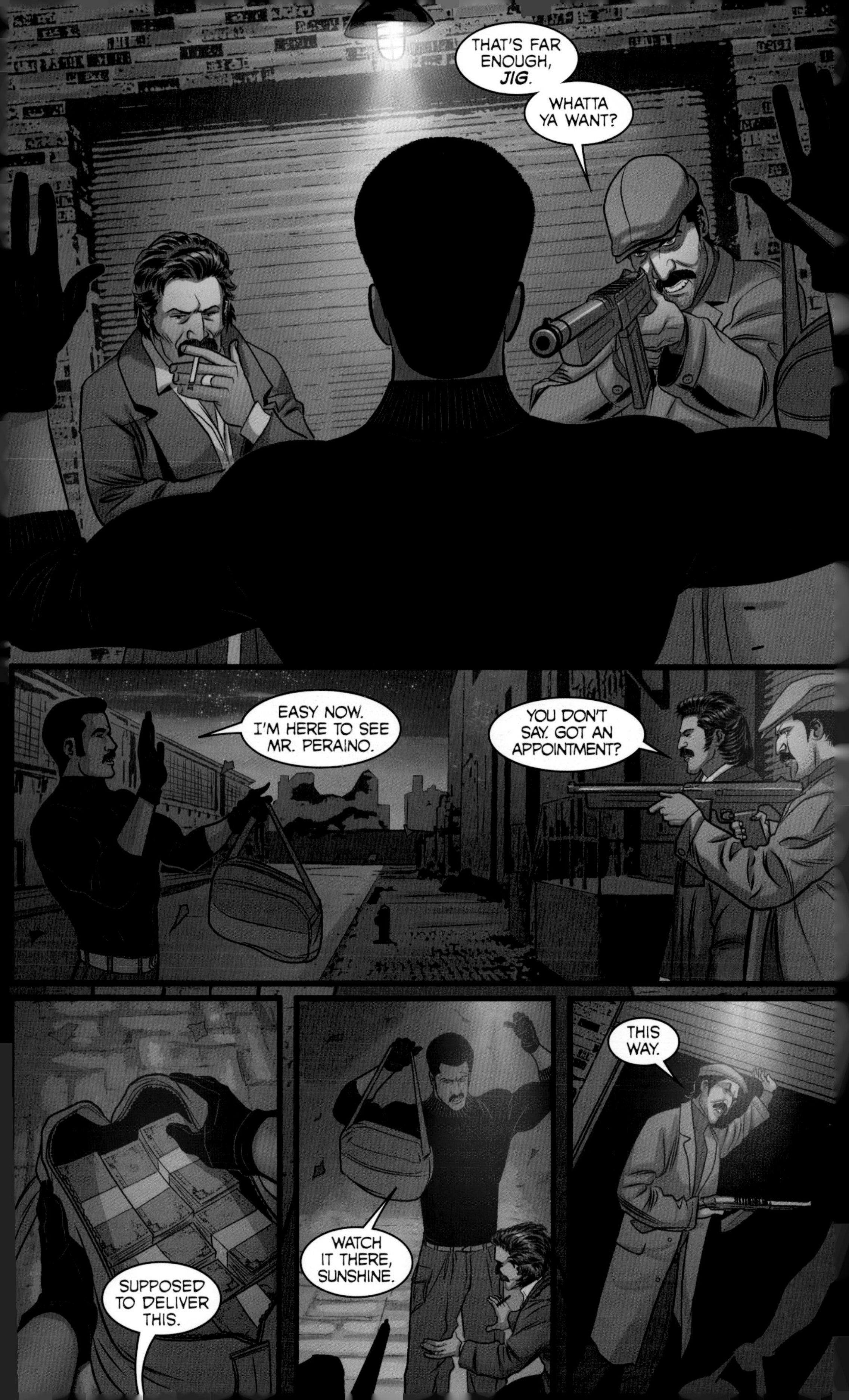
THAT'S FAR ENOUGH, *JIG*.
WHATTA YA WANT?
EASY NOW. I'M HERE TO SEE MR. PERAINO.
YOU DON'T SAY. GOT AN APPOINTMENT?
SUPPOSED TO DELIVER THIS.
WATCH IT THERE, SUNSHINE.
THIS WAY.

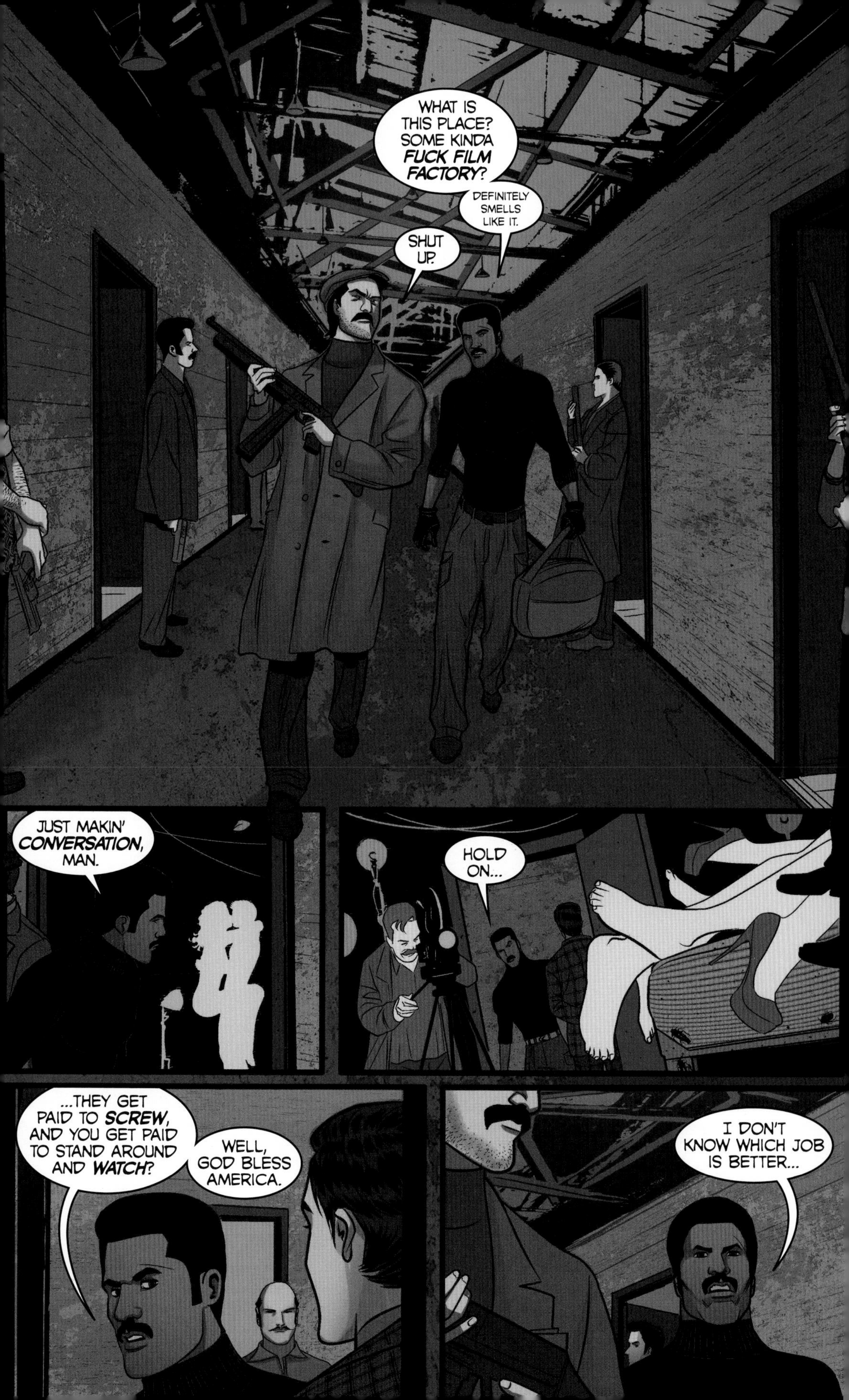
WHAT IS THIS PLACE? SOME KINDA FUCK FILM FACTORY?
DEFINITELY SMELLS LIKE IT.
SHUT UP.
JUST MAKIN' CONVERSATION, MAN.
HOLD ON...
...THEY GET PAID TO SCREW, AND YOU GET PAID TO STAND AROUND AND WATCH?
WELL, GOD BLESS AMERICA.
I DON'T KNOW WHICH JOB IS BETTER...

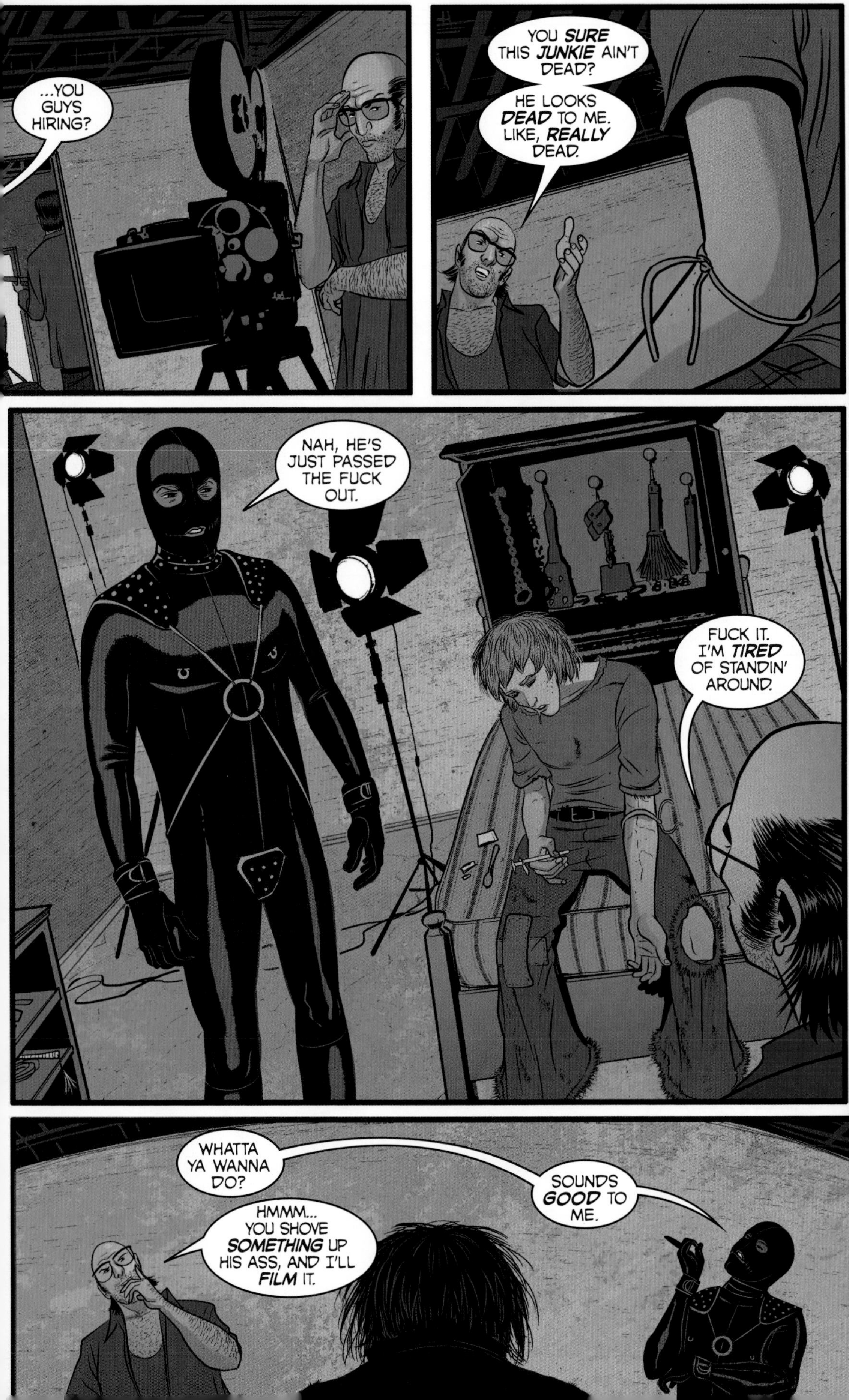
...YOU GUYS HIRING?
YOU SURE THIS JUNKIE AIN'T DEAD?
HE LOOKS DEAD TO ME. LIKE, REALLY DEAD.
NAH, HE'S JUST PASSED THE FUCK OUT.
FUCK IT. I'M TIRED OF STANDIN' AROUND.
WHATTA YA WANNA DO?
HMMM... YOU SHOVE SOMETHING UP HIS ASS, AND I'LL FILM IT.
SOUNDS GOOD TO ME.

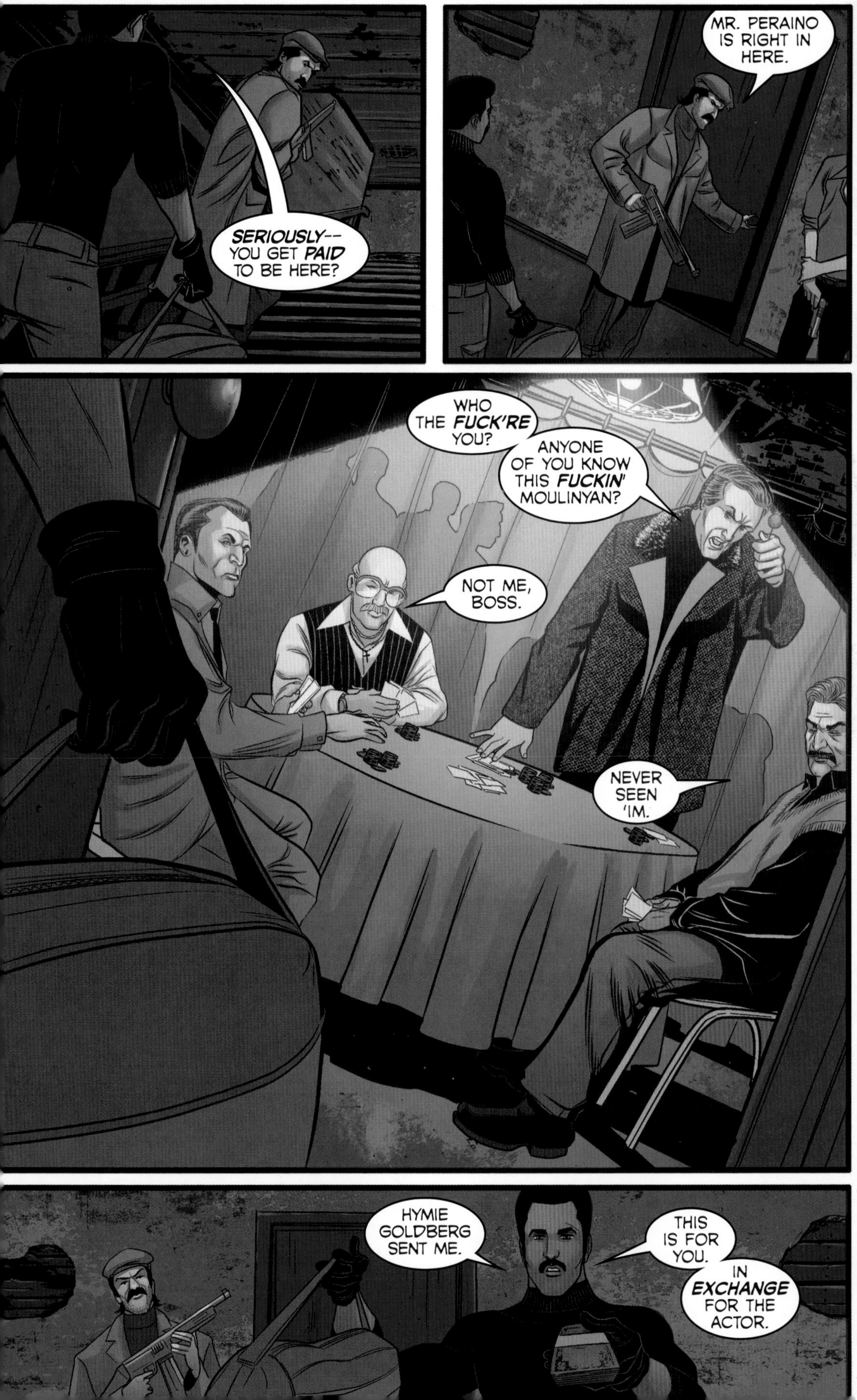
SERIOUSLY-- YOU GET PAID TO BE HERE?
MR. PERAINO IS RIGHT IN HERE.
WHO THE FUCK'RE YOU?
ANYONE OF YOU KNOW THIS FUCKIN' MOULINYAN?
NOT ME, BOSS.
NEVER SEEN 'IM.
HYMIE GOLDBERG SENT ME.
THIS IS FOR YOU.
IN EXCHANGE FOR THE ACTOR.

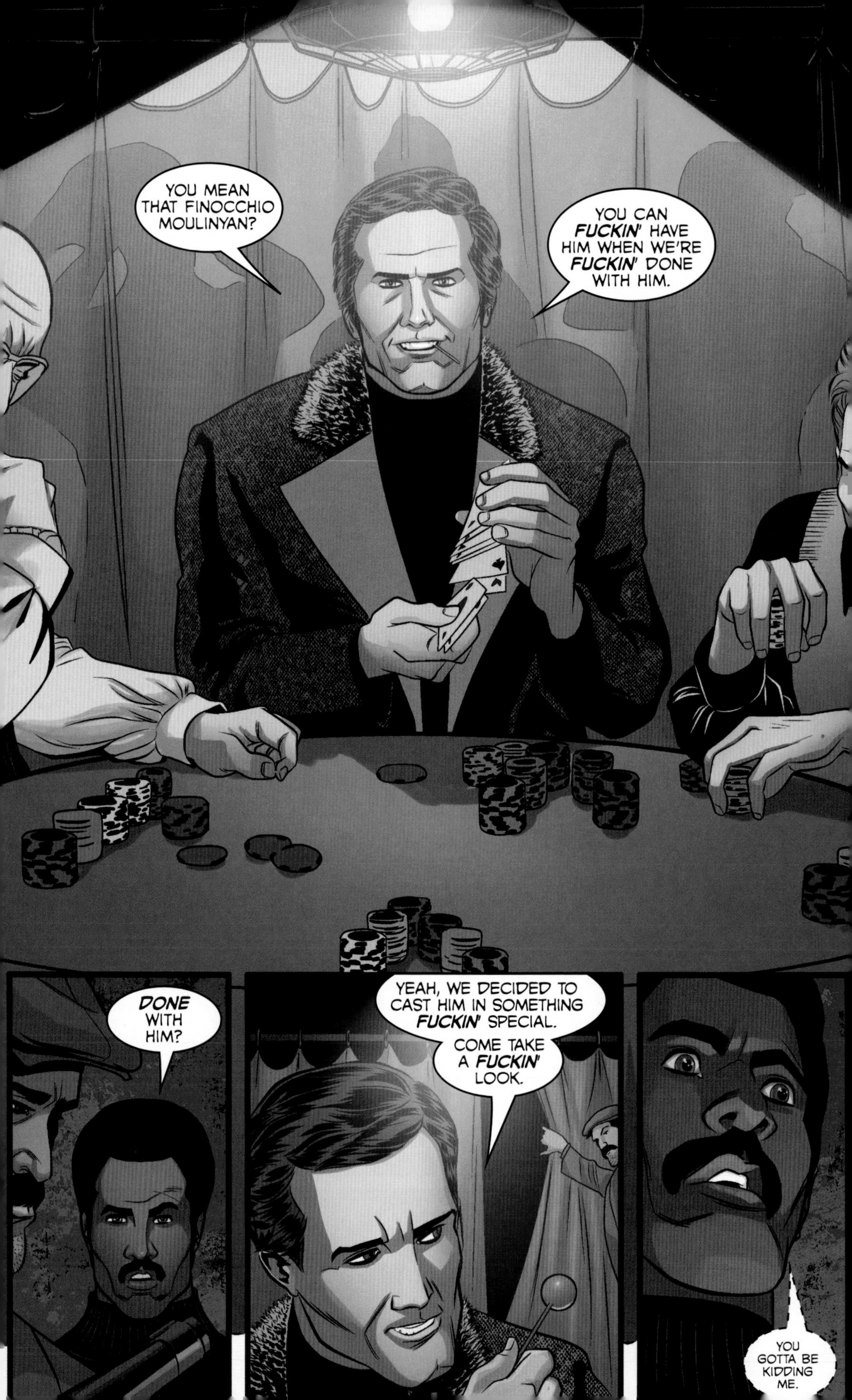
YOU MEAN THAT FINOCCHIO MOULINYAN?
YOU CAN *FUCKIN'* HAVE HIM WHEN WE'RE *FUCKIN'* DONE WITH HIM.
DONE WITH HIM?
YEAH, WE DECIDED TO CAST HIM IN SOMETHING *FUCKIN'* SPECIAL.
COME TAKE A *FUCKIN'* LOOK.
YOU GOTTA BE KIDDING ME.

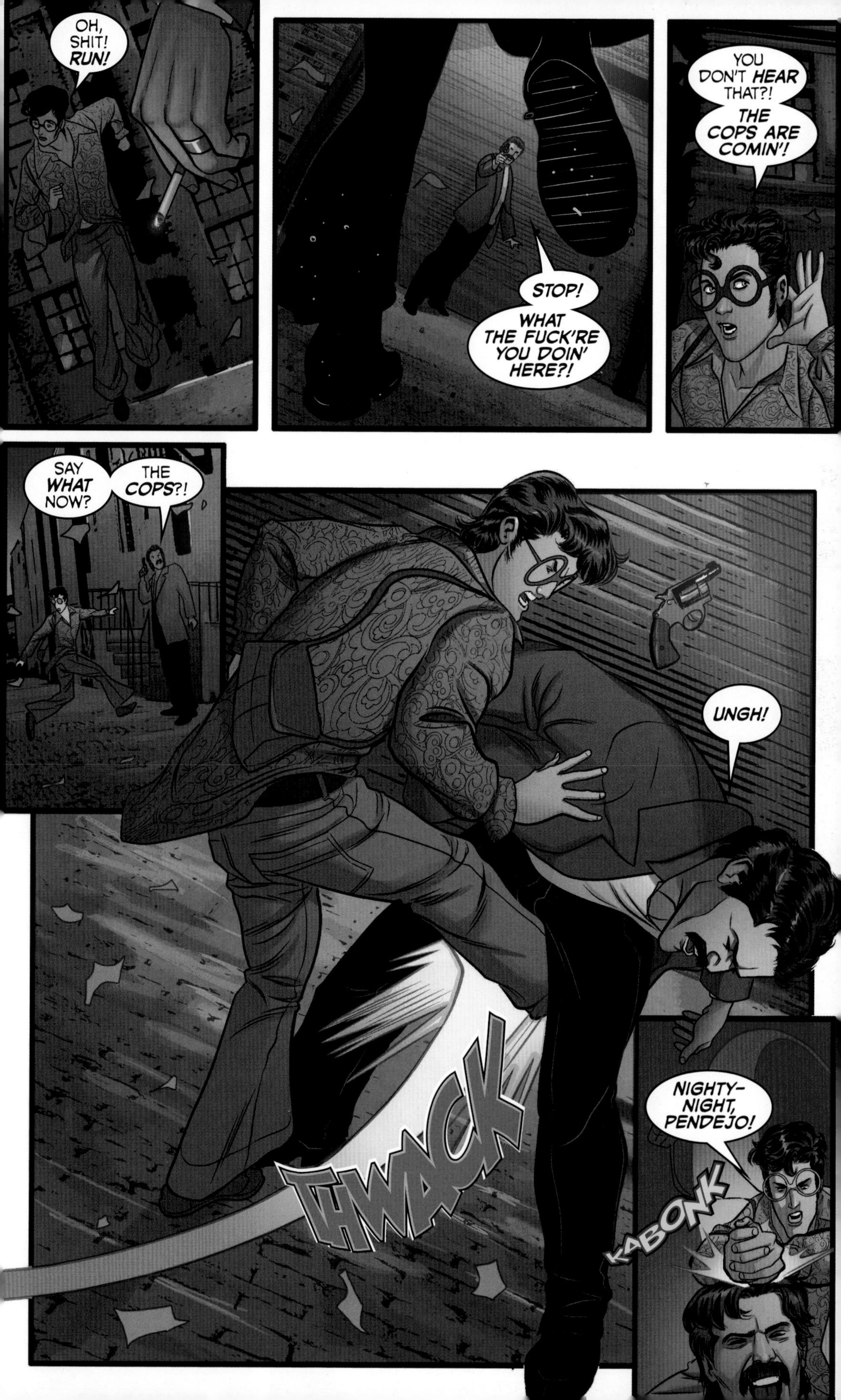
OH, SHIT! RUN!
STOP! WHAT THE FUCK'RE YOU DOIN' HERE?!
YOU DON'T HEAR THAT?! THE COPS ARE COMIN'!
SAY WHAT NOW?
THE COPS?!
UNGH!
THWACK
NIGHTY-NIGHT, PENDEJO!
KABONK

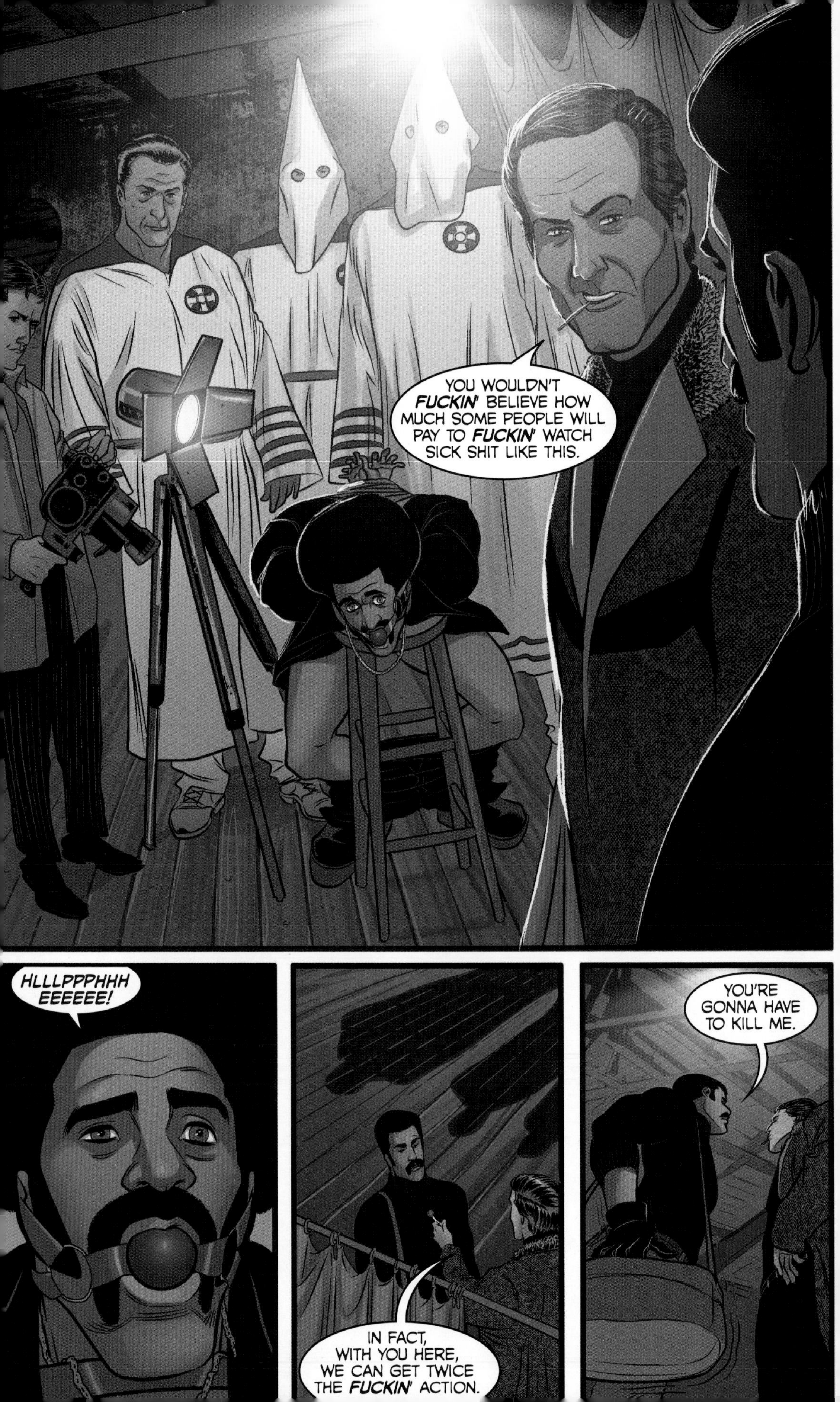
YOU WOULDN'T FUCKIN' BELIEVE HOW MUCH SOME PEOPLE WILL PAY TO FUCKIN' WATCH SICK SHIT LIKE THIS.
HLLLPPPHHH EEEEEE!
IN FACT, WITH YOU HERE, WE CAN GET TWICE THE FUCKIN' ACTION.
YOU'RE GONNA HAVE TO KILL ME.

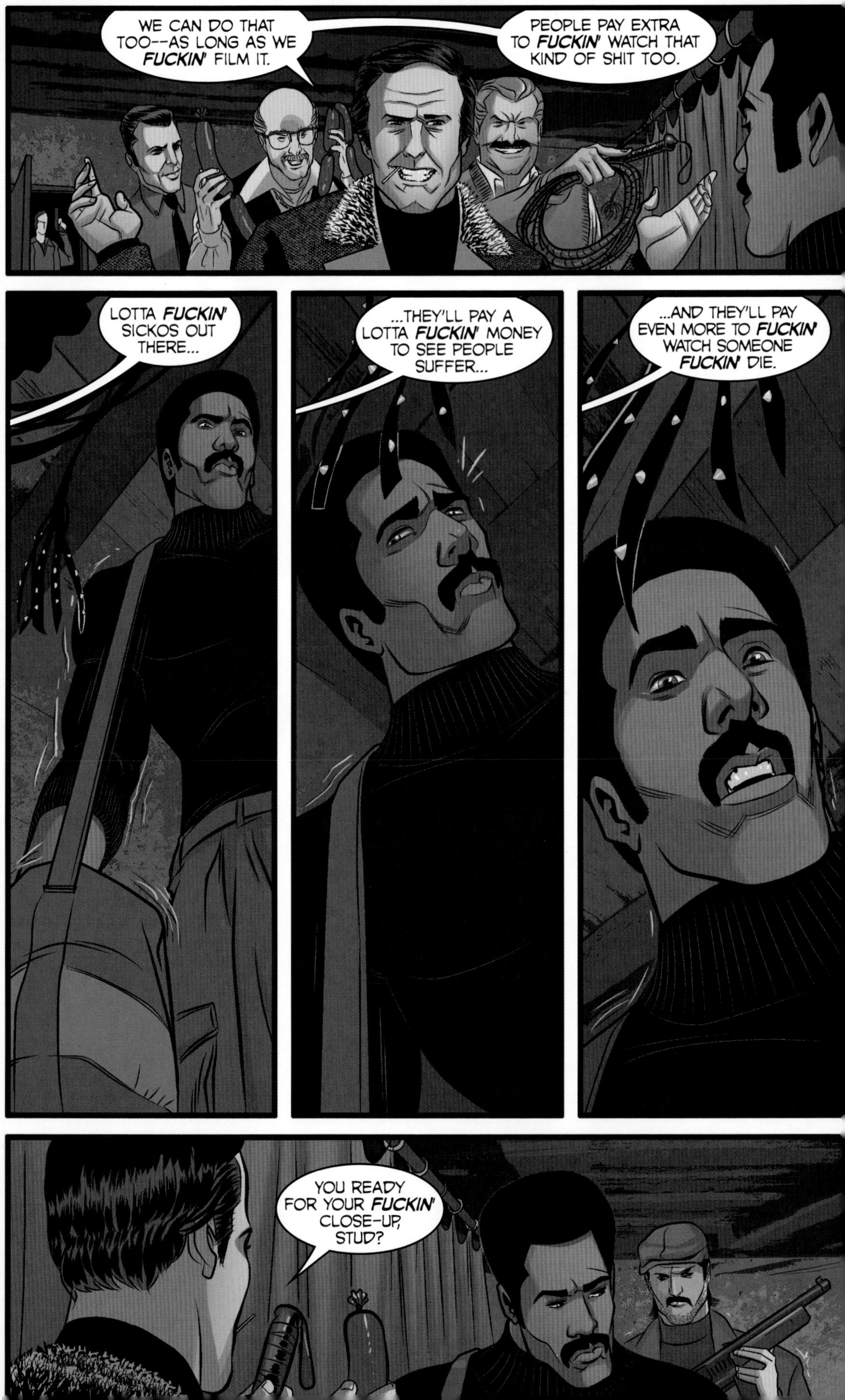
WE CAN DO THAT TOO--AS LONG AS WE FUCKIN' FILM IT.
PEOPLE PAY EXTRA TO FUCKIN' WATCH THAT KIND OF SHIT TOO.
LOTTA FUCKIN' SICKOS OUT THERE...
...THEY'LL PAY A LOTTA FUCKIN' MONEY TO SEE PEOPLE SUFFER...
...AND THEY'LL PAY EVEN MORE TO FUCKIN' WATCH SOMEONE FUCKIN' DIE.
YOU READY FOR YOUR FUCKIN' CLOSE-UP, STUD?

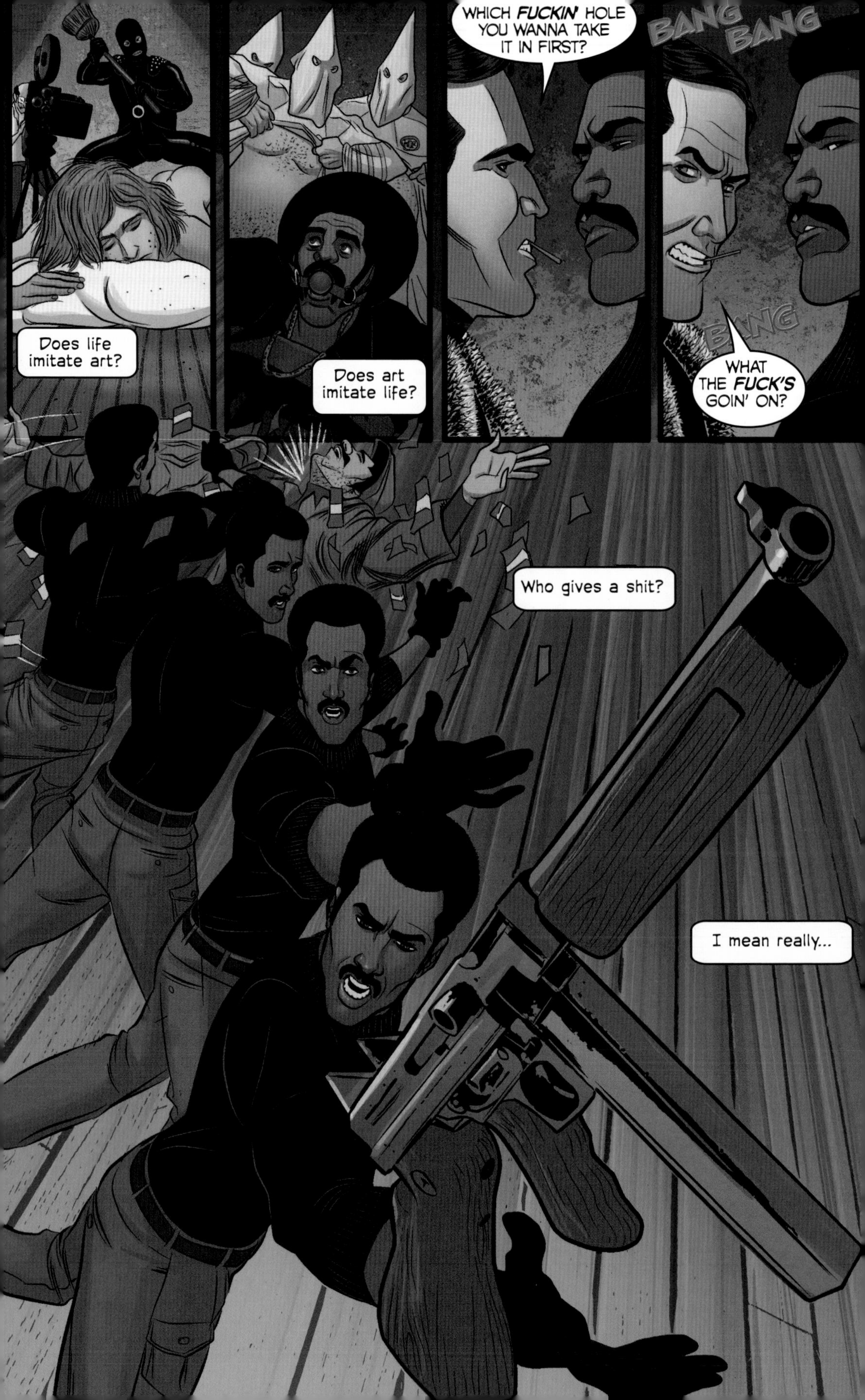
Does life imitate art?
Does art imitate life?
WHICH FUCKIN' HOLE YOU WANNA TAKE IT IN FIRST?
BANG BANG
BANG
WHAT THE FUCK'S GOIN' ON?
Who gives a shit?
I mean really...

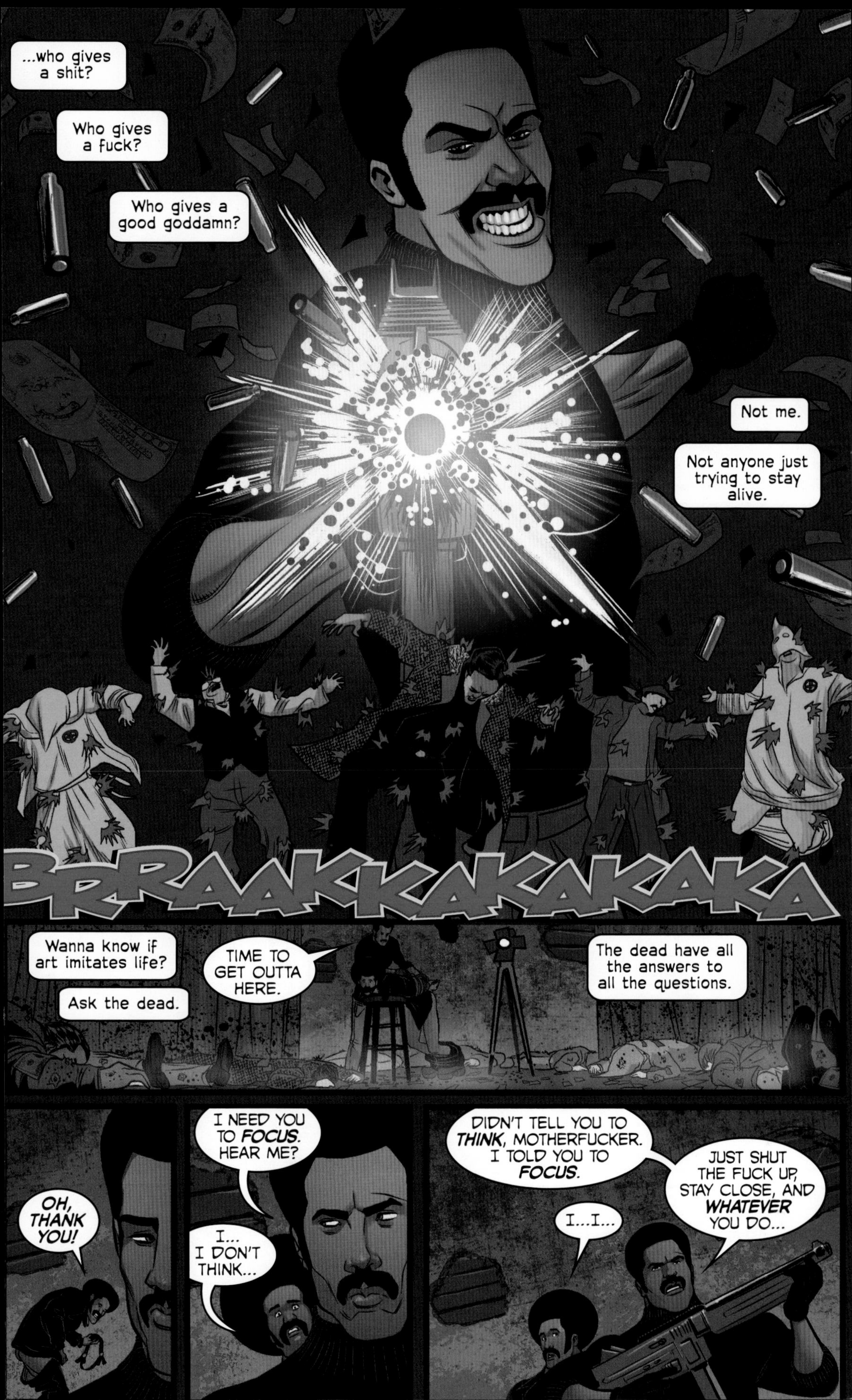

...who gives a shit?
Who gives a fuck?
Who gives a good goddamn?
Not me.
Not anyone just trying to stay alive.
BRRAAKKAKAKAKA
Wanna know if art imitates life?
Ask the dead.
TIME TO GET OUTTA HERE.
The dead have all the answers to all the questions.
OH, THANK YOU!
I NEED YOU TO FOCUS. HEAR ME?
I... I DON'T THINK...
DIDN'T TELL YOU TO THINK, MOTHERFUCKER. I TOLD YOU TO FOCUS.
I...I...
JUST SHUT THE FUCK UP, STAY CLOSE, AND WHATEVER YOU DO...

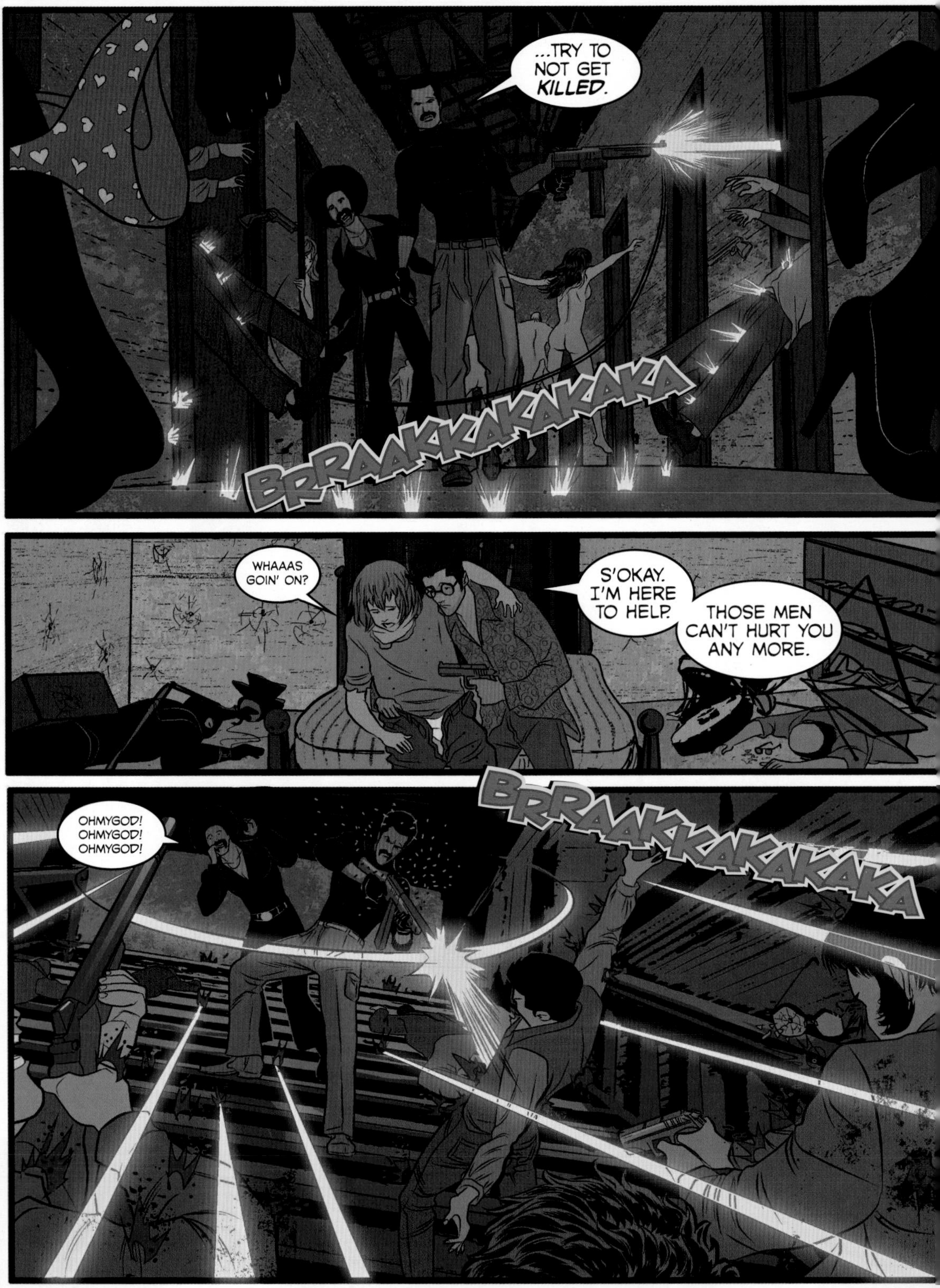

...TRY TO NOT GET KILLED.
BRRAAKKAKAKAKAKA
WHAAAS GOIN' ON?
S'OKAY. I'M HERE TO HELP.
THOSE MEN CAN'T HURT YOU ANY MORE.
BRRAAKKAKAKAKAKA
OHMYGOD! OHMYGOD! OHMYGOD!

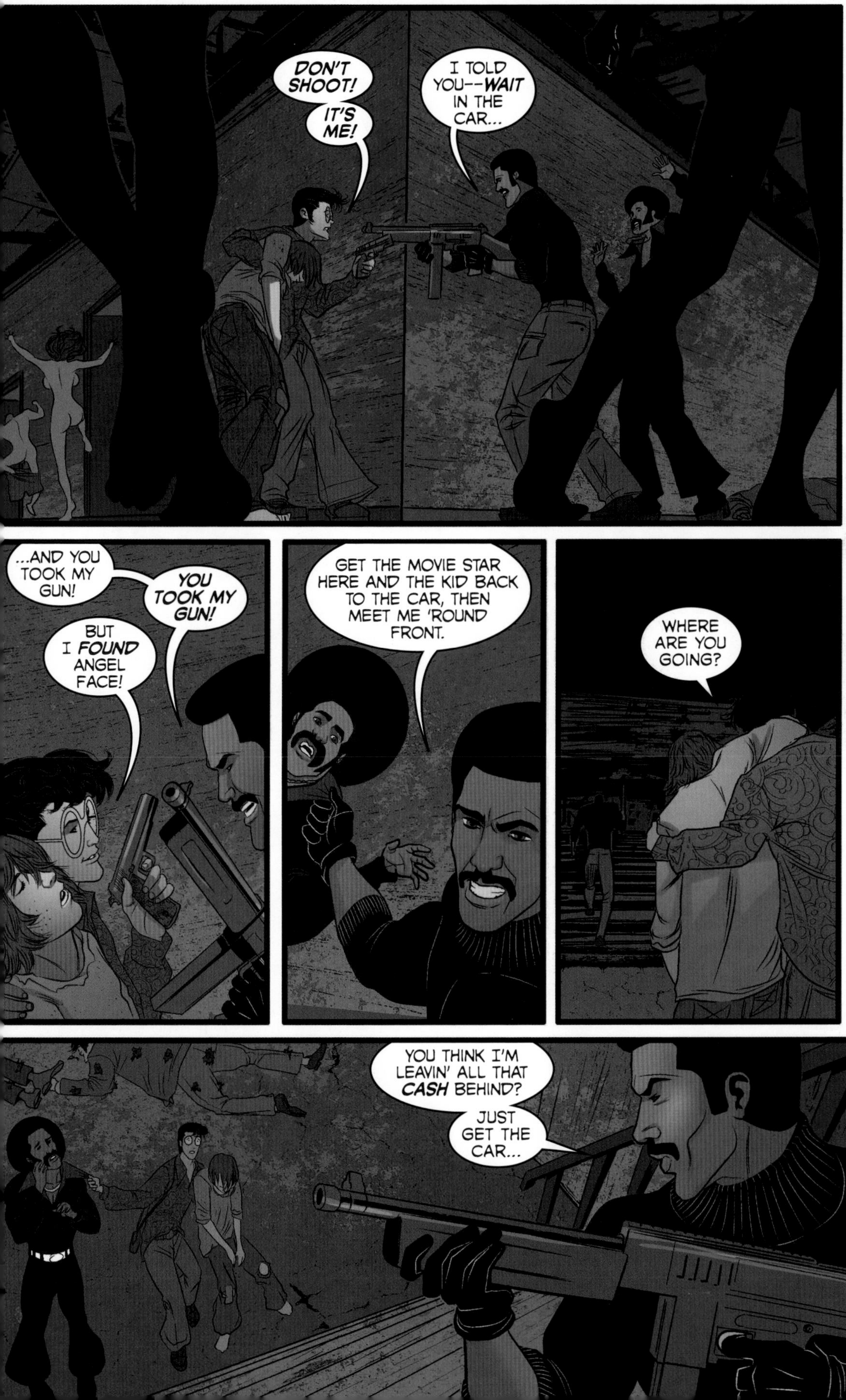
DON'T SHOOT!
IT'S ME!
I TOLD YOU--WAIT IN THE CAR...
...AND YOU TOOK MY GUN!
YOU TOOK MY GUN!
BUT I FOUND ANGEL FACE!
GET THE MOVIE STAR HERE AND THE KID BACK TO THE CAR, THEN MEET ME 'ROUND FRONT.
WHERE ARE YOU GOING?
YOU THINK I'M LEAVIN' ALL THAT CASH BEHIND?
JUST GET THE CAR...

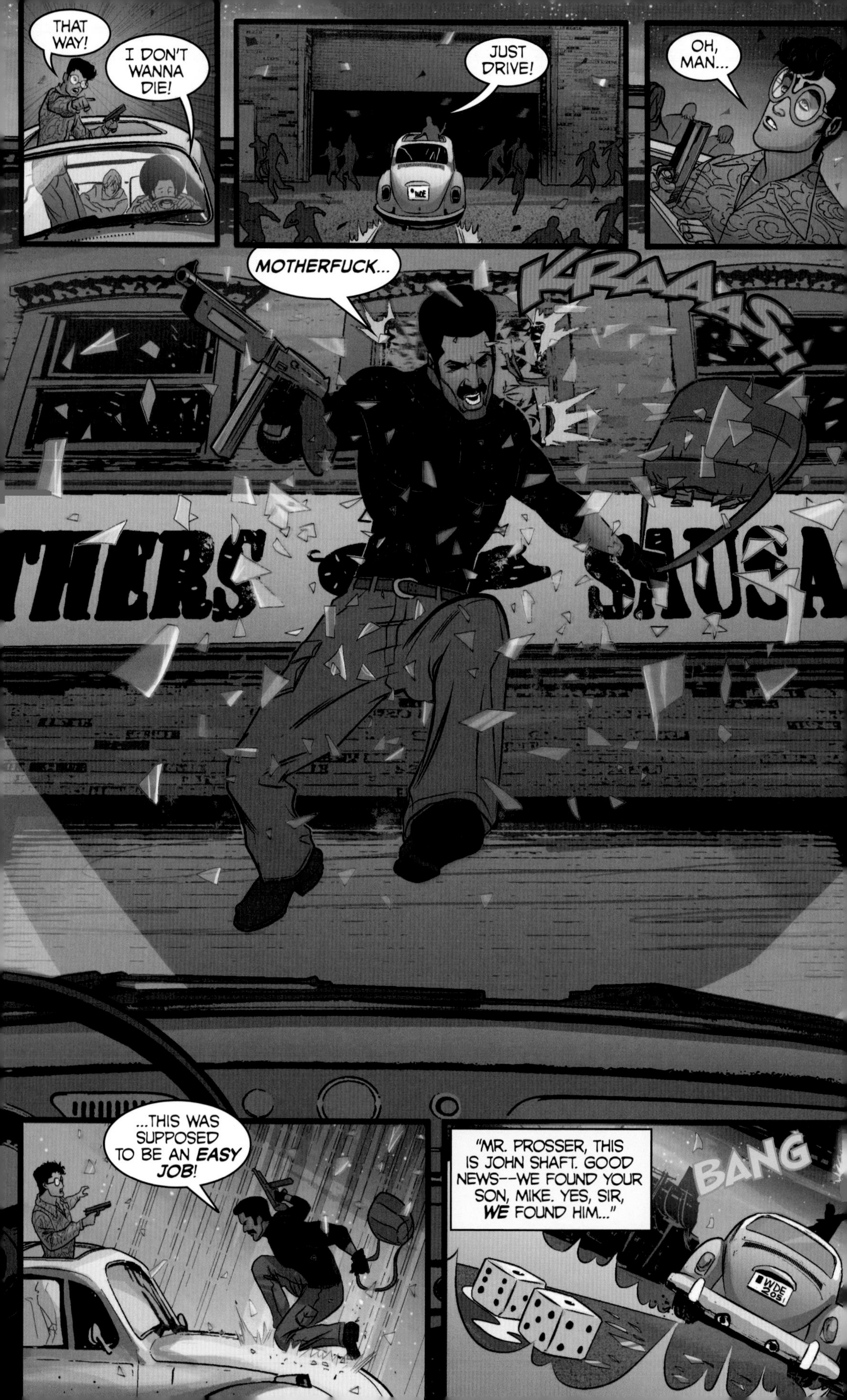
THAT WAY!
I DON'T WANNA DIE!
JUST DRIVE!
OH, MAN...
MOTHERFUCK...
KRAAASH!
THERS
SAUSA
...THIS WAS SUPPOSED TO BE AN EASY JOB!
"MR. PROSSER, THIS IS JOHN SHAFT. GOOD NEWS--WE FOUND YOUR SON, MIKE. YES, SIR, WE FOUND HIM..."
BANG
WDE 205

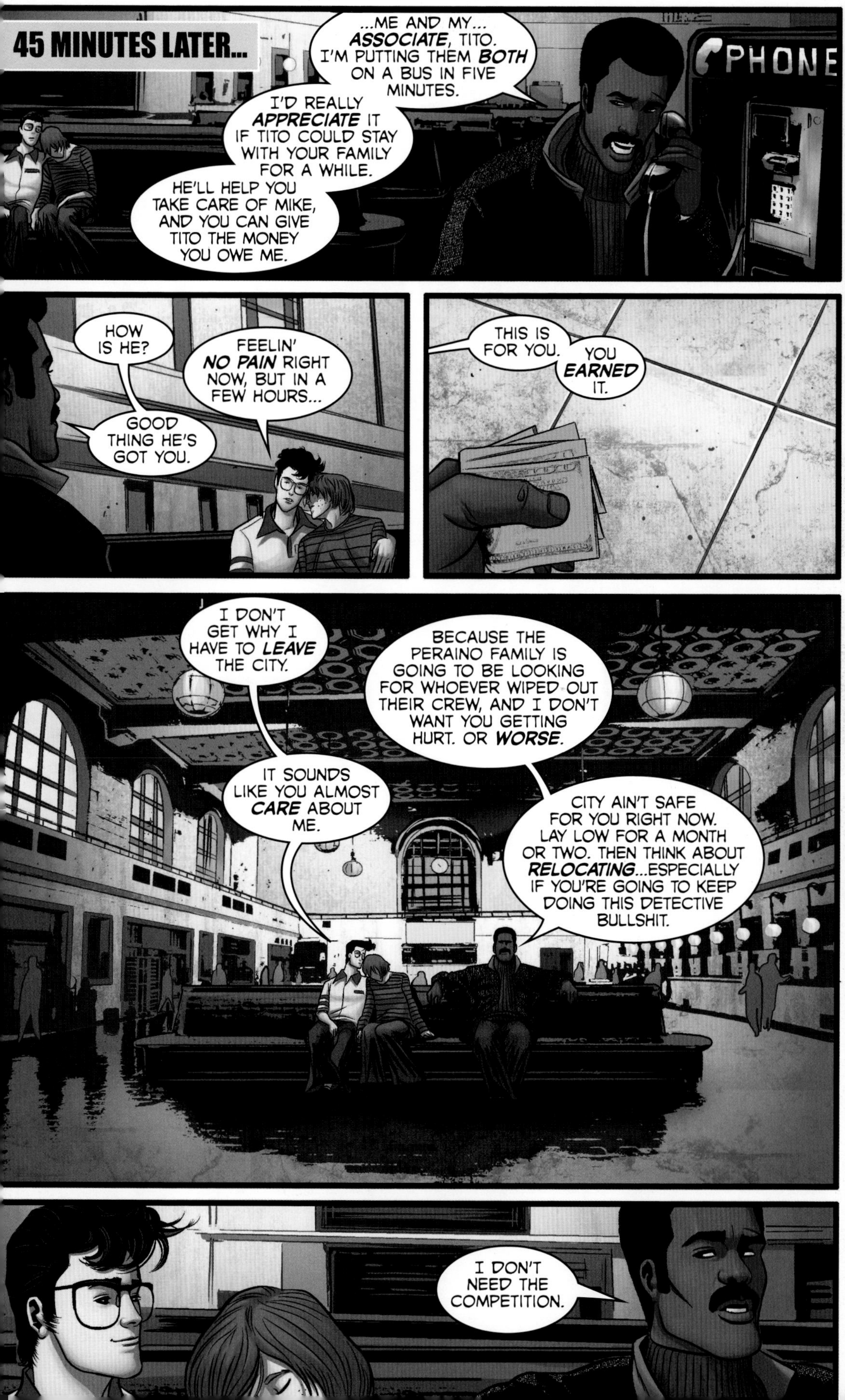
45 MINUTES LATER...
...ME AND MY... ASSOCIATE, TITO. I'M PUTTING THEM BOTH ON A BUS IN FIVE MINUTES.
I'D REALLY APPRECIATE IT IF TITO COULD STAY WITH YOUR FAMILY FOR A WHILE.
HE'LL HELP YOU TAKE CARE OF MIKE, AND YOU CAN GIVE TITO THE MONEY YOU OWE ME.
PHONE
HOW IS HE?
FEELIN' NO PAIN RIGHT NOW, BUT IN A FEW HOURS...
GOOD THING HE'S GOT YOU.
THIS IS FOR YOU.
YOU EARNED IT.
I DON'T GET WHY I HAVE TO LEAVE THE CITY.
BECAUSE THE PERAINO FAMILY IS GOING TO BE LOOKING FOR WHOEVER WIPED OUT THEIR CREW, AND I DON'T WANT YOU GETTING HURT. OR WORSE.
IT SOUNDS LIKE YOU ALMOST CARE ABOUT ME.
CITY AIN'T SAFE FOR YOU RIGHT NOW. LAY LOW FOR A MONTH OR TWO. THEN THINK ABOUT RELOCATING...ESPECIALLY IF YOU'RE GOING TO KEEP DOING THIS DETECTIVE BULLSHIT.
I DON'T NEED THE COMPETITION.

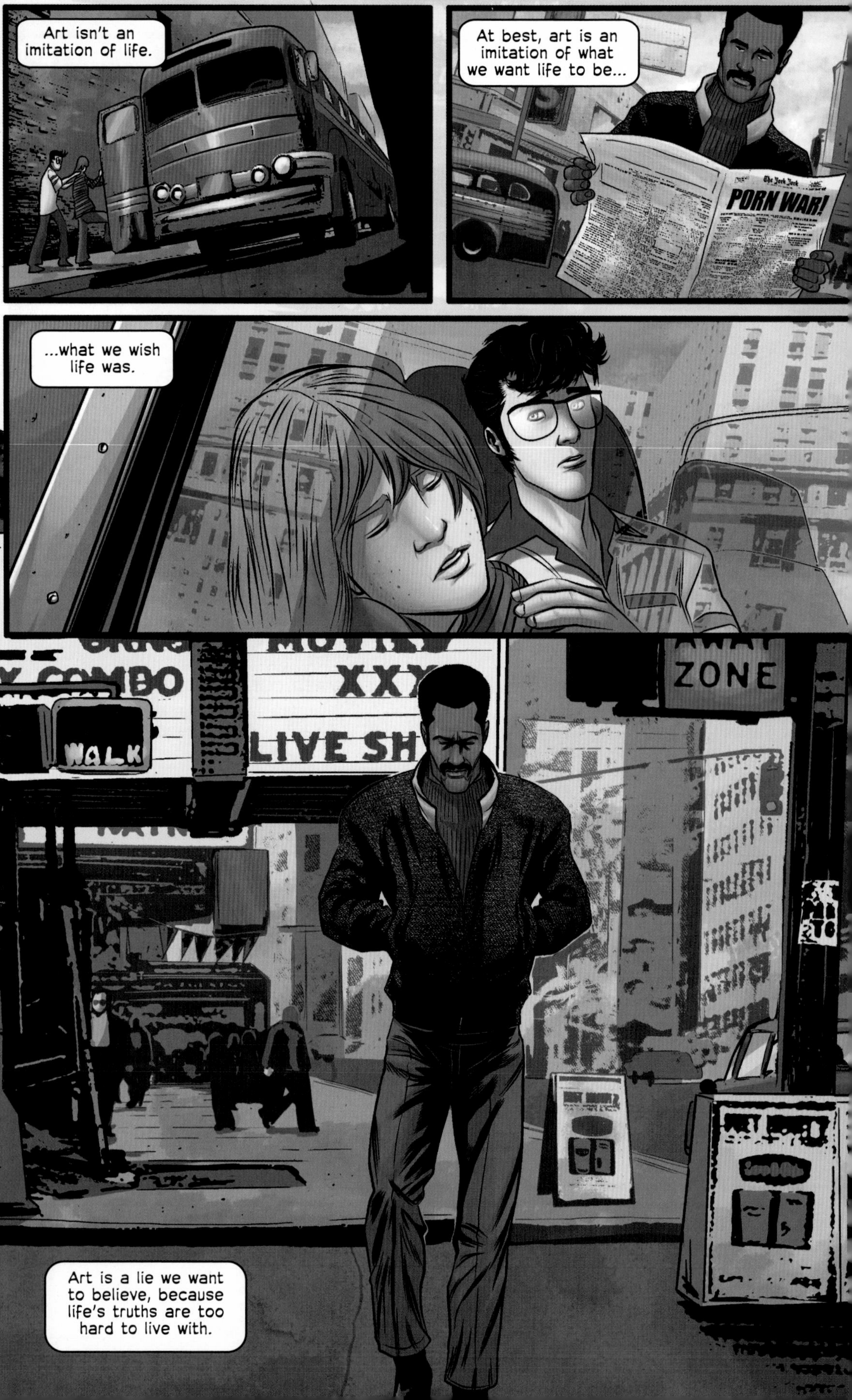
Art isn't an imitation of life.
At best, art is an imitation of what we want life to be...
PORN WAR!
...what we wish life was.
X COMBO
XXX
LIVE SH
WALK
ZONE
Art is a lie we want to believe, because life's truths are too hard to live with.

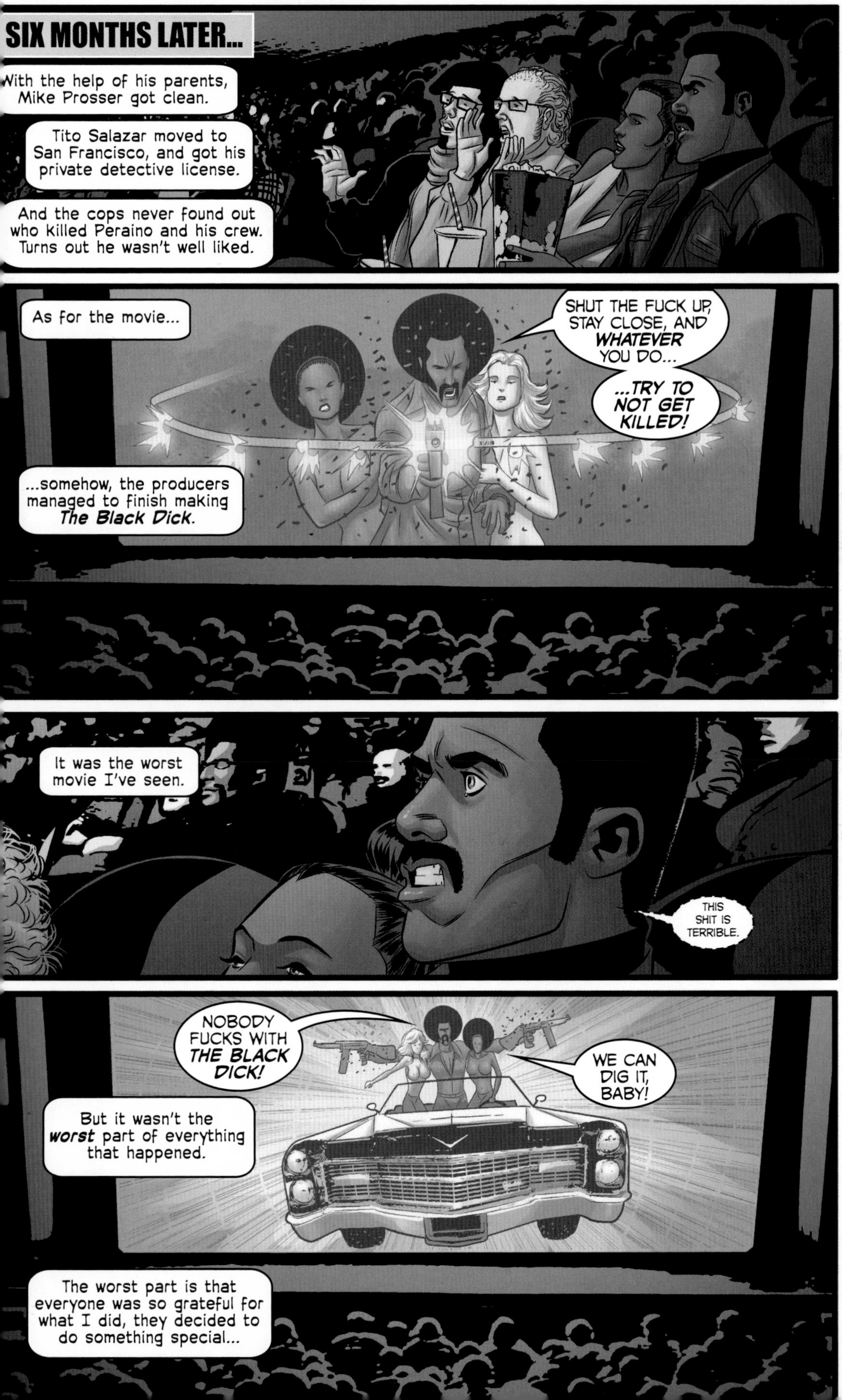

SIX MONTHS LATER...
With the help of his parents, Mike Prosser got clean.
Tito Salazar moved to San Francisco, and got his private detective license.
And the cops never found out who killed Peraino and his crew. Turns out he wasn't well liked.
As for the movie...
SHUT THE FUCK UP, STAY CLOSE, AND WHATEVER YOU DO...
...TRY TO NOT GET KILLED!
...somehow, the producers managed to finish making The Black Dick.
It was the worst movie I've seen.
THIS SHIT IS TERRIBLE.
NOBODY FUCKS WITH THE BLACK DICK!
WE CAN DIG IT, BABY!
But it wasn't the worst part of everything that happened.
The worst part is that everyone was so grateful for what I did, they decided to do something special...

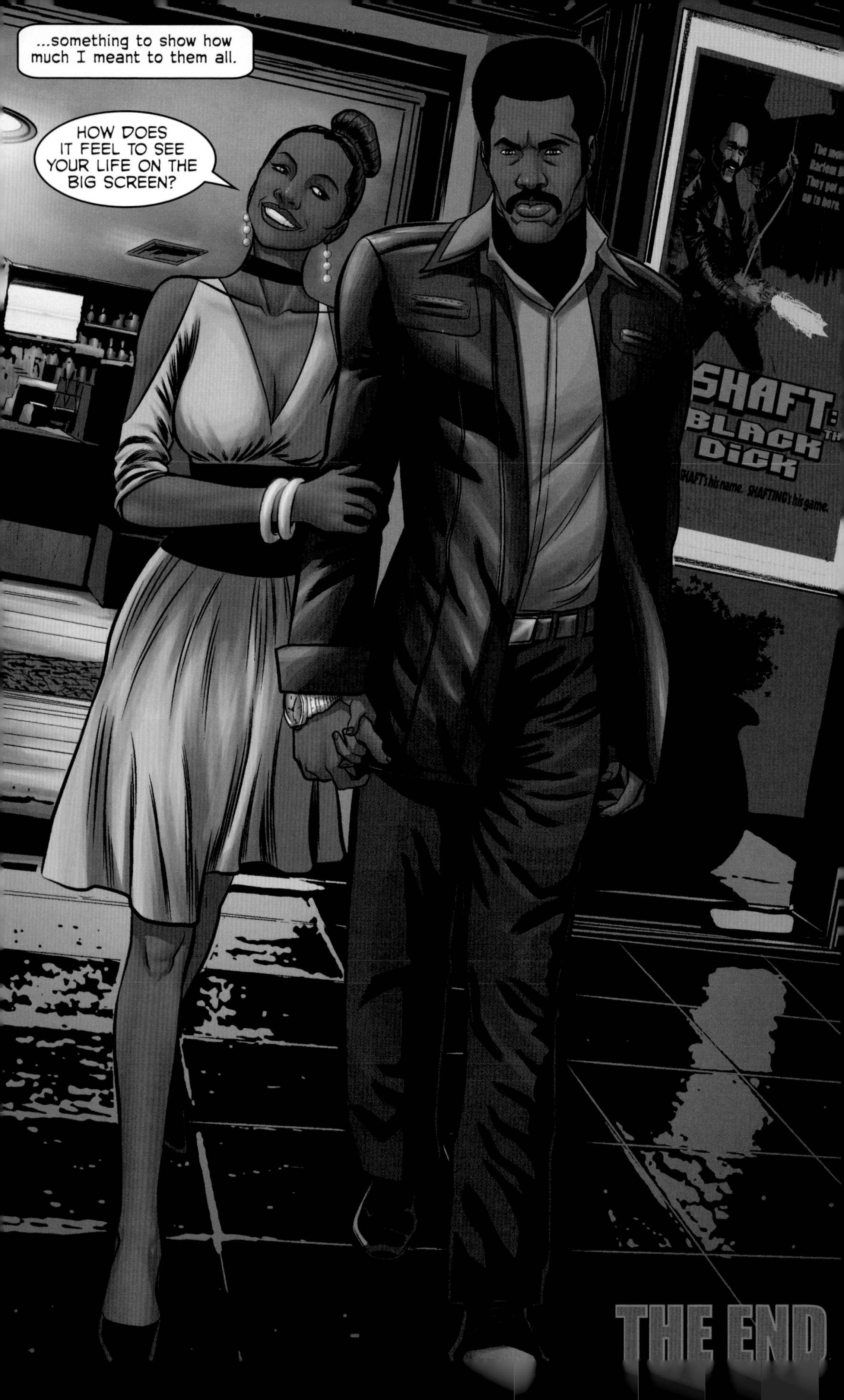
...something to show how much I meant to them all.
HOW DOES IT FEEL TO SEE YOUR LIFE ON THE BIG SCREEN?
SHAFT: BLACK DICK
SHAFT's his name. SHAFTING's his game.
THE END

SHAFT

Dynamite Proudly presents the 1970 original and unabridged tour de force of hardboiled crime fiction that introduced an unsuspecting world to a cultural icon.

Written by Ernest Tidyman:
ACADEMY AWARD-WINNING SCREENWRITER
OF THE FRENCH CONNECTION!
Cover by Robert Hack

from the Academy Award-Winning screenwriter of *The French Connection*

A DYNAMITE NOVEL · $9.99 US

ERNEST TIDYMAN
SHAFT

SHAFT HAS NO PREJUDICES.
HE'LL KILL ANYONE–BLACK OR WHITE.

"Ernest Tidyman created one of the most iconic and enduring pop culture characters in John Shaft, a legacy that has reached across multiple mediums, and sparked the imagination of millions of people, myself included." – David F. Walke

Shaft's Revenge
by DAVID WALKER
GLYPH AWARD-WINNING WRITER OF THE SHAFT: A COMPLICATED MAN GRAPHIC NOVE
Cover by Francesco Francavilla

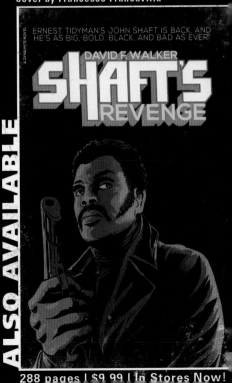

A DYNAMITE NOVEL

ERNEST TIDYMAN'S JOHN SHAFT IS BACK, AND HE'S AS BIG, BOLD, BLACK, AND BAD AS EVER!

DAVID F. WALKER
SHAFT'S REVENGE

240 pages | $9.99 | In Stores Now!

ALSO AVAILABLE

288 pages | $9.99 | In Stores Now!

DYNAMITE

Online at www.DYNAMITE.com On Facebook /Dynamitecomics
On Instagram @Dynamitecomics On Tumblr dynamitecomics.tumblr.com
On Twitter @Dynamitecomics On YouTube /Dynamitecomics
SHAFT is ™ and © 2016 Ernest Tidyman. Dynamite, Dynamite
Entertainment & its logo are © 2016 Dynamite. All Rights Reserved.

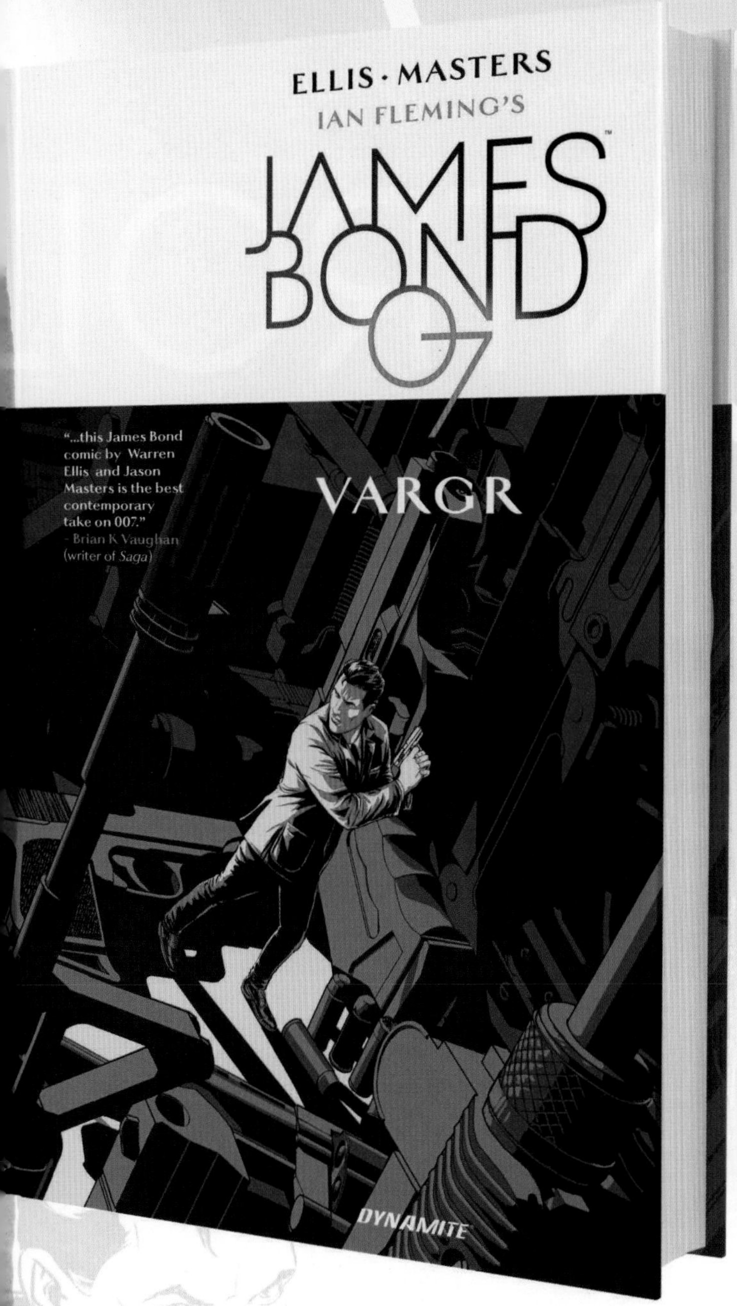
ELLIS · MASTERS
IAN FLEMING'S
JAMES BOND 007
"...this James Bond comic by Warren Ellis and Jason Masters is the best contemporary take on 007."
- Brian K Vaughan (writer of *Saga*)
VARGR
DYNAMITE

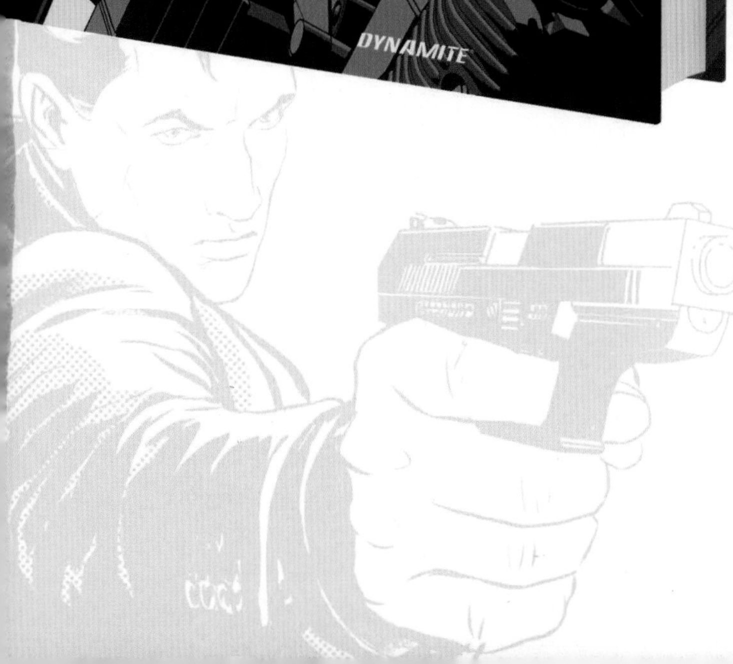

Cop or criminal, power is about control, applied top-down from the penthouse elite to the hustlers on the street.

But what happens when the street pushes back...?

CONTROL

741.5973 Walker v.1
Walker, David F.
Shaft.
30519009888655

andy diggle
angela cruickshank

CONTROL

andrea mutti
vladimir popov

dynamite · mature readers

A new hardboiled trade paperback from

Andy Diggle
Angela Cruickshank
Andrea Mutti

Coming March 2017
Available in print & digitally

DYNAMITE. www.dynamite.com
/dynamitecomics @dynamitecomic